THE WILD - TYPE

THE WILD ■ TYPE

Jeffrey Ivan Victoroff

Crown Publishers, Inc., New York

To my father

Copyright © 1989 by Jeffrey Ivan Victoroff
All rights reserved. No part of this book may be reproduced or transmitted in any form or by any means, electronic or mechanical, including photo-copying, recording, or by any information storage and retrieval system, without permission in writing from the publisher.

Published by Crown Publishers, Inc., 225 Park Avenue South, New York, New York 10003.

CROWN is a trademark of Crown Publishers, Inc.

Printed in the U.S.A.

Library of Congress Cataloging-in-Publication Data

Victoroff, Jeffrey Ivan.
  The wild type.
  I. Title.
PS3572.I284W5 1989   813'.54   88-18924
ISBN 0-517-57127-7

10 9 8 7 6 5 4 3 2 1

First Edition

THE
WILD - TYPE

— ■ PROLOGUE ■—

D r. Harkus was ordinarily a calm man. This was not an ordinary night.

The professor's eyes blazed with a feverish excitement as he drove into the parking lot. He killed the car's engine and grabbed some papers off the seat. Quickly, almost frantically, he stuffed the papers into the top of his briefcase. Then he locked the car and rushed toward the rear entrance of the Stanford Medical School.

"Applications," Harkus muttered. Jerking open the door of the Animal Facilities, he made his way rapidly straight to the bank of elevators. He punched a button, and punched it again, and paced in an anxious circle waiting for the car to come down.

"They want human applications," he went on, "they'll get their goddamn applications this time!" A bell rang above the steel-clad doors, which slid apart with a groan as the elevator arrived. The gray-haired doctor lunged into the car and jabbed the button marked 5. As he was carried up through the silent school, he clenched tight the handle of his disintegrating leather briefcase, overflowing with its untidy batch of handwritten sheets.

Dr. Harkus's Neuroanatomy Labs occupied most of the fifth floor. In their way, they represented the achievement of a lifetime. After winning the Lasker Award in 1955 and sharing the Nobel in 1967, Harkus had been given carte blanche by the university to assemble the minds and technology he needed for his work. Grant money gushed from the federal cornucopia; young scientists were lured from Berkeley, from MIT, from Columbia and Yale. His fifth-floor labs had become a legendary research center, searching for the genes that control the nervous system.

But the past several years had been hard. With the belt tightening of the eighties, the emphasis had shifted toward clinical research—practical research—as funding organizations threw their support to projects that might quickly bear the sweetest fruits of medical science: human applications.

"A golden chariot driven by myopic baboons!" was the doctor's metaphor. He told Washington, again and again, that you simply cannot do good human research without a solid foundation in basic science. They listened to him sympathetically as they chopped his grant money year by year. And now Harkus was internationally revered as a giant, in decline.

"Goddamnit!" he complained as the elevator opened to reveal an utterly dark hallway. The cleaning people had turned off the lights at midnight. Harkus stepped out into the blackness, shuffling his feet and extending his hand until he felt the cool obstruction of the cinder-block wall. Sliding his free hand along the wall as a guide, he began tracing his way through the labyrinth of halls toward his office. There were no windows, no other sources of light except the dim disembodied glimmer of a red Exit sign far down the first side hall he passed. As he shuffled along, the whir of the air replacement fans added an eerie hum to the silence of the building.

Proteins! Could we find the genes by finding the proteins? I've got to know! he thought. That was the thought, the inspiration, that had impelled him out into the night. He had leapt from his bed, burning with this new idea, and driven to the lab to set up a pilot experiment without delay. He could hear his own quick breath as he moved along the wall. He became aware of the dull pounding of his heart. Rounding the last corner, the doctor was instantly relieved to see a wedge of light spilling from under the door to his office. The light allowed him to speed ahead, and he reached for the doorknob in a moment.

A heavy-set stranger was standing over his desk, where a file lay open. The man looked up to face Harkus. The two stared at each other in mutual amazement. Suddenly, the man at the desk reached for a metal cylinder strapped to the wall. He tore it loose and rushed at the staring figure of the scientist. Harkus choked, "No!" just as the steel tube crashed through the pitiful defense of his old hands and drove an inch into his head. Shards of broken skull sliced into the soft pink meat of his brain, ripping open the vessels, flooding his head with a gush of hot red blood. He fell, a storm of electrical chaos exploding in his dying brain as nerve cells frantically flashed their final signals of memory and pain and, in that bloody storm of consciousness, something like a thought. For a moment he knew. Then he was dead.

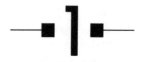

Dr. Jason McCane slammed the door of the taxicab and turned to face the huge brick building on the hill.

Before him stood the Clinical Center. The massive medical research building rose above him, dominating the campus of the National Institutes of Health. All around him, white-coated figures strolled across the rolling landscape in the heart of Bethesda, Maryland, making their way over the clipped green lawns and private roads of the world's largest biomedical research complex. He paid them no attention, but stared instead at that enormous building.

The young doctor's expression was unreadable. Long brown hair and a blond beard framed a face that was perhaps a bit too rugged for society's notion of a young physician. Deep-set blue-gray eyes pierced out from under the shadow of his brow. His stance was quiet, barely hinting at a reined energy. He stood for that moment, silent and unmoving, contemplating his new life. Then he stepped up to the glass-walled guard's booth, signed in, and briskly walked into the Center.

NEW FELLOWS

The sign hung over a table in one corner of the modern lobby, where a small crowd was gathered. Jason quickly strode up to the table and introduced himself to one of the men who sat behind it.

"Ah, yes, Dr. Jason McCane!" the man responded. "Here, won't you take this little information packet . . ."

As the man assembled a mountain of registration forms, Jason glanced with curiosity at the group around him. All of them, he suspected, were thinking the same thing. So this is it: the National Institutes of Health.

Each year, a handful of young scientists are brought to the NIH to do research. The selection process is veiled in the secret ways of the government science establishment. Jason had received the notice at Stanford announcing his fellowship appointment just a week before. He had quickly packed his belongings for shipment, thrown some clothes into his old duffel bag, and flown from California to NIH.

Jason accepted the hefty registration packet and asked directions to his branch office. As he began to turn away, a strikingly attractive young woman appeared at the table. Jason saw her long hair swing down across one eye, catching the light with its red and golden hues. She flipped her hair smoothly back, uncovering a face of singular Irish-featured beauty. She looked up and met Jason's eyes. Then she looked away, an almost imperceptible shift of vision, slow and gradual, as if she wished to make it appear that the moment had never occurred. He smiled.

Jason turned again toward the elevator lobby. As he waited, the tawny-haired young woman joined the excited group waiting for the elevators. He asked, "Your first day as well?"

"Oh." She seemed surprised to be addressed. "Why, yes. I'm joining the Clinical Psychobiology branch."

"I'm headed for Clinical Neuroscience." He smiled and extended his hand. "The name is McCane. Jason McCane."

"I'm Jennifer," she replied as they briefly shook hands, "Jennifer Darien."

"And what's your research interest, if I may ask?"

"Primatology," she said, shrugging. "Monkey behavior. I just got in from Wisconsin." She glanced around with a hint of distraction, a kind of nervous energy, not exactly haughty, but clearly distant.

"You're from the Wisconsin Regional Primate Center?" Jason asked.

"Oh, you know it?" The tawny-haired young woman looked at him as if for the first time.

"Are you joking?" he said. "That lab has been doing the best animal work in the country for twenty years. Who doesn't know it?"

Jennifer nodded, accepting his comment. "And you, Dr. McCane? Will you be doing psychopharmacology?"

"Good guess. Actually, I'm involved in gene mapping."

He was surprised by her reaction. She riveted her gaze on his face. Then she looked away. "Oh, the elevator!"

They both hurried to squeeze their way onto the crowded car. Neither spoke as the car moved up through the building, and Jennifer was the first one off. He called after her, "Good to meet you, Dr. Darien . . ." But the young woman had already turned away.

As he stepped out onto his own floor, Jason realized that even the National Institutes had not emerged unscathed from the budget-cutting enthusiasms of the last two administrations: Now that he had left the polished reception areas, the physical plant appeared marginally maintained. Cardboard cartons were stacked in the hall, the paint was peeling in spots, the green linoleum, despite its well-buffed patina of varnish, had lifted and cracked. As he walked down the gloomy corridor, anonymous white-coated figures strode past him, heads bent in arcane discussion. He was about to turn west when a voice came from behind.

"Excuse me, may I help you, sir?" A burly young man with a crew cut, dressed in a sort of orange-jacketed uniform, stepped around Jason and planted himself squarely in the doctor's path. His tone was a challenge.

Jason was rather taken aback. "I'm Dr. McCane, a new Fellow with Clinical Neuroscience. I'm heading for a meeting with the branch chief now."

The man nodded in grudging approval. "Ah, yes, Dr. McCane. You've been expected." He took a step forward and looked the young doctor up and down. "It's just that we're not used to people without whites on up here."

Jason stepped around the man and said, "I'll remember

that." As he turned down the west corridor, he could almost feel the man's eyes boring into his back.

A gangling gray-haired gentleman dressed in a long white lab coat was pacing directly toward him up the hall. The man smiled, sighting Jason. "Dr. McCane!"

Jason walked forward to meet him. "Dr. Murray?"

"Right. I'm Ben Murray." The branch chief extended his hand as he reached Jason, the sleeves of his white lab coat riding up over the cuff of the cashmere sweater he wore beneath it. "We've been expecting you."

"Yes," said the young doctor, glancing momentarily back down the hall, "I see." It was then that he noticed the glint beneath the guard's half-open jacket. The handle of a gun.

"Oh, don't mind Billy," said the chief, strolling back toward his office beside Jason. He explained that a new security force had recently been brought to NIH to protect classified research. Dr. Murray grinned, pushing open a frosted glass door marked Clinical Neurosciences and gesturing for the younger doctor to precede him.

They entered a large outer office where three secretaries were working, a buxom middle-aged lady, who sat at the largest desk, and two younger women. The two younger ones exchanged a private smile when they saw the new Clinical Fellow. Murray introduced Jason to the three women, then led the way toward another door. The branch chief's enclave was entered through a middle room, a storage area overflowing with reprints and boxed files with labels such as Brain Development and Mood Regulation. The men passed through, stepping around the haphazard obstacles, and into an office crammed to the ceiling with books and papers.

"Have a seat," said Murray, "if you can find one."

Jason shifted a pile of journals off a chair and sat across from the older scientist, who was fiddling with an electric coffee machine behind the desk. "Have some?"

"Please. Black's fine."

The branch chief passed Jason a steaming cup, then turned back to prepare his own. As Jason sipped the strong black coffee, he glanced around the office. It was cramped, chaotic at first glance, but clearly the center of activity in the branch.

Something like the chief: Dr. Murray looked to be in his late forties, a tall man who moved like a former athlete. He looked just slightly disorganized at first, tieless, one corner of his collar tilted up, but his casual facade did not succeed in concealing the drive, the fierce intelligence that danced behind his piercing black eyes.

Dr. Murray sat down and addressed his new Fellow. "Dr. McCane, you've just come from Stanford. Before we get you set up, I want to express my personal regrets. I know that you worked closely with Dr. Harkus. I understand you actually found the . . . body yourself. It must have been quite a blow."

Jason turned his eyes to the chief. "Yes, thanks. Dr. Harkus's murder is actually very much on my mind." He shook his head. "The fact is, I simply can't understand how such a thing could happen. I keep trying to figure it out, but there's something to it that just escapes me."

"Oh?" The chief watched him carefully. "So you're involved with the murder investigation?"

"Well, no. Not exactly. But I'm convinced that it wasn't just a random act of violence. A lot of data was stolen from the lab on the night of the murder. There must have been something about the work we were doing; I've been looking through some of Dr. Harkus's papers, trying to find a clue."

"Ah, yes." Murray leaned an elbow onto the desk, looking intently across at his young colleague. "We all feel the loss. But,"—he pursed his lips, searching for the right way to say it—"if you'll forgive my curbside psychotherapy, aren't you taking an unfair share of the burden on yourself? I mean, I hope you won't give yourself more responsibility for this investigation than you ought to." His tone was measured, kindly. "Perhaps you should leave it to the police."

Jason sighed. He knew that Murray's statement made sense. But he also knew that he couldn't leave it to the police; not only had Dr. Harkus become almost like a father to him, but the violence of his death reminded him of his own parents' deaths many years before. He responded to Murray: "I suppose you're right, although I would probably feel even more guilty if I did nothing."

"Of course. Well, just a suggestion." Murray's eyes were fixed on Jason. "Think about it." The chief stood up, smiling again. "Now, how about a tour?"

The west wing was better lit and maintained than the administrative corridor, and Jason was a little relieved to see the brightness. There was still a sense of too much work in too little space. Huge freezers and ultracentrifuges all but blocked the corridor where bustling groups of scientists scurried past one another like dancers at a crowded ball. As the two doctors walked, several more of the orange-jacketed security men were in evidence. They scrutinized Jason carefully as he passed. He tried to ignore them. The chief pointed out individual laboratories one after another and described the projects being pursued in them. The array of hardware was staggering. Crammed awkwardly into every square foot of bench or shelf space was the latest model of every sophisticated analytic device that Jason had ever seen, and several he'd only read about.

Murray stopped one hunched and straggle-haired man whose curly mustache nearly covered his mouth. He introduced the man as Dr. Larry Guttman, a third-year Fellow. Dr. Guttman nodded once, seeming not to see Jason's outstretched hand, and briskly continued to trundle his cart of test tubes down the corridor.

"Friendly bastard, actually."

Jason turned to see the speaker, a thin, dark-haired man in his early thirties who had come over to join them.

"Oh, Tom," said Murray, "let me introduce Dr. McCane."

"Hi." The man smiled unaffectedly and offered his hand. "I'm Tom Sherrington, third-year Fellow." The young men shook hands. "What I meant to say was, don't get the wrong idea about Larry. He's usually a prince, but he's in the middle of a new assay right now and he hasn't had time to piss in the sink for the last three days."

Jason smiled back. "I can imagine."

"Look, Tom," interceded the branch chief, glancing at the Rolex on his wrist, "do you have some time to show Jason around? I was due at a Human Experimentation Committee meeting five minutes ago."

"Sure, I think I can manage that," answered Tom.

"Thanks. Sorry to farm you out like this, Jason, but I'll see you at the research meeting tomorrow morning. Welcome again." He waved as he strode off down the corridor.

Thirty feet farther on, however, he almost collided with a blond technician, who had suddenly backed out of a door balancing a tray of ice buckets. The young woman caught the tipping buckets, and Jason was a bit surprised to see Murray laughing boyishly as he helped her rebalance the load.

"Ah, yes. The perks of office," said Tom, who had also watched the scene. Jason looked at him speculatively. Tom explained that the young blond woman had come to NIH last year as an entry-level lab technician. However, since she had discovered the charms of the branch chief, and vice-versa, she had virtually been catapulted into the position of director of Laboratory Services. "Big Ben is a sly old dog." Tom chuckled, looking after the branch chief.

"Big Ben?"

"That's what we call him." Tom turned with a smile to face him. "Well, why don't I give you a tour of the research ward? It's just a flight up."

They pushed through a door into a dimly lit stairwell and climbed together up through the relative dark, finally passing out of the stairwell into a broad corridor. The corridor dead-ended at a large wall of green painted metal, marked with a plastic sign: NIH PATIENT DIVISION. AUTHORIZED PERSONNEL ONLY. Tom turned toward a small chrome panel built into the side wall. He keyed a number on a ten-button board, which beeped in response to his touch. A mechanical voice addressed him from a hidden speaker:

"Please state your name."

"Dr. Thomas Sherrington."

"Thank you, Dr. Sherrington," the wall responded politely.

An electric whirring began as the heavy green steel door slid open before them. It closed behind them quickly when they'd passed, sealing with a final and very solid click. Jason bent to examine the chrome electronic panel on the inner wall, identical to the one outside. Tom explained that it was a voiceprint lock, designed to maximize security.

"Isn't all this slightly elaborate, even for a locked ward?" Jason asked.

Tom nodded his agreement but said that there was a reason for the security. Two months before, a young woman had suddenly become psychotic. She had managed to fight her way off the ward, and then she simply disappeared. "Suicidal, we guess." Tom frowned. "It's a shame. She'll probably wash up someday out of the Potomac. Pretty girl. Bright too, although she acquired some rather far-out delusions by that time."

"Oh, what sort?"

Tom shook his head. "Something about being sexually assaulted as part of an experiment."

Jason looked at him, then back at the steel door they had entered. It was invisible. The corridor appeared to end in a blank green wall. Escape looked rather unlikely now.

"Come on," Tom said. "Most of the patients are in Group Meeting right now, so we have the run of the place."

Tom led him down the corridor, a brightly lit and carpeted hall with semiprivate rooms off each side. In contrast to the floor below, the ward was informal and warm, carpeted throughout, almost plushly outfitted. The two doctors passed a conference room, a small laboratory, and several patient rooms, comfortably decorated in pleasing shades of beige and tan.

They came to a door marked TREATMENT ROOM, which Tom unlocked. He explained that the room was designed for patient examinations and certain drug experiments, pointing out the EKG, the EEG, the automated blood sampling equipment, and the video camera beside the examination table. He gave Jason a moment to look around, then closed the door again. Next, Tom walked Jason down the hall to the glass-enclosed nurses' station where he introduced him to the head nurse and the social worker. Finally, the men rounded a corner to emerge in a large common room, furnished like the living room of a private home.

A pretty auburn-haired girl who appeared to be about nineteen or twenty was sitting at a table playing solitaire.

Tom caught Jason's questioning look and said, "Oh, Cindy's

not a patient. She's a Normal Volunteer.'' He led the way over to the table.

The girl heard them approach and turned with a bright smile. "Hey, Dr. Sherrington."

"Hi, Cindy. This is Dr. McCane, a brand new Clinical Fellow. First day here. Jason, Cindy."

"Well." She bounded up with that energy unique to her age and shook hands with the young doctor. "Welcome to the Clinical Center!"

"Thank you. I hope we're not stealing you from your game."

"Oh, that's nothing," she said, gazing up at his blond-bearded face. "I'm just waiting for someone."

"Tom says you're a 'Normal Volunteer.' What does that mean, exactly?"

She smiled, and explained that Normal Volunteers are college students who come to NIH for a few months to serve as controls for human experiments.

"Generally pre-meds," added Tom.

"What sort of experiments?" Jason asked.

"Oh, drugs and things," she replied. "We take the same experimental stuff as the patients, and go through the same testing. They said nothing painful or really dangerous. And in my spare time, I get to meet all the scientists, and go all over Washington, concerts and museums and everything!" Her eyes twinkled with enthusiasm.

"Speaking of 'everything,' " Tom asked her, "where's Tony?"

She half blushed, suddenly uncomfortable. "I think he's lifting weights down in Physical Therapy."

Just then, an enormous shirtless young man came around the corner. His skin was covered with sweat, which gleamed like a polish on the overdeveloped muscles of his big chest and bulging arms. He frowned when he saw the doctors with Cindy, and quickly walked to her, placing a huge hand possessively on her shoulder. Veins stood out in blue knots up his forearm. Jason suspected that his costume was deliberate, intending to demonstrate his grossly swollen muscles to the girl.

"Hey Tom," the weight lifter nodded, eyeing Jason suspiciously. He towered over even the new doctor.

"Tony, this is Dr. McCane, a new Fellow." To Jason he explained, "Tony's another Normal Volunteer. And, I might add, the last Eastern Division college wrestling champ. Heavyweight."

"Pleased to meet you," said the doctor, offering his hand.

Tony grabbed the hand, shook down once, and began to squeeze, eyeing Jason as he did. The grip went well beyond the point of politeness. He smiled. He persisted, his hand working like an iron machine built for this single task, to crush. Jason looked at him squarely. "You certainly are strong."

Tony grinned and let go. "Yeah, I guess." He stood with his feet apart, the hand returning to Cindy's shoulder. "You gotta stay in shape, you know what I mean?"

The lanky doctor examined his hand, on which the red indentations of Tony's fingers were fading across the back. "I think I do," he replied.

———■———

Tom quickly completed the ward tour and returned with Jason back down to the laboratory wing. He guided the new Fellow to the room assigned to him. Just before opening the door, he admonished Jason not to call the piano movers: The grand would have to stay at home.

Jason laughed. "I see what you mean."

The office he'd been assigned was really just a cubicle, part of a larger room, separated from the other Fellows' offices by a wall of olive steel filing cabinets. Light came over the cabinets from the single window shared by the three junior scientists. Other than a desktop computer terminal, the only furniture was the scarred, government-issue wooden desk and an old vinyl-clad secretarial chair on wheels. Tom plopped himself down in the chair and put his hands behind his head.

"Ah, the life of luxury," he said, leaning back. The chair began to tip over backward.

"Watch it!" Jason leapt across the room, catching the chair as it fell. He lifted the other man back to a sitting position.

"Thanks!" Tom stood up, shaken, glaring at the chair. "I should have known. About half of these things do that." He looked at Jason. "Hey, are you some kind of acrobat, or what?"

Jason didn't answer. He had turned to exploring the cubicle, opening cabinets, looking through drawers.

Tom continued eyeing Jason as he moved about the tiny office, following each movement with a new sort of interest. His brow came down to shade his narrowed eyes. Finally, he shrugged. "Anyway, this place isn't much for creature comforts, but the work is fun. By the way, what did you say you'll be working on?"

"Well, I suppose I'll continue working on the project I just started at Stanford. Gene mapping of manic-depressive illness." He tapped experimentally on the keyboard of the computer terminal on his desk.

"Dynamite! Right up my alley."

Jason stopped and turned to face Tom. "Oh? I didn't know anyone else in this branch was involved in gene mapping."

Tom smiled. "Actually, that's a fairly recent change for me. Funding has been beefed up for genetics studies here in the last year or so. There's a real push from the powers that be."

"And what is your research area now?"

"Gene splicing." He checked his watch. "Say, Jason, I have to take off." Tom offered his hand. "Anyway, welcome to the Center!"

Jason watched him go. He was somewhat surprised to learn that others in his group were also involved in the new field of behavioral genetics.

He lifted the chair up onto the desk and tightened a loose bolt with his fingers. Then he returned the chair to its place. He sat, lifting his heels onto the desk, and folded his arms. For a moment, he was lost in thought as the events of the past week filled his mind. His mentor, Dr. Harkus, had been murdered. Data had been stolen from the Stanford labs. And suddenly he was in Bethesda, three thousand miles away, lost without a clue to his mentor's bloody death. He admitted it: For the last three years Dr. Harkus had been like a father to him. An expression of sharp private pain flashed across his face. He squeezed his eyes shut. Then he opened them and took a deep breath. Perhaps his new job would help to divert his thoughts.

From his seat, he could see out the window to the rolling lawns of the NIH campus. As he stared into the green distance, his mind wandered through events of his first hours in the Clinical Center. The orientation, the tour through a strange mix of luxury and dilapidation, the scientists, the armed guards, the amazing labs . . . He was left with a montage of impressions, struck by a sense of incredible possibility.

Then he remembered. A young female primatologist from Wisconsin.

■ 2 ■

The fat red-faced man swung open the office door and began to shout, "Goddamn it, Julie, I told you not to—" His mouth worked silently, then slowly shut as he saw the square-jawed visitor who was in the reception room, feet planted wide, standing silently before the secretary's desk. "Yes, I see. It's all right, Julie." He cleared his throat. "Uh, won't you come in, Mr. . . . . ?"

"Williams."

"Yes, of course. Mr. Williams. Please." He stood aside for the man to pass through the door into his office. With a show of polite control, he asked the secretary to hold his calls for the time being. Then he swung the door shut with a dull clump, leaving the secretary staring in confusion at its brass nameplate.

"What the—"

The man who called himself Williams silenced his host with a quick gesture and rapidly crossed to the marble-topped bar. He pressed a panel; it opened with a click to reveal a stereo receiver. The visitor quickly switched it on and left the volume somewhat above medium. He turned to face his host. "Speak quietly, please. This conversation is not intended for posterity."

16

The beefy host worked his jaw a moment in tightly restrained anger, then said icily, "You were not to come here. I will not tolerate it. How will I explain this to my staff?"

"Actually, we leave that to your famous capacity for fabrication." Williams smiled at his host. He removed a pair of glasses with heavy rims, revealing a mole that protruded from under his left eye. Without the distorting glasses, the contours of his face were also better revealed: His dark hair was trimmed unfashionably short atop an almost rectangular head. His clean-shaven chin could not escape the bluish cast of remaining stubble, which covered a jaw as square as a brick. "Forgive the subterfuge," he said, slipping the glasses into a case. "Simple but effective. Have you heard about our western adventure?"

"What are you talking—"

The square-jawed visitor drew a newspaper clipping from inside the jacket of his plain blue suit, letting it flutter onto the desktop. He stood silently before the desk, feet planted wide as before, something military about the stance.

His host scowled as he snatched up the clipping. He read through it quickly, noting that it was from the *San Francisco Chronicle*, dated a week before. His expression changed as he read. "Jesus." He dropped the piece of newsprint onto his blotter and planted one hand flat over it, as if he wanted it to disappear.

"Jesus, indeed," Mr. Williams said. "Fortunately, the Agency acted quickly to influence the course of the investigation."

The red-faced host moved around his desk, his corpulent frame so heavy that he tipped from side to side as he walked, and grunted into the chair. "I see," he said with an air of profound annoyance. "So I take it the Director is getting impatient. Now, what does this have to do with me?"

His visitor turned to sit in the facing chair. For a moment, he regarded his host with a look approaching contempt. Tenting his fingers, he answered, "The Director is concerned. It seems that our new acquisition, Dr. McCane, has taken a personal interest in the murder investigation. His suspicions must not be aroused. If McCane gets in the way—"

"You wouldn't dare!"

Mr. Williams glared back at his host. "The project must go forward. Interference will not be tolerated. Whatever or whoever gets in the way will be . . . let's just say neutralized."

The fat man stood up. "What the hell is the Director going to get out of eliminating—"

"Nothing! But if young Dr. McCane becomes suspicious of our plan, the entire project is in jeopardy! I'm sure you wouldn't want that. And I'm also sure," he said, almost sneering, "you wouldn't want to lose your access to the, shall we say, fringe benefits of our arrangement?"

The host swallowed. He began to knead his hands together, moving his pudgy fingers in a continuous nervous clasp. "Well, what do you think we should do?"

"To begin with, we must monitor Dr. McCane. Naturally, my organization will continue our watchers, and you will continue your electronic measures, but we need someone closer. Does your team have the manpower for that?"

"You mean," the fat man asked, "assign someone from my team to close surveillance?"

"Precisely. Someone who can get to him, talk to him. Someone who can take action if the need arises. Have you got a good man?"

The host frowned a minute. Then he slowly began to smile. "Yes. I believe I can arrange just the right personnel for this. I'll take care of it tonight."

"Good." The square-jawed visitor who called himself Williams rose rapidly. He replaced his distorting glasses, then walked straight to the door. He paused with his hand on the knob. "I'll expect you to make contact at the usual time." Without waiting for a response, he opened the door, stepped through, and closed it behind him.

The reluctant host exhaled slowly. He paused a moment in thought, his thick lips bent in a frown. Then he got up and turned off the stereo. He returned to his desk with a book of matches. He lit one, lifted the small clipping from his desk, and pushed it into the flame.

The newsprint image of Professor Harkus flared yellow for

a second, then quickly went black, and finally became a thin gray ash.

———■———

As the shadows lengthened in the early evening light, Jason gathered up his papers off the carpet and bundled them into a folder marked Harkus. He jogged up the stairs of his town house and shoved the folder into a cardboard box in the back of the bedroom closet. Then he laced on his old track shoes and set out for a run.

As he ran out of his cul-de-sac and left his town house behind, his mind kept wrestling with the question that had tormented him since the night of Dr. Harkus's death. Why? Why was the lab broken into? Why would someone want to steal that data, kill for it? What was it in the projects at the lab that was so valuable? As it had turned out, on the night of the murder a number of items had been stolen from the Harkus labs: protocol books, data sheets, private memos. Before leaving for Bethesda, Jason had quietly compiled notes relating to the research projects that had been violated, as well as photocopies of several handwritten sheets that had been found on the floor beneath Dr. Harkus's fallen body.

He kept coming back to those last cryptic notes left by Dr. Harkus, a rambling list of proteins thought to be important to brain development, ending with the frantic scribble: "Check with PPP!"

Who or what was PPP? he asked himself for the hundredth time. What did Harkus mean to check? What was it about that list of proteins that had so excited the old professor, had driven him to his extraordinary nighttime visit to the laboratory, had driven him to his death? He shook his head. Maybe his new branch chief, Dr. Murray, was right. Maybe he should leave the investigation to the police. All of his speculations left him with the same questions, and the same infuriating lack of a clue to his mentor's brutal murder.

In the fading light, Jason tried to memorize the street names as he ran northwest, out toward the Potomac area. Soon he no longer bothered to check the names, intending instead to remember the sequence of turns he took as he explored the neighborhood. Pounding along the sidewalks and tree lawns, he inhaled deeply, taking in the smells of the summer. Late-blossoming trees in residential yards lent their perfume to the aroma of fresh-cut grass. A few crickets began to sing as night came on. Traffic was light, so he shifted off the sidewalk and ran in the street. The houses and yards became progressively larger as the young doctor ran, with white pickets giving way to spiked fences of wrought iron, and short tarmac driveways yielding to broad semicircular drives or even private roads. Jason could not help marveling at the immense wealth of the area, startling in contrast with the primitive jungle outposts where he had spent his own childhood, following his anthropologist father from dig to dig.

A pair of headlights appeared around the curve ahead, and the doctor shifted off the crown of the road into the leaves along the curb. He breathed easily and began to lift his knees to bring his feet down more securely into the crackling debris. As the road began to climb, he deliberately accelerated to feel the effects of the hill.

Jason could now hear the engine of the approaching car, the deep outraged rumble of a powerful V-8. He kept his eyes on the lights, approaching down the hill with what seemed to be excessive speed. They grew bigger, slicing out of the night, as the car roared around the long curve, tires starting to shriek. Too fast, he thought. Much too fast.

The doctor realized with a start that the car was angling directly toward him. Its engine became a whining roar. The headlights pinned him, the vehicle charging at him like a wild beast.

Jason left the ground, jackknifing his body in a twisting leap behind an elm. The car slammed into the tree, caromed off, and fishtailed back onto the road, where it smashed into another car coming up the hill. Tearing loose molding from the other car, it straightened and roared off around the curve. In a moment, even the roar of the engine was gone, leaving only the sound of the breeze, singing through the leaves above.

Jason had landed heavily on his chest, a thick root knocking the wind out of him. He heard the damaged car's door creak open and running footsteps approaching. He painfully rolled onto his back, hands reflexively poised. But his eyes would barely focus. Quick steps crunched across the leaves.

A woman's voice said, "I saw that! You could have been killed! Are you all right?"

Jason looked up. He saw a long pair of legs disappearing up a light cotton dress. Looking higher, he took in the narrow waist and the breasts pressed braless against the clinging fabric. A cascade of flowing ebony hair fell around a high-cheekboned face. Even in the fading light, her looks were extraordinary.

"Fine," he replied. His rough breathing evened out. Then he flexed his limbs individually to test them before clambering to his feet beside her. The raven-haired girl was almost his height.

She was looking down the road. "Those bastards! They almost hit me head on! I ought to call the police. No," the woman said, turning to him, "you should call. You're the one they nearly ran over."

"Perhaps I will, although I don't think it even had a license plate. Listen, did you happen to see what kind of car it was?"

"I'm sorry, no. But it was a fairly large one, blue or black, I guess." She turned toward her own automobile, eyeing the shattered headlight. "What a mess!"

Jason walked over to her car, a dark green Lincoln, and inspected the damaged front. Although the left fender was crumpled and the light smashed, there was still space between the tire and the wheel well. He knelt and peered beneath the body. Nothing seemed to be leaking below the engine, and the undercarriage was intact.

"Perhaps it's not too bad," said the doctor, rising slowly, still loosening up from his fall. "Try to start it."

The girl climbed into the driver's seat and turned the key. The big engine immediately roared to life. She backed off the lawn and straightened the car. Leaving the engine running, she leaned over and lowered the passenger window facing the doctor.

"Look, I really am concerned. You might be injured. Is there any place I can take you?"

"No," he answered. "It was very good of you to stop, but I'm really fine."

"But I can't just leave you out here. Do you live nearby?"

"Well, five miles I would guess. In fact," he said, peering into the gathering dusk, "I'm not entirely certain of the way."

"Well, then. That settles it." She pushed open the passenger door for him. "I know just about everything in this area. Really, I insist." She looked up at him with a pretty pout.

Jason needed no further encouragement. He climbed in beside her.

After asking the address and swinging the car around, the girl introduced herself: "I'm Layla Kalia."

"My name is McCane. Jason McCane. New to the area, actually."

"Jason McCane? Listen, I don't mean to pry, but do you have anything to do with the Institutes?"

He looked at her quizzically. "Why yes, as a matter of fact. I'm a new Clinical Fellow."

"Oh, *Doctor* McCane. Now I know where I heard your name. My dad was talking about you."

Jason was quite amazed. "I beg your pardon, but may I ask, who is your father?"

She laughed, a bright carefree sound, the accident apparently forgotten. "My father is Paul Kalia. He's on the Selection Committee for the Center. I heard him talk about you a couple of times. You must be pretty hot stuff."

"Kalia? Oh hell, I should have recognized . . . You mean *the* Paul Kalia, as in brain development?"

"That's the one." She nodded.

Jason sat silent, thinking as the young woman drove on. Paul Kalia was certainly one of the principal living figures in brain science, a winner of the Nobel prize, possibly the most honored neuroscientist in the free world. His early experiments on the behavioral effects of social conditions were masterpieces of insight. He was the one who built large plexiglass rat communities, then demonstrated how stresses such as crowding would rapidly affect the rats' behavior, increasing the frequency of cannibalism and homosexual couplings. His work had often been taken to explain what some saw as the impending decline of Western civilization.

Jason nodded to himself. A large piece of the NIH budget went to support Dr. Kalia's enormous new Laboratory of Brain and Behavior. And, although he had always kept his laboratory closed to visitors, the entire scientific community fully expected that remarkable discoveries would come from the new facility. His standing in world science was colossal. Finally, the young doctor said, "He must be an extraordinary man."

The tall young woman laughed lightly at Jason's reference. "Oh, don't be too overwhelmed. He's just another scientist, like you. He's only human, you know."

The young doctor, among many other feelings, was quite aware of his own humanity as he sat dressed only in running shorts beside this elegant young lady. She maneuvered the heavy car expertly down the boulevard, and without hesitation picked out the entrance to his cul-de-sac, where she pulled the car over and killed the engine.

Turning toward him, she appeared thoughtful for a moment. Then she asked, "Well, how would you like to meet my dad?"

Jason smiled and replied immediately, "I'd like to very much."

"Great." She picked a slim black notebook out of her purse and flipped it open to a calendar. "Look, we're having a few people over for drinks on Saturday night. Nothing fancy. Would you like to stop by?" Her slender body was twisted toward him as she searched his face.

"Yes, I'd be delighted to," he answered.

Layla wrote out the address on a card and handed it to him. Jason took the card and began to open the car door. Before getting out, he said, "Thanks for the ride. And I look forward to Saturday."

The girl reached out and laid her palm lightly on his bare thigh. "So do I."

——■——

"Who is calling, please?" The woman's tone was clipped.

"You never the hell mind who's calling, young lady! Just rouse that bastard wherever he is and have him call me damn fast. The number is . . ."

The portly figure finished reciting the number and slammed down the receiver. He stood, huddled in the phone booth, shivering. The streets were nearly empty of cars, though each set of headlights seemed directed straight at him. He shifted anxiously this way and that, trying to place the shadow of the aluminum hinge of the door directly over his face. His features, he worried, might be recognizable even with a casual glance from a passerby. He didn't want to be seen at all.

He lurched forward, banging his head against the glass door, startled as the phone rang. "Shit! Goddamn . . ." he cursed as he reversed himself in the booth, grappling the phone off the hook and up to his ear. "Is that you?"

There was a brief silence on the other end. Then a voice came on the line—the voice of the man who had called himself Mr. Williams. "My dear Senator, may I ask whatever has possessed you to use the emergency number?"

"I'll tell you what's possessed me! Your Agency friends are trying to fuck up the whole operation, that's what!"

"Please, please, such language, and from a man of your stature . . ."

"Don't you patronize me. Just tell me why the Director has taken to running over our neuroscientists in the street."

"What?" Williams's voice became sharp. "Who . . . which one?"

"Calm down. No one was killed. At least not yet."

"But how do you know . . . ?"

The senator explained that Dr. McCane had just phoned the Bethesda police. He had been obliged to leap off the road to avoid an automobile traveling at high speed. The doctor had described the car as a large, dark sedan with no visible license plate.

"Oh, hell." Williams cursed. "Believe me, I had no idea that the Director was going to do this. I'll speak to him as soon as I can."

"Great!" The senator spat the word sarcastically. "Take your time! And meanwhile your precious Director buries a scientist it's taken us six months to find and recruit. I thought we were just going to *watch* the bastard!"

"All right!" There was a pause as Williams gathered his

thoughts. "Look, clearly the Director considers McCane a threat. As we discussed, the young doctor has taken it upon himself to try to unravel the Harkus . . . event."

"So what? What is he, a fucking Sherlock Holmes? We need him!"

"Yes, I'm well aware of that," said Williams. "Perhaps there's a way we can both get what we want out of him and eliminate him as a threat to the project." Williams took a minute to outline his plan to the senator. Then he said, "I'll speak to the Director at once. In the meantime, it is essential to find out what McCane's up to. Do I have to assign my own surveillance?"

"Hell no! I told you I'm going to assign someone from my team. We're talking about a relationship, damn it! This thing will take time to develop. You just keep the Director off my back."

Mr. Williams began to answer, then thought better of it. He closed his eyes, briefly rubbing at the mole under his eye, and shook his head. Finally, he said, "Senator, I will do what I can."

"You'd better—"

"Please," he interrupted. "I'm sure we would not want to deprive your dear wife of your conjugal attentions any longer. Good night."

"You . . ." The obese politician released a string of expletives. But the line was already dead.

■ 3 ■

Psychiatry is bullshit. Bullshit, bullshit, bullshit!" Dr. Larry Guttman regaled the assembly with his outburst, waving the remains of his sandwich in the air for emphasis. "This pitiful bastard of a science, staggering blind through a morass of useless theories,"—a speck of spittle appeared in his mustache with the last word—"it's bullshit!"

"What's going on?" Jason arrived at the cafeteria table with his tray and the others squeezed closer to make room.

"Oh, Larry's waxing poetic again," Tom Sherrington answered with a grin.

"Ah, I see." He nodded to the group from his branch who were gathered to share the lunch break: Linda, the lab supervisor; Cindy and Tony, the two Normal Volunteers; and his fellow researchers, Larry and Tom.

The last couple of days had been hectic. Jason spent the time getting used to the Clinical Center. He learned how to find lab space, how to requisition equipment and animals, even how to survive the perils of the cafeteria. He was also attending rounds on the ward to learn more about the human research. The Fellows Tom and Larry quickly learned to respect his consultations. Cindy, the young volunteer, regarded him as

26

her own discovery. The only irritant was the gargantuan Tony, who, despite Jason's efforts to reassure him, continued to harbor a black jealousy, missing no opportunity to confront the doctor with mute hints of physical harm.

As he placed his tray on the table, he couldn't help but notice Tony wrapping one of his overdeveloped arms around Cindy and casting him an acid look.

"What do you think, Dr. McCane?" Cindy asked. "Do you think psychiatry is . . . well, bullshit?"

Jason smiled. "I think psych research has always been tough to do. For one thing, we don't have animal models. Rats just don't go crazy the way humans do."

"And then there's the ethics problem," Tom put in. "We just can't get away with experiments on humans. No way."

"Human experiments, right on!" Larry grinned.

"I think you're all ignoring something." Linda, the lab supervisor, spoke up. The others looked to her with interest. Her cheeks colored briefly as she went on. "Well, I think there's something else that messes up research: These patients upset people."

Cindy began nodding. "You're telling me. I mean, I'm sleeping up on the ward, and even if I really feel sympathetic, sometimes these patients are just plain scary."

"Like, what's there to be scared of?" Tony interrupted her. The big wrestler lifted his carton of milk to his mouth, finishing it in a gulp and drawing his forearm across his mouth. "This whole thing is bullshit." He glanced sidelong at Jason as he crushed the carton in his hand.

"Tony," Linda responded, "if you think it's all bullshit, why did you volunteer for the Clinical Neuroscience branch?"

"Hey, I didn't choose this branch. I got chosen to be in a 'special experiment.'"

Tom and Larry looked at each other, wondering what experiment Tony was referring to. "What sort of experiment, Tony?" Linda asked.

"I dunno. Something to do with 'adaptation to high environmental stress.' Said I was the perfect physical specimen." The big wrestler favored Cindy with a theatrical wink.

Cindy's face took on a flustered expression. She pushed

back her chair and began to rise from the table. "I better get back to work."

"Yeah, I got stuff to do too." Tony lifted his tray and stood up rapidly, shooting his chair into a neighboring diner. "Hey, watch it, okay?" he addressed the surprised target, an Indian doctor who looked up with confusion. American social conventions never ceased to baffle him.

"Hey, you two," Tom said, stopping them. "Heard about the lecture on Monday? Dr. Kalia himself is coming!"

"Wow," the girl responded, "I read about him."

"You coming, Cindy?" Tony called back.

Tom picked up his own tray. "We better all get back up there before Big Ben starts his afternoon tour."

As the group rose from the table, Jason asked Tom, "Have you ever heard Kalia speak?"

"Jason," Tom answered, grinning at his new colleague, "Dr. Kalia is going to blow your mind."

—■—

"Well, Jason, how goes it?" Dr. Murray leaned into the doorway of the cubicle, a solicitous smile drawing up the corners of his lips, a pipe cradled in one hand. "Can you spare a minute?"

"Sure."

The chief led the way down the hall to his own office, his face set in his trademark tight smile. He pushed the door open for Jason. "You know, Jason," the older man said as he fiddled with the coffee machine, "I've been meaning to speak to you about your project."

"Yes?"

"Well," Murray said as he settled in his chair, "I was wondering . . . are there any other behaviors you'd be interested in mapping?"

Jason was a little surprised. "You mean, map behavioral genes other than those for manic depression?"

"Precisely." Murray toyed with his pipe and looked reflectively at the young doctor.

It was a question that Jason had considered often. The problem was markers. In order to focus his search for the manic-depressive genes, he had needed a clue, a marker in the genome. That clue appeared when two research groups found markers in the genome of large families with manic-depressive illness. Those genetic signals were like beacons, lighting the way to the secrets of the human chromosome. The genes for other behaviors were bound to have their own markers. But so far, no one had found them. "More easily said than done, I'm afraid." Jason shook his head. "Without a good marker . . ."

"Ah, but that's not necessarily true," Murray interjected. "Of course markers would help. However, there's another way."

The young doctor watched as the branch chief refilled his pipe. Murray took his time, gently working the tobacco down into the bowl. Finally he asked, "Dr. McCane, have you ever done any genetic intervention work?"

"You mean, genetic engineering?"

"That's right." Murray smiled. "Although that particular phrase always puts me in mind of shirt-sleeved draftsmen busily drawing up blueprints for chromosomes."

The young doctor grinned back. "Right. Out west we call them 'designer genes.' "

Murray laughed aloud, throwing back his gray head. "Designer genes! Yes! I'll remember that. . . . Well?"

Jason said he was fairly familiar with the techniques of genetic engineering and asked what Dr. Murray had in mind.

The branch chief was still smiling. "Well, up to now we've been talking about finding the genes directly. Instead, what if we looked for the proteins?"

"Find the proteins that control behavior? How do you mean?"

Murray smiled again and outlined a research plan: First, find a group of neurons important for behavior. Then analyze every protein made by those cells, and inject them into the brain, one after another, until you produce the behavior you're looking for.

"Incredible! Dr. Murray—"

The chief stopped Jason with an upheld hand. "Incredible, but possible."

Jason stared at the older scientist. "But even then, the question remains, how would you find the gene?"

"Ah, here's where we do some real genetic engineering!" Murray chuckled. He leaned back in his chair and folded his arms. "We could simply reencode the protein sequence into DNA, clone the DNA, and use the clones to probe a DNA library!"

The young doctor kept staring for a silent moment. "Find the genes by finding the proteins . . . yes," he finally agreed, "it could be done. But how could we be sure that the gene actually worked?"

Murray was still smiling. "Oh, that's the best part. You know, it would be interesting to see what behavior changes you get by inserting these genes into the genome of small mammals." He turned in his chair and looked casually out the window. "The only problem would be mapping the exact gene site. Your specialty."

Jason exhaled slowly. "Dr. Murray, I agree it's an interesting idea. But can you imagine the number of experiments this would take? We're talking about an immense project . . ."

"The Center is an immense place." Murray let the statement hang in the air. "We have the resources. All we need is the expertise. Just think, Jason,"—he leaned forward across the desk—"consider the potential: manic depression, alcoholism, schizophrenia, many forms of mental retardation. Theoretically, we could wipe them out in a generation." The branch chief leaned back in his chair, tenting his fingers. "You see, among other things, the professional rewards could become rather generous, if your work fits in with our new project." He paused for emphasis.

Jason's eyes met the older man's. He already knew Murray's authority as a scientist. He began to appreciate the branch chief's reputation as a politician. "Well, I'll certainly think about it."

"Good," Murray answered. "Do that."

—■—

Jason walked down the hall, leafing through a stack of articles that Dr. Murray had given him to copy. All of them related to finding the proteins that controlled behavior. Some of the projects were familiar to him, like the mouse experiments at UCLA, some of them were quite surprising, like the incredible monkey research of Steven Shay, but all of this material was brand new. These were original manuscripts, the latest work of the country's top scientists. Obviously, Murray was in an ideal position to watch over the field, picking and choosing the best.

"Hi, Dr. McCane!"

The orange-jacketed guard appeared directly in front of Jason as he turned the corner, blocking his way. "Oh, please, after you." Billy jumped to the side and bowed grandly. The grin that twisted the security guard's mouth had a surly edge.

Jason passed without comment. It had happened too often. He remained disconcerted by the presence of armed guards in a research hospital. He tucked the papers under his arm and continued down the corridor, away from the ripe organic smell of the laboratories.

The Neuroscience photocopy room was just a converted closet with a high-speed copier wedged into one corner. The room was empty when he arrived. He set down the pack of articles and turned on the machine.

"Excuse me, will you be using it for a while?"

He smiled as he turned to face the doorway. "Dr. Darien, I presume?"

"Oh." The young woman seemed surprised when she saw who he was. "Dr. McCane."

"Call me Jason, please." He abandoned his task for the moment, leaning back onto the workbench, facing the young primatologist from Wisconsin. "How are you doing, Jennifer?"

"Fine, thanks. And yourself?" She crossed her tanned arms over her breasts, a gesture of modesty that subverted itself as she leaned into the doorframe, her bright hair hanging over one eye, the curve of her slender hips well defined under her skirt.

"I'm fine, apart from trying to master the computer system." He smiled. "Just about when I figured I was competent at reading and writing, somebody invented the idea of computer literacy."

She laughed. "Oh, I think you'll get used to computing

pretty fast. Just make sure you keep a healthy balance between input and output."

"What do you mean?"

Her smile broadened, a grin that raised the freckles on her suntanned cheeks. "Well, computers are selfish. If you let them do it, they'll take up all your time inputting data, and they'll never really put out for you." She stopped, then began to blush.

"I see."

"So"—Jennifer crossed her arms more tightly—"have you decided what project you'll be working on yet?"

Jason answered that he had come to NIH with one project in mind, but it looked as if his branch chief had other ideas. He shrugged toward the articles on the workbench. "How about you? What's life like in the Clinical Psychobiology branch?"

Jennifer's eyes wandered toward the stack of articles on the workbench. "Oh, I guess things are a bit complicated for me as well."

"Really?"

"Yes." She paused. "It looks like my branch chief wants me to change my project too. . . . So, what do you think your new project will be like?"

Again Jason saw her eyes angling toward his papers. He quickly turned, lifting the pack of articles off the bench, and extended it toward her. "Can't tell exactly, but here's what my homework looks like."

Her face revealed a flash of surprise, as if she didn't expect him to be so candid. "Thanks." She accepted the packet and began flipping through the articles, reading each title in turn. "And you think computers are tough! This stuff is totally out of my . . ." Her smile froze in place. For a moment she was silent, then she finished her statement, "league." She was looking at the article by Steven Shay. She flipped to the next paper in the pack, then worked her way mechanically through the rest of them. Her smile remained, fixed and graceful, as she returned the articles to Jason.

"Find anything of particular interest?"

"Not especially," she said, shrugging. "Oh, well, come to think of it . . . ah, may I ask how you got hold of this article by Steven Shay?" Her voice was unnaturally steady, almost as if she were trying to restrain her question.

"My branch chief," Jason answered. "Would you like a copy? I'll do it right now." He turned back to the workbench and rummaged in the box of supplies for the staple remover. As he worked, he asked Jennifer if she was familiar with Dr. Shay's research.

"Dr. Shay . . . worked at the Wisconsin Primate Center."

"That's right, the lab you came from!" Jason recalled. "You know, I heard Dr. Shay speak at the Chicago neuroscience meetings last month, but I don't think he announced this research project. It must be very new."

"You were at the Chicago meetings?"

Jason turned to face her, struck by her tone of voice. She was staring at him with incredible intensity. He didn't flatter himself. It was not a merely social appraisal. He held the sheets on the glass with his fingers and copied them one at a time. "Yes," he replied, "I was at the meetings. Did you know Dr. Shay?"

Her chest lifted with a breath, "Yes, I knew him. But I didn't know . . . I haven't seen this article."

"I see." He pulled the copies from the tray and presented them to Jennifer. "With my compliments."

"You're sure it's all right?"

"Dr. Murray will probably shoot me for distributing unpublished data. Go ahead."

She accepted the sheets and immediately folded them into her arms, pinning them against her chest. "I promise I won't tell a soul."

"Didn't you plan to use the machine? I'll be done in—"

"No." She stopped herself, one long leg already crossing the threshold of the room. "That's all right. I'll come by later. Good to see you again, Dr. McCane."

"Jason."

"Jason." She turned her head quickly to give him a smile. Then her hair swung in a golden wave, following her head around the corner. Jason kept his eyes on the doorway. Like a thing seen in bright light, an afterimage of the young woman at the open door lingered in his mind's eye.

———■———

Jennifer entered her cubicle-office, clicked on the light, and locked the door behind her. She set the photocopied article on the desk beside her computer terminal. Pulling the desk drawer open, she extracted a pair of scissors. Then she sat down and peered carefully at the first page of the article. Her eyes ignored the print. Instead, she systematically scanned the edges of the paper. Not satisfied, she examined the second page. Again she looked at the dark borders of the page, the areas where the photocopy paper extended beyond the size of the original. She turned to the third page.

After a moment, she lifted the scissors and quickly cut out a small square of the mottled hazy border. She opened the drawer again and placed the scissors and the copied article inside. Then she laid the square of paper on the desk.

She flipped up the power switch of her computer. The screen awoke in its odd green light. She pulled the keyboard closer and began to type quickly. A menu of options appeared on the screen. Using her cursor, she made her choice, rapidly working her way through three progressively narrower menus until she arrived at the list she wanted.

"Employee Records, Clinical Fellows" lit up in the center of the screen.

"McCane, Jason, M.D.," she typed.

"Classified. Enter personal code" appeared below the name.

"Trial entry," Jennifer typed. "000,000."

The screen blanked. "Classified. Enter personal code" appeared again.

She typed, "Trial entry, 000,001." Then, below it, a series of additional words. "Routine H: Query: Suc Ordinal Trial: Sort: Query, Prompt, Query. Return sequence: Limit 999,999. Record: Save Code." She drew her hands back from the keyboard. Her eyes appraised the vertical list of commands. Then they closed.

For a minute, she sat still, silent, resting her delicate fingers on the edge of the desk. Her lips were pressed in a line. A pulse was visible where her bright hair crossed her temple. She opened her eyes. She pressed the key marked Execute.

The screen blanked. Then Jason's name reappeared, followed by the six digits 000,001. The word *Classified* appeared below the name, but immediately flashed off as the number changed to 000,002. Again and again, the display alternated between numbers and words, and with each successive trial, with gathering speed, the number beside the name increased. 000,003, 000,004, . . .

She twisted a knob, dimming the display on the screen until it appeared to be off, while the program continued, testing one number after another, looking for Jason's private code.

The young woman swiveled away from the terminal and rose from the chair. She lifted the square of mottled paper off the desk and held it close to her eyes. She tilted it to catch the best of the light. Clearly reproduced in the center of the square was a complex of tiny lines, whorling around one another, climbing toward a minuscule peak. It was a perfect photocopied image of a fingerprint.

Jennifer tucked Jason's fingerprint in the breast pocket of her blouse and left the room.

■ 4 ■

In the depths of the Clinical Center, a cage door opened. Two black-suited figures blocked the light as they leaned into the cage, their thick hands reaching. To the big chimpanzee that cowered in the corner of the cage, it seemed as if they were about to attack.

It tried to leap away, but the men grabbed its legs and jerked it out of the cage. The ape looked up in terror to see a third figure, dressed in a long white lab coat, towering above it.

The chimp twisted and turned, screeching at all of them, its frantic eyes flashing everywhere. It kicked ferociously at the two men, who were trying to straighten one of its legs. It almost broke free, but one of the men caught its ankle, slamming the hapless animal to the concrete. The ape felt a sharp jab in its thigh.

Then it went limp.

The chimpanzee began to awaken on the floor of a speeding van. It opened its eyes but could only make out a dark uneven blur, interrupted at times by the quick flash of a streetlamp as the van made its way through the night. Awareness came and went while the drug slowly cleared from its brain. The vehicle turned, and the ape slid into the corner like a sack. Then it was jostled and shaken about as the van careened down a rugged road. It tried but could not move its limbs to protect itself from the beating of the metal floor against its limp body. It whimpered weakly on the floor. Finally, it slid forward as the vehicle came to a halt.

It felt itself being lifted by two pairs of hands. It heard their words and sensed the hostility in them. For a short time, it felt the coolness of the summer's night. Then it was warm again.

A pain shot through its ribs as it was dropped onto a cold, flat surface. There came a hum, and it sensed a downward movement. Then its limbs were jerked up as it was lifted once more and carried, bumping from side to side against the men's legs. The next time they set it down, it felt a strange uneven surface at its back. Its eyelids slowly parted. It saw only blackness.

Rope webbing wrapped around the ape's body and it felt itself being hoisted rapidly into the air. It gave out a feeble screech. It vaguely recognized the feeling, from an earlier time, of being placed in a net and lifted by a crane. There was a pause as it hung suspended in space.

A click sounded. The net moved sideways. Suddenly the ape sensed a rush of hot moist air. And the smell.

As the net was lowered, the ape's strength gradually returned. It squirmed fitfully in the webbing, clawing ineffectually at the knotted rope. When its back touched the ground, its eyes went wide. It immediately rolled over and struggled to all fours. The net was quickly pulled from beneath the ape, slamming it onto its back as the webbing rose out of sight. It turned over once more. It sniffed at the air, frightened and amazed. Even through the darkness of the night, the things it saw made its heart race in its barrel chest.

For a minute, the animal sat back on its haunches, swiveling its head about as if it could not believe where it was. For all of the mysterious and terrifying things that had happened to it, nothing in its life had prepared it for this sudden impossible change. It could hardly believe its eyes. But it could not question the smell. The smell was like no other.

A sudden tingling began in its head, a feeling that was deep and inescapable. It passed a hand up to its head and, when its fingers encountered the strange shape there, it remembered. It recalled the terror and confusion as it awoke before and first felt it. As quickly as the tingling arrived, though, it was gone, and the big chimpanzee felt an inexplicable sleepiness come over it. A calm.

A night bird called softly from a nearby tree.

The ape looked up. At the beck of some long-abandoned instinct, it rose and knuckle-walked to the moss-grown trunk of the massive tree. Shakily, it climbed. In a moment, it pulled its lethargic body into the crotch of two large branches and curled into itself. The bird called again and flew off. The ape's head came to rest on its shoulder. For several baffled minutes, it surveyed the remarkable scene before it. Then it slowly closed its eyes. Eventually, it fell asleep, comforted by that smell, strangely familiar, warm and dank and alive: the unmistakable smell of the jungle.

———■———

The bus let Jason off outside the cross-country automobile delivery office. He showed his identification and signed a form. In a moment, there came a screech and a roar as a battered gray vehicle, trimmed with a red veneer of rust, careened around the corner and pulled up before the office.

"Jesus, mister!" the attendant exclaimed as he leapt out of the car, "what you got in there?" He jerked his head toward the hood.

"Just a few modifications," Jason responded with a smile. He accepted the key and climbed into his turbocharged Land Rover.

Jason hadn't seen Washington in twenty years. He had vivid childhood memories of mountainous buildings bordering the broad green sweep of the Mall. As he drove across the Roosevelt bridge, he wondered if the city would retain the grandeur of those memories.

Jason's memories didn't disappoint him; the view down Jefferson Drive was just as compelling as he remembered. Huge granite porticoes, marble facades, and the crenulated towers of the Smithsonian still dominated the landscape with their massive presence. Early gaps in the parade of buildings had now been filled by more modern structures: the History and Technology Museum, the Hirshhorn gallery, and the Air and Space Museum. Crowds of spring visitors promenaded down the gravel paths in a bustling collage of colors, lending the scene an almost carnival air. He decided to begin his Saturday tour with some art.

The young doctor found a parking spot, then walked back to the National Gallery. Pope's neoclassical masterwork was as perfect as he remembered it, its scale somehow undiminished by his own transition from child to adult. He climbed the stairs and entered, squeezing through the crowd. His eyes had to adjust to the darkness as he made his way to the cool circle of the central rotunda. Thick columns of green-black marble, yards around, ringed the rococo fountain and stretched up to the coffered vault. He bent to read the plaque in the center of the fountain.

A whisper suddenly came from behind, "Death comes gently at the hands of the Master."

Jason began to whirl. "Hai!" He felt a hand jab into his left kidney. He rolled away from it, lowering his body and sweeping his heel around until it encountered an ankle.

The big man behind him instantly leapt over the sweeping foot and spun around to face the doctor, fists raised. He was grinning.

"Red!" Jason smiled, rising from his crouch and clasping the man's outstretched hand. "Where the hell did you come from?"

The big man chuckled lightly and laid a thick arm across Jason's shoulders, steering him out of the rotunda where a few startled visitors were staring at the unlikely greeting. "Ah, my dear Jason, if only you knew; your friends are keeping an eye on you."

Jason laughed. "With friends like this . . . Well I'll be goddamned! What's it been, four years? So how's the old Red Menace?"

Jason used the nickname of the man, Jim Gradov, perhaps Jason's oldest friend in the United States. A mammoth Slav

with flaming crimson hair and a full red beard, Jim had
inevitably come to be called "Red." The "Menace" part of
his nickname was a later addition: Red had been a notorious
middle-linebacker for Yale, whose "Red Menace" reputation
made him a source of terror for an entire class of Ivy League
quarterbacks.

"I'm fine, just fine. And you, Doctor? Still in fighting shape?"

He and Jason had met at Oxford when Jason was a student
and Red was spending a semester abroad. Neither was likely
to forget the meeting: their first day at the Kempo class,
matched to spar by the unwitting instructor. The violence of
that conflict had startled the gym into silence. "Oh, I'm in
passable shape, I guess," Jason answered. "Not much time to
work out. How about you?"

"You'll see." Red let the answer hang. Then he laughed.
"So, you're coming out here to work for the big uncle? NIH
fellowship, is it?"

"And how the hell did you find that out, may I ask?"

"Oh, we have our ways, young master Jason," Red replied
with a grin. "As you may recall, I work for Uncle Sam myself."

"You're still with the NSA? I wasn't even sure you'd still
be in Washington." Jason remembered how Red had put his
Slavik language experience to work in a job with the National
Security Agency, translating coded radio signals intercepted
from Eastern Europe.

"Well, yes and no. We'd better talk about that later. But
I came here to see some art, and I want to do this place right!
Want to show me around? You're the only artiste I could ever
stand."

Jason laughed and shook his head. "Thanks, but I doubt I
have anything terribly clever to say."

"That's okay. Lead on, McCane!"

Jason returned his grin and led the way toward the upstairs
galleries.

They toured the museum with the high spirits of two boys
on a hike, exploring the maze of galleries as they talked and
bantered about old times. On occasion, at Red's urging, Jason
reluctantly offered comments on the art, based on his own
experiments in the arts at a younger age. But mostly they just

looked. The paintings were like an intoxicant, transporting Jason back to that very early love. And they let him see a side of his friend that he never had before: For all of Red's muscle-bound roughness, he was clearly enthralled by the art.

Finally they entered the display of the Impressionists. They found themselves alone in a sudden empty calm before a large blue Monet. "Great." Red spoke the word quietly. For a minute the two sat down, staring at the canvas as if swept into the blue depths of the scene.

Then the big man cleared his throat. "So, my friend," Red spoke casually, "I hear there's some heavy stuff went down at that lab of yours in Stanford."

"You mean, what happened to Dr. Harkus?"

"Sure. I read the papers."

The doctor nodded. Of course. The Nobel laureate's death had certainly made news across the country. "I suppose 'heavy stuff' describes it well. As you know, someone murdered Dr. Harkus. Apparently whoever did it also stole a load of data from the lab."

Red looked carefully at his friend. "You have any idea why?"

Jason shook his head. "I don't know, Red . . ." There was a pause in his words, a point of decision. Red ought to know; that was the place of a friend. "But I'll tell you something: I intend to figure it out."

The big man watched Jason carefully. "And how will you do that, may I ask?"

Jason told Red about the papers found by Harkus's body, and the list of brain-active chemicals, ending with the mysterious comment, "Check with PPP!" He told Red how he was studying those papers each night at his apartment, looking for a clue. He was sure that the papers, or the projects going on in the lab, had something to do with the murder.

"You say data were stolen?" Red asked. "What kind of data?"

"Raw data, for the most part," Jason said with a shrug.

"You mean"—Red seemed to be concentrating,—"like chromatographs? Printouts from emission counters?"

"Sure, that kind of thing." Jason suddenly looked at the

big man. "Say, Red, since when did you get so clever about neuroscience?"

"Goes with the territory." Red winked.

Jason regarded his friend. "By any chance, does this have something to do with that cryptic answer you gave me about your job? What's the story? Are you still working for the NSA satellite spies, keeping America safe from—"

"God, they're gorgeous, aren't they?" Red interrupted. The big man was smiling as he gazed past Jason's shoulder.

The young doctor turned. Following Red's gaze, he found himself looking at two attractive young women who stood just across the hall, engrossed in a painting by Gauguin.

He realized with a start that he knew them: the volunteer Cindy and the primatologist Jennifer Darien.

Red was shaking his head as he watched the women. "Jason, why don't I ever meet women like that?"

"Okay, Red." Jason faced his friend sternly. "Which one are you referring to, or has your fervid fancy turned to bigamy?"

"Hey, man, unlike you, I know my limits. You remember my tastes—that dark-haired nymph, of course!"

Jason simply said, "Her name is Cindy."

Red turned slowly to face Jason, who was nonchalantly admiring the ceiling. He put his heavy hands on Jason's shoulders and said evenly, "If this is a joke, you'll be swimming in the Reflecting Pool."

Jason couldn't restrain a grin. "You want an introduction?"

"You kidding? Come on!" The big man grabbed Jason's arm, pulled him up from the chair, and began to drag him toward the women. "Wait," Red said halting. "I've got to use my secret weapon: you."

"What?"

"We've got to show off our 'cultcha'! Give them a treat."

"Red . . ."

But Red had already plowed across the hall to stand behind the young ladies, turning to Jason as he arrived and addressing him in a stage whisper, "Well, Doctor, so is this another example of Post-Impressionism?"

Jason grinned and played along. In his best Oxford don,

he intoned, "Technically speaking, yes. But at this point in his career, Gauguin was probably still torn between the Impressionist devices of his friend Pissarro and the revisionist theories of the Pont Aven school."

The women half turned at the sound of his voice, then broke into smiles when they saw that the lecturer was Jason. Cindy aimed her thumb at the men and said, "I didn't know they let motorcycle gangs in here."

Jennifer whispered back, "Maybe they're lost."

At the same time, however, a large tour group of middle-aged ladies had entered the room. An earnest matron in tortoise-shell bifocals said, "Oh please, sir, would you mind awfully if we listened?"

Red and the girls went to the verge of hysterics. Jennifer gushed, "Yes, yes, sir. Please go on."

Jason brought a hand to his forehead in a parody of serious thought, actually trying to hide his smile. He cleared his throat, then carried on with high drama, "Well, even after his voyage to Martinique, Gauguin did not fully commit himself to tropical themes and unmixed colors." He stepped over to another canvas, the strikingly sensual *Fatata te Midi*, with its trio of golden bodies, one female removing her sarong. "It probably wasn't until the first trip to Tahiti that he made a complete break with his Impressionist training."

Jennifer raised her hand like an eager schoolgirl. "Well, what exactly did he do with the natives of Tahiti? I mean,"— she paused in mock embarrassment—"what about all these shocking pictures of naked women? Did he . . . well, you know . . . ?"

Jason stared at her for a moment. Then he moved closer and put an arm around her shoulder. "Well," he said, walking her toward the door, "I'm going to tell you a true story about Gauguin and the girl undressing in this painting. . . ."

Red offered his arm to Cindy and the four of them moved away from the tour group, all of whom were straining to hear, some gasping.

Once out in the corridor, the four burst out in laughter as Jason led them rushing to the museum exit. Out on the marble steps, the doctor collared Red in a stranglehold. "How could you do that to me!"

"Wait," Red gasped, his eyes tearing from hilarity. He pointed to Jennifer. "She's your tormenter. I'm just an innocent bystander!"

"Innocent, my ass!" Jason released him.

They all caught their breath a moment and then, remembering the looks of the tour group, convulsed again with laughter. Finally, Jason managed to introduce Red to the girls. "This big character is my friend, Jim Gradov. Call him Red. Red, this is Dr. Darien—"

"Jennifer, please."

"And Cindy."

"Hi." Red extended his hand and shook with both of them, holding onto Cindy's hand a little longer than to Jennifer's. "Glad to meet you. Can I possibly convince you young ladies to join us for lemonade?" He grinned and didn't even wait for an answer. He was already down the steps, heading for one of the umbrella-shaded street carts. Jennifer and Cindy exchanged a smile. In a moment, the big man was waving them down the stairs, four tall white cups balanced in one hand. "Come and get it!"

The three of them moved down the steps to join him, then the group strolled together out onto the Mall. They found a shady spot in the clipped grass and Red passed out the drinks.

"I didn't know you were such a scholar," said Jennifer, shaking her hair back from her tanned face and looking at Jason. The young doctor was struck again by the beauty of her face, the fair skin, the tiny freckles across the bridge of her nose. She was wearing a bright yellow blouse tucked into faded blue jeans that showed her figure to good advantage. Despite her interest, Jason still sensed a willful reserve, a wariness.

"Oh, don't be fooled," he said. "I really just make it up as I go along. Red's the real expert."

Red guffawed. "Don't believe him for a minute!" He started to punch Jason's shoulder.

The doctor unconsciously dodged the blow, twisting sideways. It occurred to him that he had seen a lot of Jennifer lately. First the photocopy room, now the museum. It almost seemed like more than coincidence. "By the way," he asked the girls, "how did you two happen to end up here?"

"Well, I . . ."

"She was . . ."

The girls laughed as they both answered at once. Jennifer stretched her palm toward Cindy, who explained that they'd met at NIH and decided to explore the Mall together. "Jennifer's been teaching me about apes at the Smithsonian. I'm taking a class in animal behavior at the Center and—"

"Say no more!" Red interrupted. "I happen to be totally fascinated by the field." He ignored Jason's sidelong glance. "In fact," he went on, smiling, "I would be honored if you two would share your insights with us . . . say over dinner at a French restaurant?"

Jason paused a moment, then interrupted. "Damn the luck. I'm afraid it will have to be the three of you. I have a . . . there's something I have to do tonight."

Jennifer's eyes turned to him. She looked at him with what seemed to be a strange mix of curiosity and something else. Not exactly anger. More like suspicion. Jason noted the look with surprise.

Red grinned, undismayed. "We'll miss you, my friend."

"Uh," Cindy spoke hesitantly, "I hate to be a party pooper, but Tony wants to go someplace, I think."

Red turned toward her with a wounded look. "Tony?" he asked quietly.

"Yeah, he's my . . . my friend." She didn't look any happier than Red.

A pall came over the group, until Red spoke bravely, "Well, maybe next week!"

"Sure, maybe!" Cindy smiled. "Hey,"—she checked her watch—"I'm really sorry, but I have to get to my class at the Center."

"Can't be late." Red offered his hands to Cindy, and pulled her up to her feet. Slowly, she withdrew her hands from his.

Jason and Jennifer also stood. They faced each other, both crossing their arms. Jason said, "I imagine I'll see you at the Center."

"Perhaps." She turned to Cindy. "All set?"

Cindy was still looking at Red. "I guess. 'Bye." She shrugged at him and followed Jennifer, who was already setting a brisk pace down the sidewalk.

Red sighed as he watched them round the corner of the museum. The young women disappeared from view.

"Sorry," said Jason.

Red shook his head, then managed a half grin. "Easy come, easy go." He turned to face his friend. "Well, what say I take out this romantic tragedy on you? Want to spar?"

"Sure. I'm getting slow without a partner."

"Jason, my friend, you have no idea what you're in for. You don't have a chance!" Red arranged to meet him the next day and gave him directions to his athletic club. He slapped him on the shoulder. Then they parted, Jason walking south.

Red watched the lanky doctor move down the Mall. As he watched, the heavy muscles across Red's back tightened unconsciously. The big man's eyes narrowed, looking at Jason, as he repeated to himself in just a whisper: "Not a chance."

◾ 5 ◾

J ason pulled into the leafy debris at the road's edge and confirmed the address. The lit number on the gate was clear. He had come to the right place. Somehow, the road up to the Potomac neighborhood seemed steeper than he remembered from his run, the hedges higher, the homes larger. The night that Layla had invited him seemed part of some distant past. Certainly he had not expected this.

Looking across the grounds from the entrance to the drive, he surveyed the stately Federal-style mansion. It was distanced from its neighbors by sweeping expanses of trimmed lawn. Its two-story windows were brightly lit from within, casting the shadows of its four perfect white columns out to the grounds. It was a massive jewel, set on a rise of hill, silhouetted by the sunset. Mercedeses and Cadillacs clogged the curving drive where a few chauffers smoked, leaning against the long black limousines.

"Nothing fancy," Layla had said.

Dressing for the evening, he'd picked a standard blue oxford-cloth shirt and, respectful of the famed scientist, his navy blazer. He had decided against a tie.

The doctor drove up to the entrance and turned his rusty

Land Rover over to a baffled valet. With quick steps, he moved across the terrazzo court, up the granite stairs to the church-wide double doors. The waiting doorman examined him with poorly concealed disdain and asked his name.

"Dr. McCane. I was invited by Miss Kalia."

The man eyed him doubtfully. He instructed Jason to wait a moment and disappeared through the doors. Jason could hear a soft hum of voices through the wood, an occasional clink of glasses, muffled strains of Vivaldi.

"Dr. McCane!" The door opened wide, and he found himself facing a smiling Layla. She stretched out her bare arms in greeting. The girl was dressed in a floor-length gown of pure white, which clung close to her long body, except where the side was slit along her leg.

"Good evening, Miss Kalia." Jason stepped in to kiss her cheek. Then he offered his arm, and the pair moved past the scowling doorman into the house.

The foyer was palatial, decorated in an unrestrained Empire style, highlighted by massive statuary. A string quartet was busy in one corner. Waitresses in short lace aprons circulated with canapes, waiters offered flutes of champagne, and a chic crowd gathered under a row of chandeliers that lit the main hall. The men all wore dinner jackets.

"Perhaps I misunderstood the protocol of the evening," Jason said, fingering his blazer.

"Oh, never mind that," Layla said, obviously amused. "You look just gorgeous. Come on, you're missing the show!" Slipping her arm back into his, she promenaded with him down to the end of the hall where it opened on a huge room.

In contrast with the hall, the room was decorated in a more tempered French Provincial. Polished antiques gleamed all around, and one wall was dominated by a fieldstone fireplace as tall as a man.

Most of the guests were here, seated or standing in a circle around a large open-field Aubusson carpet. Jason recognized his chief, Dr. Murray, as well as the president of the NIH, and an array of prominent American political figures, half-remembered from newspaper photographs.

"What's going on?" Jason whispered.

"Watch!" the girl answered, squeezing his arm. "We're playing a game!"

"*D.*" The sound of a deep male voice cut through the murmurs. Attention was obviously focused on the man who had spoken, a tall patrician figure with pure white hair, enthroned in a wing-back chair. His eyes seemed to crackle with brilliance. Jason identified him instantly: Dr. Paul Kalia.

"You are, of course, the king of Persia," a man had spoken up, clearly directing his remark to Dr. Kalia.

"No, Jim." The elderly scientist smiled. "Nor did I have the honor of losing at Marathon, as Darius did. That wasn't my century. But thank you for getting us started."

"Then perhaps you are a statesman," an Indian spoke in crisp British tones, "a fitting career for the first earl of Beaconsfield."

"Beaconsfield?" Dr. Kalia responded. There was a tension in the room as Kalia's brow gathered in a collection of wrinkles. "Beaconsfield?" the host repeated.

Jason noted that Layla's eyes were riveted on her father. She was biting her lower lip.

"Well, Ambassador Subramanian," Kalia said at last, "I wish I had that gentleman's diplomatic skills. It would certainly make securing congressional funding an easier affair." There were several laughs. "In truth, however, I am not Mr. Disraeli."

Again, exclamations and grins were exchanged in the room. Layla felt for Jason's hand, and again they moved forward. The two were now standing fully in the room. Jason was not oblivious to the frank stares he drew in his casual dress.

"If you are not a warrior nor a statesman, then perhaps you are an artist?" a woman in a black velvet gown cautiously put in, drawing the eyes of the group. "Did you ever undertake commissions for the duke of Milan?"

"Yes," the scientist responded.

Immediately the room broke into boisterous discussion, with some clapping, but began to quiet again quickly. Dr. Kalia had lifted his hand. "That is, yes, I am an artist. But no, I am not da Vinci. His century preceded mine. Thank you, Mrs. Peabody. And I should also say thank you, by the way, for your generous gift to the laboratory." He bowed formally to the dowager, who returned the bow as polite applause swelled briefly.

Dr. Kalia's sharp eyes moved over his audience, grinning at each of his guests in turn, searching for any takers.

Abruptly, he stopped when he saw his daughter, who was still holding Jason's arm. He took in Jason's bearded face and longish hair, his rugged look and his casual clothing. The crowd was beginning to follow his gaze.

He spoke: "Why, Layla! Have you brought a surprise for us?"

The room fell silent, and all eyes turned to the young pair.

"Hi, Dad. You remember I invited Dr. McCane, don't you?" She was clearly entertained by the scene, and Jason wondered briefly if she had engineered it. "Dr. Jason McCane," she introduced them, "Dr. Paul Kalia."

Jason nodded to the man.

"Ah, yes. The young Dr. McCane." Kalia's deep voice filled the room like a gust. He paused and then spoke with care, staring directly into Jason's gray eyes, "Well, perhaps you should explain to Dr. McCane the rules of this game."

The double meaning took a moment to register. Then it was lost on no one. A few stifled chuckles began to rise from the crowd.

Jason's face burned. He briefly returned the scientist's gaze, then he bowed and turned, lifting his arm to guide Layla back through the crowd. They could hear the guests renewing the game as they passed out into the hall.

Jason stepped with Layla into an isolated corner.

She was grinning. "You have to admit it's pretty funny." The girl put both her hands onto his arm and smiled up at him.

"I suppose there's that element," he agreed. "Okay, Miss Kalia, teach me the rules of your father's game."

The word game was a variation on Botticelli. One player would take the identity of a famous historical figure, revealing to the others only his last initial, in this case *D*. The other players had to guess the name. They would describe possible characters, and the first player had to correctly identify the figures that were described or he would lose. It was a classic battle of wits.

"So, you can win either by stumping Dad, which is impossible, or by guessing the right name. Got it?"

"I think so." Jason took her by the hand and turned back into the room, making his way quietly through the guests to the periphery of the circle.

A man was asking, "Are you sometimes regarded as the inventor of etching?"

"No," Kalia said again, relishing the word. "Good guess, Your Honor, but I am not Albrecht Dürer."

Jason silently raised his hand at his side. Kalia glanced about the room but passed over him. He nodded instead to the president of the National Science Foundation, who sat sucking a pipe in an armchair, a young Oriental girl on his knee.

"An artist." The man puffed reflectively for a moment. "I suppose that safely eliminates Duchamp, unless you imagine that Dada is art." The room quickly burst into laughter. Then the science policy maker went on. "Instead, you must be the noted French satirist of the Second Empire."

"Good!" Kalia nodded vigorously. "Very good, Fred. I must agree with your taste. However, as much as I admire him, I am not Daumier."

Again the room was filled with groans and restive exclamations. Again the host swept his gaze around the room. Jason raised his hand higher. He was the only one. Kalia at first seemed not to see. Then he looked at him with an expression that could have been satisfaction. "Yes, Dr. McCane?"

The gray-eyed doctor spoke softly, looking directly at his host. The room quieted as he spoke: " 'It is evident that nature cares very little whether man has a mind or not. The real man is the savage; he is in accord with nature as she is. As soon as man sharpens his intelligence, increases his ideas and the way of expressing them, and acquires need, nature runs counter to him in everything.' " Jason paused. "Did you say that?"

No one moved. In the hushed room, only the distant sound of the quartet was heard, filtering in from the hall. Kalia stared at his young guest with a look that startled Jason, a

terrible, burning, passionate gaze. Suddenly, the features softened. "Yes." Kalia spoke with an air of graceful acquiescence.
"I am Eugène Delacroix."

For a moment more the room was silent. Then the old
scientist began to smile. "Well done, son."

The room erupted with applause. His back was pounded
with congratulations. Layla lifted on her toes and kissed him.
Several men strode purposefully across the salon, thrusting
out their hands to shake his. "Excellent!" "Good show, old
boy!" He shook each hand in turn, not unaware of Layla's
leg pressed against his own. "First time I've seen it!" "What
was your name again?" He accepted the congratulations, the
back pounding, and the salutations silently, keeping his gaze
above the crowd on the white-haired figure, trying to understand. Kalia looked proud.

———■———

"So, you have come to share the wisdom of the west with
your struggling eastern colleagues," smiled Dr. Kalia as he
joined Jason and his branch chief in the main hall.

"Well, I'd hardly say that," Jason said. "It's rather the other
way around, I believe."

"Nonsense. We need the input of young lions like yourself."
He grinned as he drew the young scientist and the branch
chief toward a quieter corner. "Benjamin here tells me that
you may be interested in joining our genetics program."

"Our program?" Jason asked. "Dr. Kalia, I wasn't aware
that your laboratory was involved."

"Why yes. In a way, we're at the center of the project . . .
as you could be." The old man's benign, reflective eyes turned
cold.

Jason was rather puzzled. "Actually, I'm not entirely sure
what I'll concentrate on yet. I need a little time to get my
priorities straight."

"Of course you do." Kalia reached to squeeze the young
man's thick shoulder muscle. "I just want you to know that
my daughter and I would be most grateful for your help."

"Your daughter? Layla is also involved?"

"But, of course! Didn't Ben tell you? Her rice research is
absolutely paramount. Layla!" He saw her passing and raised

his hand in a signal. "Layla," Kalia said as the young woman joined them, "we were just discussing your research. Jason, didn't you know my daughter was a botanist?"

"She didn't mention it," he said.

"Layla is doing work that will lead to a historic event: the final end of hunger."

Jason regarded Layla with interest. "And how will this come about?"

The young woman shrugged. "Rice."

"Rice?"

"Rice," her father confirmed. "Tell him."

"Most people don't realize that rice makes up more than half the diet of about two billion people on earth," Layla began.

Jason whistled softly. "Two billion . . . incredible."

Layla nodded. "But what's really incredible is the difference in rice yield in different places. In most of the third world, farmers manage to grow only half a ton per acre, but there are a few places where they're getting as much as ten!"

Jason was watching her closely. Her passion for her research had caught him by surprise. "What accounts for the differences?"

"The biggest factor," Layla replied, folding her hands before her and looking directly up at the young doctor, "is the genetic type."

Murray and Kalia had also turned to regard him. He had the definite impression they were awaiting his response.

"I see," he said. "Genetic engineering."

"Precisely!" Dr. Kalia exclaimed.

Jason had to smile at Layla. "And, may I ask, what is your project . . . in particular?"

"Oh." Her eyes flashed to her father. He nodded, and she went on. "Well, my current work is inducing genetic mutations. What I'd really like to do is to map all the genes for the highest yield and recombine them into a totally new rice genome."

Dr. Kalia cleared his throat. "That is where you could help."

"Oh?" Jason turned to his host. "How could I?"

Kalia quietly said, "The automated gene sequencer."

"But, Dr. Kalia," Jason replied, "for one thing the auto-mated gene sequencer is highly experimental." He saw Layla nodding, unperturbed. He went on. "For another thing, I frankly don't know a thing about plant genetics."

Kalia had lifted his hand. "Jason, frankly, neither do I. But Layla does. Perhaps you could chat with her about it some-time?"

"Yes," Layla added. "At least we could go over the pos-sibilities?" Her mouth formed into a hopeful, questioning grin that was impossible to resist.

The young doctor smiled.

"Good!" Kalia exclaimed. "Jason, it's good to have you aboard. It's a particular pleasure for me"—he paused—"since I once worked with your father."

Jason was astonished. "I had no idea! When was that, may I ask? Forgive me, I have no memory of it."

Kalia chuckled lightly. "Oh, I imagine you were hardly into long pants at the time. Your father and I were cochairmen at the Paris conference!"

Jason thought back. The Paris conference. In the mid-fifties, he knew his father had chaired an important meeting in Paris. Jason's father had been a renowned anthropologist, and the Paris Conference on Human Evolution was thought to be an almost historic event in his field. It made sense—that was the common ground for the research done by Kalia and by his father: the evolution of man.

"So," spoke Kalia, "the torch is passed down. I must say, Jason, that the world of science suffered a mighty blow when your parents were . . ." Seeing the young doctor's expression, Kalia didn't go on. "I'm sorry."

At the reminder of the death of his parents, Jason's face tightened. The memory stabbed into him: His family had been living at an anthropological dig in the jungle of Java. When they came down to Djakarta to resupply, they were caught in the anti-Western riots. His parents had been beaten to death before his eyes. He was barely fifteen at the time. It was a moment before he quietly responded. "It's all right. Thank you."

The old man stepped toward Jason, reaching for his hand.

"Your father was . . . an extraordinary man. It is an honor to meet the young McCane at last." Kalia locked his eyes on the young doctor's. "Consider our research program, Jason. We truly need your help."

Jason paused. "May I have some time to think about it?"

"Of course!" Kalia squeezed the young man's hands in his. He seemed to hesitate. Then he said, "In fact, before you come to any decision, why don't you come out to see my laboratory?"

The offer came as a surprise. Jason knew how extraordinarily protective both Kalia and the Institutes were of his work. Few, even among the senior scientists, had actually seen the new Laboratory of Brain and Behavior. It was discussed with a kind of hushed reverence.

Jason accepted the offer with thanks. Then an idea occurred to him. He asked if it would be all right to bring along one of the other new Fellows.

Murray and Kalia exchanged a look. The Nobel laureate answered, "Why . . . certainly. No problem at all. Of course, I'm speaking at the Center on Monday. Tuesday morning then?"

"My pleasure, sir."

Kalia bowed slightly and offered his arm to Layla. As the two of them moved off, she turned back to give Jason a secret smile.

———■———

The evening was an enlightening one. As Jason circulated through the group meeting the heads of the American science establishment, the young doctor realized that the event was more than social. The power seekers swam into pools of talk with the power brokers and their conversations turned into delicate jousts. Offers, counteroffers, smiling debates, handshakes that meant something other than friendship. He had seen social politics before. He had never seen anything like this. He felt as if he were watching America's secret government at work.

Finally, Jason retreated to explore the library, a calm spot in the center of the storm.

He was examining the leather-bound volumes lining one wall when Layla came up behind him. She lightly ran a finger straight down his back, from his neck to just short of his coccyx.

He turned and smiled. "For shame, Prudence. The children will see."

She laughed. "Dr. McCane, forgive me, I do believe I've had a bit too much champagne." She closed her eyes and opened them more slowly. "Will you promise not to take advantage of me in my vulnerable state?"

"No."

She laughed again, a musical sound, as her eyes met his. "Jason? Do you want to . . . have you had a tour of the house?"

"I've explored a bit."

"Oh." Her smile turned playful. "I'll bet you've missed a few things." She linked her hands before her waist, holding her champagne glass against her and turning from side to side. The fabric of her gown molded to her breasts.

He nodded, letting his eyes fall, then return to her face. "I'm sure I've missed a thing or two. Perhaps you should show me."

"Yes," she said. "Perhaps I should." She tossed off the rest of her champagne and took his arm.

They were approaching a side hall when they heard her father's voice.

Dr. Kalia was walking closely with a man so fat that he tipped from side to side as he walked. His beefy face was mottled red. Neither of the men saw Jason and Layla.

"Who is that?" Jason asked the girl quietly. "I know I've seen that face before, but I just can't place it."

"Oh, that's Senator Bowie. You know, Senate Appropriations Committee for Labor, Health, and Human Services. He oversees funding for the entire National Institutes."

"That's right!" Jason remembered. "The guy who torpedoed Kennedy's Subcommittee on Scientific Research. Your dad has some interesting friends."

" 'Important' is what they like to be called," Layla said, smiling. She led him around the corner into the hall, looking both ways before quickly moving through a pantry door and beginning to climb a set of wooden stairs.

Jason followed quietly.

Once on the second floor, Layla led him down the hall through a door into a thickly carpeted room. It was lit with tulip-shaped sconces of translucent marble positioned halfway up the wall. The lights cast a warm pink glow. Jason could see a bed through a door into the adjoining room.

"All right, Miss Kalia," he said as he turned her to face him. "Just what did you want to show me?"

She smiled up at him, her tongue just touching her lower lip, and lifted a hand slowly to the silk tie at her shoulder. "Guess."

He pulled her to him, pressing the length of her body against his, meeting her open mouth with his lips. His other hand reached for the silken tie. He tugged once. The knot came loose.

As he kissed her, he peeled the dress off her shoulders and down to her waist. The bare tips of her nipples grew as they brushed against his shirt. She leaned her head back to take the depth of his kisses, clutching him to her, rubbing her body rhythmically against him. Then, still kissing her, Jason placed the tips of two fingers at the nape of her neck and drew them slowly and deliberately down her spine, as she had done to him. He felt her shiver. He reached the swell of her buttocks, locked his thumb around the gathered fabric of her dress, and pulled it quickly down over her bottom.

"Oh!" she exclaimed. "Jason!"

He didn't answer. He kissed his way down her and, without stopping, pulled her tiny nylon panties and the rest of her dress straight down to her feet. He stood, and as he did so, he lifted her straight off the floor. He carried her into the bedroom, kicking the door wide with his foot. He crossed the room and laid her on the bed. She lifted onto her elbows to watch as he threw off his shirt. He finished undressing and joined her in a moment. She opened her arms, and her mouth, and her body to greet him.

She let out a gasp as he entered her. Her eyes were wide, meeting his, as he held still for a moment, poised above her, watching her. Slowly, he began to move. He kept his eyes on hers as he moved into her, filling her with the force of his muscular body. Her breasts shook with each slow, deep joining. Her breaths became deeper. Her mouth slowly parted. Then she squeezed her eyes shut and stretched her neck back, lifting her taut throat into the air. He filled her again and again, increasing his pace as the bed rocked and squeaked with each meeting of their flesh. He could sense her begin the first stage of her climax, the speeding of her, the jerking demand of her pelvis.

Her mouth formed a silent open circle. Her eyes were squeezed shut. She moaned as her orgasm began, sweeping over her like a wave rushing in to fill a beach. "Ah . . ." she cried out at last, pulsing deep inside, unable to stop the rhythm that raced her heart and overwhelmed her body and made her feel faint.

Her movements slowed. Her shaking gradually subsided. Her chest lifted, taking deep breaths. Jason rolled to the side, and Layla let her head come to rest on his shoulder.

When her breath came back, she lifted her head. "Good?"

Jason smiled, his own eyes closed. "Copacetic."

She looked at him with a rapid sequence of responses: first surprise, then curiosity, then with a second thought, distrust. Layla threw aside the covers and rolled away in one swift motion. She stood up and stepped away from the bed. "If that isn't a compliment, I guarantee you'll never leave here alive."

Jason chuckled. He lifted himself onto one of his elbows to watch her move across the room. She made no effort to cover herself, but walked naked toward the bookcase, dim light half revealing her pink body. She bent over, reading the titles, searching for the dictionary.

"Don't move," Jason said quietly.

"What?" Layla turned her head to see him. He was already off the bed, striding across the room to reach her.

—■—

Somehow, the dictionary was never consulted. She was curled beside him as they lay in bed, with the room now in total darkness, drifting toward the silken edge of sleep. Layla began to breathe evenly, her head pressed against his shoulder. One of her legs was thrown over his, covering him with her heat.

He gazed up into the blackness of the ceiling. His eyes searched the void. He tried deliberately to concentrate on the events of the evening. Kalia, his guests, his game, his passion for his research. His passionate daughter. But Jason was tired. His mind was flooded by the wave of his exhaustion, floating awareness away in a river of images, troubled by something he could not name. In the most quiet hour of the night, in that final darkness, he turned his head on the pillow and fell into a kind of sleep.

The images were formless, a shifting maze of colors that resisted resolution. He knew it was beginning. His eyes twitched in fear just as the dream began.

"Mom! Dad!"

"Jason, stay where you are!"

The boiling crowd of Javanese rioters cut between Jason and his parents. He leapt off the curb and ran toward them. A multitude of hands grabbed at him, swung fists and sticks at his face and head. He lashed out in fury, knocking aside the hands and weapons that blocked his way. "Mother, Father," he shouted, "run!"

An explosion of pain blazed in his head as a rock struck behind his ear. He blinked away the dazzling spots and fought on, guided by his mother's screams. A swarthy face thrust itself into the tunnel of his vision. The man's yellow teeth were bared in a vicious smile as he raised his ax above his head. The man's grin became a startled cry as the skinny boy shot out the heel of his hand, shattering the axman's nose. Jason leapt forward, but the mass of rioters closed in.

He was swept up in the crowd as if by a monstrous wave. His arms were pinned to his body, his feet lifted off the ground. He twisted and wrenched himself from side to side, struggling uselessly against the multitude. And as his body was lifted up, he finally saw his parents.

His father was already down. The rioters were kicking again and again at the motionless body. His mother was being tossed about, helpless, beaten and stabbed as she was passed from hand to hand. The flailing of her arms did nothing to protect her. Her pleading eyes found the boy. "Jason!" she cried.

The young doctor woke with a start. His heart was pounding, his eyes were darting about the darkened room, an expression of animal fury crossing his face. He shook his head, like a dog drying off. Gradually, his heart slowed, his breathing evened. He lay back into a fitful slumber.

■6■

K iyah!"
Red shot his foot through a short arc back toward the charging doctor's face. Jason ducked under the foot and lifted the ankle, until Red scissored his other leg up and knocked off the grabbing hand. Red landed on both feet, but his balance was off. Jason's instant sweep took him down. The big man tumbled away and onto his feet again in a single motion, facing his lean friend in a low crouch.

They circled, sweat dripping off their faces, breathing heavily. Red looked like a raging redheaded warrior, his eyes shut almost to slits, his lips curled back in a fierce grimace. Jason's look was more one of supernormal vigilance. A small group of men had gathered at the edge of the mat, watching carefully. One of the observers, a man with a thick mustache, worked his way quietly forward to see the fighters better.

Red moved in, feinted with a front snap kick, then brought the kick around into a high roundhouse. He pulled it back just as Jason reached his foot, dragging down Jason's hand and exposing his neck. Red's spear-hand went straight to the throat, but Jason's arm flashed up like a cobra, knocking it away just in time. Then Red swung his other hand around, leaning into the blow, but his solar plexus met the doctor's waiting fist.

The big man fell with a crash. Red caught his breath, then rolled over and jumped to his feet again at the far side of the mat. His teeth were bared, his thick hands opened and closed. He shifted from side to side, his weight a pendulum pushed one way, then the other by his stocky legs.

He charged at Jason with a shout. Six feet away, he leapt into the air. The doctor dropped to the ground and rolled under the flying form. But Red landed beside him, and pulled Jason's heel out from under him as he rose. This time, it was Jason who crashed to the floor.

Red was already up, drawing back his foot, aiming a kick directly at Jason's head. "You're dead, Jason!"

Jason whirled away, watching the blackened sole shoot by an inch from his temple. He jumped up to his feet. Red was instantly upon him, hammering blow after blow into the outside forearm blocks until their arms worked in a windmill blur that made the spectators grunt with confusion. The bigger man forced Jason back until he neared the corner of the mat. "Kiyah!" He leapt straight at Jason with a bellow of rage, knocking away Jason's arms, swinging a fist like an ax toward his head. The edge of Jason's foot caught him in the upper chest and he fell again in a heap.

"Goddamn it!" Red spat, "Goddamn it! What does it take to beat you?" He rose slowly to his feet, sucking in the air, dripping with sweat, watching the doctor.

A burst of applause broke from the spectators, who whistled and clapped in appreciation. The two men bowed to each other, then walked together off the mat. Jason didn't answer Red's question. He just stared straight ahead. The big man looked at him, trying to read his silence as they walked, passing through the circling crowd of men as if they weren't even there.

The fighters entered the locker room and stripped. They moved to the empty tile shower stall. Still the doctor was silent. As the showers crashed down on them, Red began in a tone of annoyance, "What's with you, man?"

"Give me a minute, Red."

"Dammit . . ."

"A minute." Jason turned his face into the shower, away from his friend. Fighting did it. He had to learn. Brought it too close, brought it back. Unlocked the vault of memory, cracked the door, unleashed the childhood recollection of that day on Java when the rioters had surrounded him and his parents. If only he'd been able to reach them. Jason closed his eyes as the water cascaded down over his head and back. He lifted his face to the stream, letting its rushing sound fill his consciousness, drowning out the world, the memory, breathing deeply, loosening the tightness of his throat, getting control.

Red made no further attempt to interrupt his friend's thoughts. He had seen it happen before, this sudden quietness. He also knew the moment would pass, and Jason would come back from wherever he had been and would shrug and look as calm as the surface of a lake on a windless day.

After they dressed, Red led the way out to the nearly deserted lounge, where they took a booth. The big man brought two beers from the bar. As he sat down he finally said, "Jason, where the hell did you learn to fight like that?"

"Well, you know I spent that year as a kid on Java, studying with Ie Ming."

"That's not what I mean!" Red made no effort to conceal the flash of irritation. "I mean when you fight, you're always so damned cool! You don't get excited or rattled or angry. You're like a goddamned rock!"

"Red, don't . . ."

"What's wrong with you, man? It's like nothing hurts you, nothing scares you, nothing touches you! What the hell does it take to get you mad?"

Jason squeezed his eyes shut. How could he say it? How could he explain the rage that roared inside of him? The rage he had fought to control since the day his mother and father were beaten to death in front of him. The rage that chased him in his sleep, that burned in his chest like a hot coal, burned, Jason sometimes thought, where his heart used to beat?

"You're inhuman!" Red nearly shouted. "You're superhuman, that's what it is! It's like you're from another goddamned species, the next step in evolution beyond *Homo sapiens—Homo McCane!*' Red chuckled, savoring the idea, until he saw his friend's expression.

Jason's face was blank. The tightness in his lips, the square unmoving jaw, the deep-set eyes were like a sculpture, fixed in speechless marble.

"Anyway"—Red cleared his throat—"that's not really what I have to talk to you about." He slid the beer back and forth between his heavy hands.

Jason lifted his eyes and looked at Red. "You have to talk to me about something?"

"Actually, I do," Red answered, fixing his eyes on those of his friend. Then the big man rose. He stepped to the jukebox, which he fed with quarters before returning to the booth. Music began to pound around the room.

Seeing Jason's questioning look, Red said, "Just a cheap intelligence trick. Helps keep conversations private."

"Intelligence?"

"Yeah. That's what we should talk about." He lifted his chin as if to stretch his neck loose from his collar. But his collar was open. "You see, Jason, I've been meaning to tell you: I'm not with the National Security Agency anymore."

Jason said nothing. He simply watched his friend, silent and motionless.

Red thrust out his red-bearded chin again in his quick way. "Yeah. I got a little tired of sitting around at NSA with headphones on all day, listening to tapes of Soviet bloc disc jockeys. I wanted to see a little more action." He pushed his beer mug to one side and spread his hands out on the table. "I switched over to work for the Company."

"The Company."

Red nodded. He watched the doctor's eyes. "I'm with the CIA now."

Jason didn't answer immediately. Then he asked, "By any chance, does this have something to do with your recent command of research techniques?"

"You got it."

Jason nodded. "Red,"—his voice was conversational—"may

I ask what the CIA has to do with neuroscience research?"

The big man chuckled. "I guess the connection isn't exactly obvious." He folded his hands before him. "Well, the CIA has a lot of different jobs to do, a lot of different divisions. Mine is involved in scientific research. It's technically called the Research Oversight Directorate—the ROD. Our job is to . . . well, to look into possible uses for science."

"Uses for science," Jason repeated the phrase.

"Yeah, you know,"—Red tipped his head back and forth, looking for words—"ways that new research might affect our national security interests. I mean, at the rate science is moving, can you imagine all the potential defense and intelligence applications? Between us and DARPA—"

"DARPA?" the young doctor interrupted. "And who or what is DARPA, Red?"

"Our sister agency over at the Defense Department. The Defense Advanced Research Projects Agency." Red explained that DARPA is one of the most secret branches of Defense, devoted to finding military applications for the latest scientific research. With their multimillion-dollar budget and their freedom from congressional restraints, DARPA was able to initiate massive projects that even the CIA knew nothing about.

"I see."

"Anyway, between us and the boys at DARPA, there's a hell of a lot of science to cover. My division actually works at the National Institutes of Health. As a matter of fact, you are one of my personal clients. When I found out you were coming to the Institutes, I asked specially to be assigned to you." He grinned.

Jason looked at him without expression. "And just what does your division do?"

Red smiled again, too broadly, and took a last swallow before putting his beer aside and launching into his spiel. He explained that his division, the ROD, was responsible for keeping tabs on American research. He described how they monitored the progress of every major laboratory, making sure that new technologies weren't stolen by foreign governments. He explained how they worked with the editors of scientific journals to censor publication of new research. "You know, this business of openly publishing every new discovery is just playing into the hands of the communists—"

"Red," Jason interrupted, "you know the policy of open publication isn't unilateral. It's an international accord. Every scientist in every country depends on it to make progress, including the Russians and the Chinese, not to mention the British, the French—"

"Sure they do. But who do you think gets the fat end of the deal? Not us, boy. We've put this enormous number of bucks into research, and who gets the gravy? A bunch of foreigners with a solid commitment to kicking the shit out of our imperialist asses! You think the Soviets would be competitive if they couldn't pick our American brains? Why, they couldn't even build a missile if it weren't for our transistors."

"Just as we couldn't build a missile until we had the help of the Germans who came in after the war. No country has a patent on brains."

"That's not the point!" Red almost shouted. "The point is, we're doing all this research and, because of your precious open scientific community, we hand it over to people who are going to use it against us. It's like giving your best weapon to your worst enemy—"

"Red, Red, hold it a minute," Jason interrupted him again. "You're talking about the National Institutes of Health. I could understand if you were talking about secret missile research or the physics of nuclear holocausts, but this is the NIH! We do medical research, damn it, with medical significance. The idea—at least the fantasy that keeps us going—is to save lives. And now you're telling me that the CIA and the Department of Defense have divisions that are specifically devoted to keeping our work secret?"

"Among other things. Jason, you just don't realize the—"

"Among what other things, Red?" The doctor eyed the government agent grimly.

Red returned his gaze, searching the doctor's face. He cleared his throat and glanced unobtrusively around the bar, eyeing the only other occupants: the barkeeper and a man with a heavy mustache who sat at the far end of the room, wearing a pair of portable earphones, nodding in time to his music. A dull throbbing drumbeat signaled the start of the next piece on the jukebox, as Red turned back to Jason.

"All right. We do more than just watch for leaks." His eyes narrowed, staring straight into the young scientist's face. "We . . . influence things."

Red described how each branch of the Institutes had its own CIA connection—a liaison officer who channeled money and projects to the Institutes, who worked with the branch chiefs to explore ways to apply their projects to defense purposes. "America trained you scientists, and now you could be our best weapons. Let me tell you, there are things going on at the National Institutes that you can't even imagine . . ."

"Like the experiments with hallucinogens on army recruits in the sixties? Like the way you tried to convert McGill University into a brainwashing research center?" Jason rose rapidly from his seat. "Like your attempt to drug the entire population of San Francisco with airborne LSD?"

"Those were foolish excesses," Red protested. "The CIA has learned a lot since that time!"

"I'm sure it has." Jason faced him coldly. "Look, Red, I don't want to be your weapon. I don't want to be your 'client.' I thought I was your friend!" He grabbed his gi and strode toward the door. Then Jason's back disappeared under the red light marked Exit.

The CIA man slammed his palm with his fist. For a moment, he sat still, glaring at the door where Jason had disappeared. Then he rose from the booth, marched to the bar, and paid the bill.

As Red left the lounge, the mustachioed figure shifted out of the far booth. He took off the small headset he was wearing, similar to the headsets for portable radios, and pocketed the tiny dishlike microphone he had been holding under the table. He made his own way rapidly toward the exit. In the vestibule, a pay phone was attached to the wall. He dropped in a coin and quickly dialed a number.

◼ 7 ◼

Hey, Doctor," Tom Sherrington said as he met Jason just as he reached the door of his cubicle, "need some entertainment?"

Jason glanced toward the mountain of papers on his desk. "Oh, how the gods so wondrously foresee our needs."

Tom grinned. "Great! I thought you'd be interested in this. Come on down to my lab." He looked at his watch. "If I get down to work, I can show you a transfer before Kalia's lecture."

The new Fellow turned from the door, and the two young men made their way into the hall. "By 'transfer,' " Jason asked while they walked, "should I presume you mean genes?"

"You presume right, my friend." Tom led the way past the big freezers that lined the long central corridor. As he walked, he spoke over his shoulder, "So Jason, what do you think of the NIH so far?"

"Things are . . . certainly interesting here."

"I'll say." Tom's agreement was emphatic. "This place is incredible."

Jason was silent. He didn't know what to say. He was still absorbing the impact of Red's announcement.

The CIA monitored the Institutes. That much was clear, a grim enough revelation by itself. But there was more to the role of this special branch of the CIA, Red's so-called Research Oversight Directorate. There was the idea of deliberate manipulation, the suggestion of a power behind the scientific throne.

What were they up to? Jason recalled the congressional hearings after the Vietnam war exposing the CIA's secret operations against innocent US citizens. He remembered the shock of the medical community when it discovered the CIA's program in scientific brainwashing. All he could do was ask himself again, what were they up to now at the National Institutes of Health?

Tom and Jason turned into the laboratory wing, where they were greeted by a wave of animal smells. Tom pushed open a door. "Come into my laboratory," he said, approximating a chuckle of Faustian evil.

The lab was divided in two. One side of the room was a work area with the usual paraphernalia of science: black-topped benches, glassware, shelves of chemicals. On the other side were tall racks of cages, housing a squealing horde of mice.

"The mice are allowed to copulate freely," Tom explained. "Over the weekend they were pretty romantic. We managed to isolate fertilized eggs from four of the females early this morning. This will be my final gene transfer."

"What gene are you transferring into them, Tom?"

The slender Clinical Fellow handed him a vial. Jason read the label: Chromosome Two; Sequence Pro-opiolipomelano-cortin. He recognized it immediately. It was an enormous molecule that was the basis for five human hormones; they included the endorphins, the brain's chemical arbiters of pleasure and pain.

Tom pulled up a chair and set a petri dish under the lens of a two-headed microscope. Jason took the opposite seat. Both men peered through their eyepieces at the glimmering image of a tiny gelatinous mouse egg. The egg seemed to glow with life as it quivered and rolled in its viscous bath.

The biologist opened a nearby drawer. He gingerly removed a metal syringe that sprouted a long projection of clear glass.

He drew a minuscule amount of a cloudy liquid up into this hollow glass needle, then locked the syringe into a micro-manipulator carriage attached to the microscope. "And now for the coup de grace."

Jason watched through the microscope. The needle tip appeared like the snout of an intruding monster beside the egg. At high magnification, it seemed to waver wildly as it moved toward the shining wall of the single cell. "Ho ho, monsieur," Tom spoke with a comical French accent, "so you wish to trifle with me? My rapier shall answer you!" Slowly, he manipulated the tip of the needle across the field, centering it flush against the wall of the egg. "Take zat!" With an imperceptible turn of the control dial, he forced the needle into the egg. Then he gently pushed in the plunger of the syringe. The egg swelled up before their eyes.

Tom drew out the glass needle and sat back with relief. "I'll tell you, when I get my new laser, these gene transfers will be a cinch."

"When will that be?" Jason inquired.

"Just two more days!" Tom covered the petri dish and returned it to an incubator. Then he turned back to face his new colleague. "So how's your own research going?"

"Well, I suppose I expected to carry on with my project to map the gene for manic depression, but I guess Dr. Murray has some rather grander plans for me." Jason paused. "He wants to expand the project. Map other behaviors."

Tom nodded, seemingly unsurprised. He said, "You know, Dr. Murray asked me to speak with you about that."

"Oh?"

"Yeah." The skinny researcher shrugged apologetically. "He wanted me to find out how you feel about the genetics project. Think you'll join us?"

Jason stared at Tom. It seemed that a lot of people were interested in that same question. He just said, "I must admit, the idea has its attractions."

"Great." Tom grinned. "You map 'em, and I'll transfer 'em!" He checked his watch. "Hey, just in time. Dr. Kalia starts his lecture in a couple of minutes."

Jason stopped him. "Tom, after your mice are born, just what effect will those new genes have?"

The other man leaned against the incubator, arms folded. "Well, a variety of effects, depending on how many of the new genes get into the mouse DNA. A lot of the mice die young from strange mutations. Like I said, the problem is mapping. If you could just help us map the genes a little better—"

"What about the mice that lived?" Jason interjected. "What are they like?"

Tom looked at the ceiling a moment, then across at Jason. "Of the six mice born so far, there's been only one consistent effect. They're almost totally invulnerable to pain."

—■—

An army in white was marshaled in the Masur Auditorium. Scientists from every one of the ten Institutes had come to the Monday noon lecture. It was an event not to be missed. Dr. Kalia's lecture was entitled "Animal Behavior: The Secrets of Motivation" and every behavioral and neuroscientist in the region had awaited it eagerly.

They were not alone. A pack of science reporters and photographers had gathered at the front of the auditorium, milling about, juggling their cameras and recorders, jockeying for the best views.

Tom and Jason worked their way through the eager crowd and secured two seats near the center. Around them, a babble of languages filled the air as the multinational group stole a few moments to chat. Jason searched the auditorium but saw no sign of Jennifer.

A gavel was banged on the podium as the deputy director of the Center brought the room to order.

Tom leaned over to whisper, "The lecture should be good, but the real fun comes afterwards during the discussion period. I've seen many a lion bearded in this particular coliseum."

"Oh? And whom should I root for? The lion or the gladiators?" Jason asked.

"In this case," Tom replied, "I think a few docs are going to turn into cat food."

A rush of applause sounded through the auditorium as Kalia took the stage. The lights of a dozen cameras flashed. He wasted no time but strode to the podium, gripped it on both sides, and launched directly into his address.

"Friends and colleagues, this is a forum of fact. We are men of fact, and it should always be so, for science must remain true to the evidence, wherever it may lead us.

"But today, I come to speak of principles, not just facts. Certain basic principles lie at the heart of the natural order. We discover these principles by boldly examining the facts of life. Though some men are terrified of such discoveries, we are not. We seek only to understand these natural principles, and by understanding, to grow strong."

Jason tapped Tom. "Is he running for senator?"

Tom whispered back, "No. I think archangel of Maryland." They both chuckled. A voice shushed them from behind.

"Why does an animal act? What is the cause of its behaviors? Before attempting to answer, let me propose that we agree to certain basic definitions, certain ideals.

"First, what is life? I will try to spare you more philosophy." Quiet laughter swept through the crowd, then Kalia went on.

"Life, from the scientist's point of view, is simply the tendency to reproduce. To make new copies of DNA. Although there is so much more to say, although life is a jewel blessed with many facets, we must define its essence. The essence of life, then, is this extraordinary tendency to perpetuate genes.

"Second, what is behavior?" His eyes swept over the audience with a look of fierce resolve that captured the attention of every listener as the famed scientist went on.

— ■ —

"Password, sir?" The duty officer grinned as Red approached the steel barrier at Langley, Level 3. Red forewent his usual joke and simply stepped up to the ID booth, aligning his eyes with the retinal pattern detector. A beep announced his clearance and he moved through the opening door into the Research Oversight Directorate data center.

"Red." A middle-aged woman bustled over and confronted the CIA man with a bundle of computer paper. "You really want me to go through all this? There are over forty major funding sources for Neurosciences alone, and that doesn't even include private donations."

"Yes, Mrs. B.," Red interrupted as he walked quickly through the data center, "I know it's a lot of auditing. Bring in a couple of the boys from Technical Services if you have to." He thanked the senior data analyst and tapped a young man on the shoulder as he came abreast of his cubicle. "Jimmy, what you got for me?"

The man looked up from his computer terminal. "Nothing. Nada. You were right, it isn't just one Normal Volunteer. Two patients have also disappeared without a trace, supposedly escaped from the ward. And for the last two years, throughout the NIH there've been a whole lot of security irregularities, lab work disappearing, software disks, even raw data, but there's no pattern to it that I can figure out. Look at this." He called up a display on his terminal. "Psychobiology, receptor chemistry, molecular bio . . ."

"You think it's an effort to disrupt our projects at the Institutes?"

"That's the thing, Red. It's not like the labs we support are being singled out." He tapped several keys and the CIA's projects lit up on the screen in boldface. Each one was a basic science project that probed the frontiers of medical science and promised spin-offs with potential value for defense or covert operations. There was the program for rapid detoxification of Soviet chemical warfare agents. There were pills that could block the effect of drugs used for interrogation. There was research on a binary aerosol weapon that would render an enemy army unconscious long enough to capture it bloodlessly.

The big agent leaned over to examine the list. "Nothing in common? You're sure no single lab has been hit harder than the others?"

The younger man shook his head. There was no relationship between the NIH labs that had been tampered with and the ones performing CIA-funded work. "You know, it's not like the research is being disrupted. In fact, it's almost as if the

work is just being *monitored,* that whoever is behind it actually
wants the research to continue."

"What about the Soviets?"

The data analyst again shook his head. He called up another
display. It listed scientific laboratories in the Soviet Union,
coded by the main focus of their research. The CIA agent
had meticulously evaluated the most recent intelligence reports. He told Red there wasn't a single recent case of a
sudden Soviet breakthrough on a subject about which data
had disappeared from the NIH. "Sir, if you don't mind my
asking, are you sure that it's the Soviets who are behind this?"

"Well, if it isn't the Soviets, then who the hell is it?" And,
he thought to himself, why? Half to himself, he said, "Maybe
it's time we got some Company field agents involved."

"Ah, sir, I don't mean to cause trouble but . . . could this
whole thing be a covert op by another CIA division?"

Red was silent. His brow came down to hood his eyes.
Slowly, he shook his head. "Keep on it, Jimmy."

As the data analyst turned back to his task, Red strode
quickly across the room. He passed through the security checkpoint and left the ROD data center. "Jason," he muttered to
himself as he walked, "you bastard . . ." He rapidly made
his way down the carpeted corridor. He finally arrived at the
door marked DDST, the office of the CIA's deputy director
for Science and Technology.

—■—

Dr. Kalia gripped the lectern as he reached the climax of
his speech.

"We all know the basic facts: Long strands of DNA are
packed into every living cell. Short sections of DNA, which
serve as blueprints for proteins, are called genes. By chance
mutations, new genes appear in the DNA. If those genes
improve the animal's ability to survive and reproduce, those
genes will be perpetuated. If not, both the genes and the
animal will disappear. That is evolution.

"Why do I review these simple facts? To make an equally
simple point. Some of these genes determine the structure
and the *function* of the brain. Thus, *some genes control behavior.*

Through eons of time, behaviors have evolved to improve the survival and reproduction of living things. Why? To perpetuate the genes themselves. In a way, animals do not exist for their own sake, but only to serve as the vessels for genes in search of immortality. If a behavior serves this ultimate goal, fine. The genes for it continue. That's why there are genes that make the animal eat and drink and flee danger and, especially, seek sex. If not, that gene will die, and that behavior will die, as dead as the dinosaurs.

"Thus the genes give purpose to the life of the animal. Thus the gene strives to perfect itself, to raise itself up from individual mortality, to transcend, by endless reproduction, the bounds of time.

"What then is the Final Cause of animal behavior? It is life. Life itself. Life in its essence as we know it to be: the drive to reproduce. The drive to make the animal serve that relentless mastermind of evolution—its own genes. Thank you."

There was a moment of silence. His summary was so crisp, so complete, that its significance took a few seconds for even that august crowd to absorb. It was nothing less than a new explanation of behavior. The applause began. It grew. "Dr. Kalia!" The pack of reporters leapt to its feet as one. "Dr. Kalia, your laboratory . . ." they cried, filling the stage with the flashes of their cameras, waving their microphones in the air.

Dr. Kalia acknowledged the applause with a slight tilt of his head, then raised his hands insistently to signal for quiet. "We have time for possibly one or two questions." He looked beyond the frantic reporters and signaled instead to one of the scientists. A frail-looking old man came to his feet, supported by a cane.

"Dr. Kalia," the man began, his mustache twitching, "you speak most eloquently of the contribution of nature to animal behavior. But what about the role of nurture? Doesn't life experience play a role?" Noisy debates rose from the crowd as the old man sat down.

Kalia smiled. "Ah, Doctor Lorenz, so we renew our old discussion. Nature versus nurture. Which one plays the critical role? Of course life experience is a crucial factor. If the baby sparrow does not hear its father's song during a critical period of its youth, that sparrow will never sing, and it will never find a mate. Yes, experience is desperately important.

"But what does experience do? It stimulates the waiting DNA. Only a sparrow, with the sparrow's genes, can learn the sparrow's song. If the brain were not genetically primed to learn, the experience would be meaningless. You can teach a dog to fetch your slippers, because it has a brain that can learn the lesson, but you can't teach a clam to do it any more than you can a rock. The behavior of every animal is constrained by its DNA."

"You say 'animal,'" a voice came out of the middle of the auditorium, and three hundred heads turned to see the impetuous speaker. It was a tall black-haired man of middle age whose shrill voice belied the firmness of his words. "But I am obliged to wonder if you include humans in this theory?"

Kalia eyed his questioner with a stern look, almost a glare, and did not answer until the murmuring of the crowd quieted again.

"Forgive me, Dr. Wilson,"—Kalia nodded to the man—"but I cannot answer. I think it best to limit my discussion to things that can be resolved scientifically—by experiment. Therefore, I cannot speak about humans. The experimental data, thank God, can never be obtained."

"But, Dr. Kalia," a feminine voice interjected from one of the front rows. Again the room's attention shifted to the speaker. Jason saw the slender tanned arm and followed it down. It was Dr. Jennifer Darien. Her voice grew more intense as she spoke. "The question remains: How does your theory account for *human* behavior—all the art and poetry and philosophy of humanity, all the inspired thoughts and brave deeds of the species *Homo sapiens*? How can your theory reduce these wonders to a strict biological equation?"

Kalia looked nonplussed. The question was challenging, possibly all the more difficult having been delivered by this striking young woman. The reporters swung their cameras her way. Jennifer paid no heed to the stir she was causing.

Finally, Kalia smiled down at her. "Ah, Dr. Darien, isn't it? Perhaps we humans are a bit like Narcissus: We want to admire ourselves forever. Humans used to think that their Earth was the center of the universe. Copernicus upset that narcissistic fantasy. Humans also used to believe that we had a different origin from other animals. Darwin forced us to give up that self-centered delusion." The lecturer paused for effect, dropping his voice a little, forcing the audience to concentrate on every word.

"Maybe we have been living for too long with the final narcissism: that our minds are something supernatural, something that goes beyond the complexities of the brain. Now, modern neuroscience is shaking the foundations of that grand self-delusion."

His voice rose in a crescendo. "We are poised at the brink of the last frontier. Let us not be afraid of the facts. We will discover what we will discover. Join me, and we shall search together for the truth!"

The roar of applause was immediate. The audience stood to honor Dr. Kalia, an almost unprecedented response to a scientific address. "Dr. Kalia!" Instantly, the reporters were clamoring at the base of the stage. "Dr. Kalia, why can't we see your laboratory?" ". . . secret laboratory!" ". . . when will you open . . ." Jason felt the hairs on the back of his neck rising.

"What did I tell you!" Tom had to shout the words over the noise of the crowd. "Lion ten; gladiators nothing!"

Kalia took a single bow and walked straight to the left edge of the stage, the press corps shouting behind him. The applause went on. Jason half expected the white-maned scientist to return for a curtain call. He didn't, and gradually the excited assembly quit their applause and turned to each other in a hundred spirited discussions.

"Well," Tom asked finally in a normal tone, "what did you think, Dr. McCane?"

Jason's gaze was on the ground as they both sidestepped toward the aisle. He was almost frowning. When they were at last clear of the row of seats, he looked seriously up into his new colleague's face. "I think," he said solemnly, "that I'd like to make a date." Then he winked.

"What?" Tom asked, bewildered. But Jason was already making his way quickly through the crowd. Toward Jennifer.

— ∎ 8 ∎—

It was another warm clear day, the few white clouds sat randomly in a blue sky, and the rolling Virginia countryside moved past the Land Rover's open windows like a fragrant and ever-changing painting. They were heading southwest of Washington, off the beltway now, tracing secondary roads toward the rise of the Blue Ridge Mountains.

Jennifer was smiling slightly, looking out the window on the passenger's side, her hair waving freely in the wind. She clasped her hands over her head and stretched, her feline body lifting high off the seat, her breasts outlined roundly in the light cotton blouse. She grinned and settled back.

"Happy you came?" Jason asked, watching her for a moment.

"I think so." She paused. "Look, I'm sorry I hesitated about coming along with you. I . . . well, there are some things that have been on my mind. But I do want to see Kalia's lab."

Jason drove silently for a minute, then asked gently, "Do you want to talk about it?"

"No." Then she softened a bit. "I mean, not right now. Oh, look at those horses!" she exclaimed with the glee of a child. They drove past a long row of stables where grooms were exercising tall sleek horses, trotting them around the paddocks in dressage routines. The scene was gone in a moment. The car continued down the well-paved highway until they reached a fork. Jason consulted the map and angled left. The tires flung some gravel as he turned, then bit into the macadam surface.

Originally, Kalia's labs took up a good portion of the lower two basements of the Clinical Center. However, when Kalia came to the Construction Committee with the proposal for his expanded facilities, they realized there was no way to accommodate a project of that size on the Bethesda campus. Kalia hadn't argued when the trustees suggested purchasing a tract of land forty miles out in the hills of Virginia. Now the renowned Laboratory of Brain and Behavior was an autonomous complex, hidden away in an isolated forest, reached by a drive of more than three-quarters of an hour.

Wildflowers bloomed in profusion along the roadside, and richly cultivated fields of tobacco alternated with dairy farms and horse pastures. As they moved up into the foothills of the Blue Ridge, the fields were separated by progressively larger patches of forest.

The two young scientists traded stories about their current labs, comparing impressions of personalities they'd both come across. They agreed that the resources were incredible, the personnel impressive, and the cafeteria appalling.

Jason asked, "Have you met Dr. Kalia?"

"Well, no, not in person. But he called me at the lab on Friday. He . . . he wanted to know if I'd be interested in helping with a project of his." She hesitated. "Actually, he asked me not to discuss it too widely."

Jason didn't respond.

Jennifer folded her hands in her lap and turned them over, running one finger back and forth across her knuckles distractedly. Finally she spoke. "Well, since you're . . . I mean, I don't see any harm in talking about it. He asked me to help write a computer program."

"I see." Jason paused. "You know, I thought your field was animal behavior. Is programming your major interest?"

Jennifer shook her head. She explained that she developed

her computer skills by working with computerized animal observation equipment at the Wisconsin lab. Dr. Kalia apparently wanted her help with similar equipment.

"Any special type of animal?"

Jennifer smiled. "Oh, primates, of course. They're my specialty."

Jason was about to ask another question when the car flashed past a dirt road almost hidden in the dense woods. He checked the odometer reading from the last turn and said, "I think this is our stop." After backing the car, he pulled onto a dirt lane, narrow and deeply rutted from the tires of heavy equipment. The trees were close on either side, a dense green colonnade that filtered out most of the sun. Bouncing and skidding along the track, he was thankful for the four-wheel drive.

After more than a mile and a half, the trail suddenly opened onto a clearing. They found themselves staring at a freshly painted hut before a high-fenced gate. The chain-link fence stretched into the woods as far as they could see in either direction. It was topped with a thick roll of barbed wire. A uniformed man stepped from the hut and waved them to a halt. He wore the same short orange jacket as the Institute guards.

"IDs please." He held out his hand.

Jason and Jennifer looked at each other. They passed over their Institute cards, and the man disappeared into the hut where they saw him reach for a phone.

"This is quite a checkpoint, Charlie," Jennifer quipped. Jason didn't answer but watched as the man spoke into the panel, apparently similar to the voiceprint lock on the ward door. The big gate slid open on chained gears with a noisy rattle. The guard signaled them through.

After about two hundred more yards, the track broadened and leveled, turning around under a low concrete portico, which thrust out directly from the ascending curve of a tree-covered mountain. They drove into the shade under the portico beside a cluster of parked vans and climbed from the car to face the entrance. A small bronze sign was bolted to the wall: LABORATORY OF BRAIN AND BEHAVIOR—NA-

TIONAL INSTITUTES OF HEALTH. It appeared as if the entire facility had been built like a huge bunker directly into the mountainside. The only sign of habitation seemed to be the flat car shelter, which they could see was covered with sod on top; the lab would be quite invisible from the air.

"Hello!" A tall, well-dressed woman in her midthirties was hailing them from the glass double doors of the entrance. "I'm Dr. Kalia's secretary. You must be Doctors McCane and Darien." She smiled and held the door for them, then ushered them through a modern lobby past potted plants and low benches into an office. Jason noted the panel on the door: Public Relations.

"Please, make yourself comfortable. I'll let Dr. Kalia know you're here." She left them alone in the room.

The pair walked around the office, looking at the framed photographs and news clippings neatly arrayed along the walls. There were articles from the *Washington Post* proclaiming, "Environmentally Conscious Government Building in Rural Virginia" and an editorial praising the way the laboratory harmonized so well with the land. There were scenes of a winter ground-breaking for the lab, with Dr. Kalia sharing the handle of a shovel with the chief administrators of NIH. A heavyset figure stood directly behind them, his reddened face partly obscured by Kalia's shoulder. Jason saw one blueprint of a computer room and several peripheral labs. There were no interior photographs at all. He turned back to the photograph of the ground-breaking ceremony. The partly hidden figure looked familiar somehow. He started to read the caption.

"Well, there you are!" Kalia stuck his head into the open door, then entered, carrying a black cloth bundle under one arm. "So, you managed to find us. Please come down to my office."

Kalia led the way down the carpeted corridor back past the lobby. They turned one corner, and then another, and came to a door marked Administration. Passing through it, the group moved through a reception area, coming at last to a broad oak door bearing a discrete rendering of the doctor's name in gold Gothic lettering.

"Please sit down." Kalia gestured at two tufted leather chairs opposite the massive desk. As he entered, he dropped the black bundle he was carrying onto a settee. The large office was fashioned in the same grand manner as the scientist's home, thick carpets warming the floor, dark mahogany paneling the walls from top to bottom, silk-shaded lamps casting a bright yellow glow. There were two matched Oriental tapestries hanging side by side covering half of one wall, lit from above by an angled spotlight.

"Now, I understand that you are probably eager to see the laboratory. But before the tour, I just want to prepare you people for what you're about to see." He sat at the desk chair, and punched a button on a panel inset in the desktop. A projection screen rolled down with a whir in front of the hanging tapestries. The white-haired doctor pushed more buttons and the room was plunged into darkness, until a slide projector lit the screen.

"What you see here is the design of the first Brain and Behavior Lab. As both of you know, our earliest work was with rats, and at that time it was possible to contain a complete colony in a space the size of a typical medical laboratory." The slide showed a white-tiled room entirely filled with a strange plexiglass structure. Hundreds of white Norwegian rats were visible inside.

"But this approach has certain limitations. It is one thing to observe behavior in the artificial world of a plexiglass cage; it is quite another to watch the animal living in its natural environment. We solved that problem as follows."

The slide changed, and they were now looking at a much larger room, brightly lit, the floor a brown landscape of ridges and mounds, with low foliage scattered about and dark holes dotting the earth. Jason saw what looked like an owl perched high up in one corner.

"This is Brain and Behavior Lab number two. We created an environment for the rats that roughly resembles their original home: the temperate zones of central Asia. We used hidden cameras to eliminate the observers. We reproduced the dangers of their natural life by providing the rats with both prey, in the form of mice and shrews, and predators, in the form of two young barn owls. You can just see one, to the upper left."

"Oh, yes. Now I see it," Jennifer said.

"Of course," Kalia continued, "we were still faced with a major problem: the species. Rats are excellent for brain-behavior relations at a primitive level. However, our real interest is in the behavior of higher creatures, especially primates: monkeys and apes."

Kalia snapped on the light and rose. "And now, allow me to show you the final solution: the current Laboratory of Brain and Behavior. I'd like you both to put on one of these before we go down to the lab." He untied the dark bundle and handed them each a black jump suit.

As they stepped into the zippered garments, Jennifer asked their purpose. Kalia explained that they would be observing animals from close range, and the suits would minimize the chance that the animals would see their observers just feet away.

They moved into the hall, and the elder scientist guided them down two short corridors to find what appeared to be a dead end. Set into the side wall, however, was one of the voiceprint analysis devices that had now become familiar to Jason. Out of curiosity, he positioned himself to watch while Kalia rapidly punched in a sequence of buttons. Jason watched the wall trundle sideways when their host announced, "Dr. Paul Kalia." The door politely thanked him. They entered what appeared to be an ordinary elevator.

Kalia pushed the only button, and they began a rapid descent. The elder scientist explained that the labs had been built deep into the mountain to protect them from climatic variations. Jason was struck by the length of the elevator ride.

The elevator silently came to a halt and the door slid open. They were facing into a short empty hall; its only features were the voiceprint lock panel on the near wall and a plain hinged door at the end, thirty feet away. Kalia led them to the unlocked door and through it.

They entered a spacious chemistry laboratory. Although it was unoccupied, signs of activity were present in the blur of a magnetic stirring rod and the plinking of fluid from the bottom of a tall glass column. Kalia strode through the room without comment, guiding them down another short hall, which opened onto a second lab.

Unlike the first, the benches of this room were crowded with gray metal cubes the size of small ovens. Along the walls stood work chambers, fronted with glass, filled with rows of petri dishes.

"Cell culture?" Jason asked.

"Exactly," the lab director responded. Jennifer peered through the glass and asked what the dishes were for. Kalia explained that each dish contained a clone of cells, each of which contained the exact same genes as every other one.

As Kalia spoke, Jason looked around the abandoned laboratory. For a lab of this size, the eerie lack of human activity was surprising.

"Now, if you'll come this way." Kalia turned away from the chamber and led the way into another hallway. It branched in three directions. One door stood at the end of each corridor. The elder scientist walked down the tunnel to the right-hand door. He knocked twice, then held it open for his young colleagues. "This is the hydroponic garden."

Jason and Jennifer stepped past him into the room. Somehow, the architect's rendering had not prepared them for the scale. The room stretched before them for nearly a hundred yards, outfitted with row upon row of tanks filled with tall green clusters of rice shoots, making an even terrace of rice reaching into the distance like an army of green soldiers on a field.

"Jason!" A slender figure in a white coat appeared from behind a tank.

"Layla," he answered.

"Layla?" Jennifer asked.

"My daughter," Kalia explained.

The dark-haired young woman swept across the floor to join them. Jason could feel Jennifer's eyes on him.

"Layla, I know you have met Dr. McCane," Kalia said, "but I don't believe you've met Dr. Jennifer Darien."

"Pleased to meet you." Layla began to offer her hand, then

drew it back, wiping it against her coat. She extended it again with a smile and the two women shook.

"Good to meet you, Layla," the primatologist responded. "I take it you work here?"

Dr. Kalia quietly said, "Layla runs this division of the laboratory. The rice research is her program."

"Oh! I see." Jennifer colored at her own presumption. "I didn't realize . . ."

"That's all right," the young botanist said with a grin. "It's really more a democracy than that. We all pitch in."

Jennifer looked at her, taking in her finely sculpted features, the shining mane of dark hair falling in a wave beside her face, her lithe form held proudly. She glanced again at Jason, who was asking a question.

"You know, somehow I had imagined your experimental plot would be outdoors, to get proper sunlight, if for no other reason."

"That's exactly it," Layla said. "If we tried to do this outdoors, we'd never be able to control things like light. Here, we can produce any amount of sunlight we want." She pointed to the bright grow-lights above. "We can control temperature, humidity, a wide range of soil conditions . . . there are even fans to reproduce the wind." She laid a hand lightly on Jason's arm and pointed over his shoulder. Her hand remained an instant longer than was quite necessary.

"But," Jennifer put in, studiously ignoring the contact, "how is this research related to the purpose of the lab, to the brain and behavior?"

Dr. Kalia chuckled, saying that even though most of the work was with animals, it was sometimes easier to see genes working in organisms that would grow quickly . . . and hold still for observations.

"Of course," Jennifer agreed.

"Now," he went on, "may I propose that we move on to the computer room? Thank you, Layla."

"My pleasure," his daughter responded. "Nice to meet you, Dr. Darien. Oh, and Jason,"—she turned her eyes up to him—"we have a date?"

"We do."

Layla nodded to him with a grin.

Dr. Kalia strode before them as they left the hydroponics lab and moved down the second branch of the hall. Jason could not fail to sense Jennifer's cool gaze. Nonetheless, both of them matched Kalia's quick pace until they arrived at another door, identical to the first.

"And here, Dr. Darien, is your domain," he said, bowing them into a room.

Jennifer stopped at the threshold. "I didn't realize you had a mainframe here." The room was a large white space, split in two by a wall of glass, bathed by the lambent ceiling lights in a glow that met the eye like a snowfield. Only the red bulbs of the power indicator lights broke up the disorienting whiteness. The wall of glass enclosed a massive mainframe of a computer, mounted on a raised platform. In the middle of the opposite wall was a simple white desk with a keyboard, a terminal, and two printers.

"Well, Jennifer," Kalia asked as he gestured with his hand, "do you suppose this will do?"

"Dr. Kalia, this is superb!"

"It will serve." Kalia favored her with a wink. "And now, if you will,"—his hand stretched back toward the door—"let us delay no longer."

Jennifer and Jason followed Kalia out of the computer room. They exchanged a glance, both wondering the same thing: How could Dr. Kalia conduct the animal research he was known for in these eerie labs buried deep in a mountain? What did he mean by calling this his "final solution"? This time, Kalia led them down the central hallway to the third door. He opened it for them, and bowed them through. They stepped across the threshold into darkness.

At first, the blackness seemed complete. When the door closed behind them, they saw nothing but the residual images on their retinas, heard nothing but each other. But as their eyes adjusted, Jason and Jennifer saw that they were looking into a narrow corridor, dimly lit by a single row of round, green, phosphorescent patches that marked the edges of the floor. The effect was like an airport runway lit in the black of night. Walking between the patches, they shuffled their way about forty feet until Dr. Kalia halted them before another plain door. In their black outfits, they were almost invisible to each other, and Jason felt Jennifer's body bump softly into his back, then recoil. "Oh, excuse me," she said.

"I'll ask you both to keep your voices as low as possible." Kalia spoke softly. He opened the door quickly and ushered them through it.

Jennifer cried out, almost by reflex. She received a quick hush from Kalia, but Jason couldn't blame her. The scene before them was fantastic.

They stood in a faintly lit control area, the floor again outlined in glowing green spots. To their left stood banks of electrical equipment, floor to ceiling, marked by blinking lights and shining meters.

But to their right, like a panorama from an awesome dream, was a jungle.

Enormous hardwood trees towered up a hundred and fifty feet from the lush undergrowth, their majestic trunks hanging with vines and dappled with flowering epiphytes. The trees stretched out in massive stands across a broad valley, its limits lost in the distance. A tangled net of creepers and lianas laced in sweeping arcs between the trees like dark and verdant webs. Huge green ferns spread open in twenty-foot fans, their leaves glistening as from a recent rain. A turbid stream snaked before them, banked with reedy plants, washing the rotting flotsam of the jungle past their eyes before disappearing back into the heavy bush. The high thick canopy of green formed a dense barrier to all but a few refracted shafts of light, penetrating down through the branches from a height that was hardly visible in the receding distance, casting the scene in a uniform twilight. A clear plexiglass wall separated them from the jungle, seeming to enclose the entire valley in a single enormous dome.

"Incredible." Jason said it quietly. Jennifer was speechless.

"Ah yes, Jason. I thought you would be pleased! The monsoon forest of southern Asia, the equatorial jungles of East Africa—the very places your father did his research. You must feel at home here."

As they stood staring through the almost invisible plexiglass wall, their eyes accommodated to the low light and details began to emerge. Brown lizards clung to branches projecting over the stream from the mossy trunk of a fallen tree. A butterfly floated into view, startling the eye with its brilliant colors, then disappeared into the impenetrable green depths.

"I simply never imagined anything so . . . enormous!" Jennifer found her voice.

Jason finally asked, "Dr. Kalia, just how big . . ."

Kalia was enjoying the moment. "The dome is nearly three miles long, more than a mile across, and over six hundred feet high. All built underground, enclosed by this wall of armored plexiglass."

"But, this isn't just a laboratory," said Jennifer. "It's a world!"

"Biome is the word, my dear," Kalia said. "It is complete. A self-contained ecosystem. There are microbes, grubs and insects, birds, fish, amphibians, reptiles, and mammals of every size."

"Which mammals?" she asked, attempting composure.

They could hear the scientist move a few feet toward the electrical panels. He said, "Lenny, turn on the monitor speakers a minute."

"Sure, Dr. Kalia."

Jennifer started at the sound. The voice had come from so close to them, speaking from the darkness like a ghostly echo. Jason peered carefully into the gloom, and now saw the shapes of at least two men, black silhouettes seated in chairs, outlined by the glowing lights of the console they faced.

Suddenly the air was alive with sound. The calls of birds rang raucously. The chirps and rattles of a thousand insects sung in a clamour chorus. But the loudest sounds were the high piercing screeches that Jason knew could come only from Old World monkeys. His eyes searched the branches, and he realized that a fair-sized troupe of monkeys was leaping and scrambling high in the trees.

"You asked about mammals, Dr. Darien," said Kalia. "Look up above you. Now do you see them?"

Jennifer spotted the monkey troupe. "Yes! Until I heard the sound, I didn't even look. Colobus monkeys, aren't they?"

"You have a good eye." Kalia nodded.

She watched with fascination as they brachiated through the trees, swinging about like a crowd of furry infants at play. "Are there other mammals as well?"

"Yes. Follow me. The best is yet to come." The famed biologist led them forward, stepping through the dark with practiced ease, guiding them between the faint green spots that lit the path.

As they walked, Dr. Kalia explained the purpose of the dome: Animal psychologists had always wanted to find some way to observe animals in the state of nature without intruding upon them. This was the solution. By building a completely enclosed biological world, they could directly watch animal behaviors with almost no observer impact. "The idea is to duplicate the state of nature and then watch the animals at will."

Jennifer interjected, "But can we really duplicate the state of nature in a huge underground chamber? What about simple natural events, like the rising and setting of the sun?" Though she spoke to Kalia, her eyes never left the scene before them.

"Ah, quite right," Kalia agreed. "To bring our experiments under ideal conditions, we re-create life in a setting which differs in some ways from nature. But we think we've made an acceptable copy." He smiled, bringing them to a stop at a small jungle clearing. With one hand on her shoulder, he gently steered Jennifer to stand at a point where a shaft of light pierced the tent of leaves above and shot through the wall itself. She shaded her eyes and looked up. A ball of incredibly intense light was blazing in a brilliant blue sky.

"Our sun," he declared. He made no effort to conceal his pride. "It rises in the east and sets in the west. It is actually a bank of solar lamps, mounted on a moving platform above the inner roof."

"Incredible." Jennifer looked down again, trying to blink away the red afterimage.

"And the moon?" Jason asked.

Kalia dropped his hand from Jennifer's shoulder and turned. His grin banished twenty years from his age. "You've just missed it. Yes, we have a moon, and stars appropriate to the seasons."

Jason let out a breath. He looked at his host politely, but could not maintain the pretense of attention very long. His eyes were drawn to the thrilling scene before them.

As the trio resumed their tour, Kalia continued to describe the technical wonders of the dome, the systems for reproducing the torrents of the rainy season, the natural variations in cloud cover and temperature. He pointed out a thin catwalk suspended forty feet up the wall that provided better views of the creatures living in the trees and allowed the only access to the dome through several small ports. He showed them black video cameras mounted inside the wall, whirring quietly as they tracked the animals' movements via heat sensors, watching the jungle day and night. Most of all, he spoke of the thrill of bringing the project from conception to fact and finally seeing nature rage before their eyes in all its wonders. Jason and Jennifer only half heard the words. No words could do justice to what they were experiencing as they walked around the underground world.

New sections of the jungle appeared, a huge mosaic of thickets and clearings and imposing stands of trees. The jungle seemed to go on and on, surrounding them with its strong green light, their presence in a separate world marked only by passing another cluster of instruments, the electronics of the second observation post.

The stream swung closer to the wall. As they approached the bend, Jennifer stifled a gasp. A large crocodile rose from the stream, water trickling down its scales. It crawled directly toward them until it was only feet away.

"You are quite safe," Kalia spoke. "The plexiglass is armored, built to army specifications. It would stop bullets."

The crocodile lunged toward the wall. It snapped its powerful jaws over the body of a small rodent, squirting blood. Jason felt Jennifer reach for his arm. She held onto him a moment, then seemed to realize what she had done and pulled away. Jason deliberately reached for her hand. She stiffened but did not let go. The lab director continued guiding them past one fantastic scene after another.

Finally, Kalia halted them a moment. "We are coming to the spot that is my personal favorite. The third observation post." The view along the wall was obstructed by a dense copse. After rounding that screen of foliage, the scene suddenly opened broadly. Jason and Jennifer could hardly believe it.

They were facing a lake. The water glistened with reflected light of the "sun" that blazed down from its morning height. At the far end of the lake, hundreds of yards away, a rugged stone cliff rose like a gray battlement at least seventy feet above the level of the bank. A large waterfall cascaded over the lip of this cliff, spraying in a dozen rivulets over the water-darkened rocks, leaping out from the wall and finally crashing as a thick white shower into the dark green water. The lake was rimmed with tall emerald grasses and tropical flowers.

Diagonally across the lake from them, in a broad, flat clearing, four chimpanzees were sitting on their haunches, grooming each other on the buff-colored shore.

"Why, this is beauti—" Jennifer stopped. "What's coming out of their heads?"

"Dr. Darien! Your voice!" Kalia rebuked her. "Jason, perhaps you can answer the lady's question."

The chimpanzees looked like any others, apart from the tops of their heads. There, rather than the expected coarse black hair, were bald patches that circled large bulges of shiny pink material. It looked as if their brains were exposed from the top. Protruding from the center of each pink bulge was an inset cap of gleaming metal.

Jason answered slowly. "If my guess is correct, you're looking at a system to record brain activity. Probably a small set of depth electrodes planted in their brains, stabilized by the pink cement that's attached to their skulls. I suspect the metal device is an antenna for radio-monitoring. The surgery isn't all that unusual. I've seen a similar setup in Reiker's lab at Colorado."

"Very good, Doctor, as far as you go," the elder scientist said, nodding. "Yes, these are electrodes implanted in the brains of the apes. And you are correct that there is recording capability. We can check pulse rate, blood pressure, and five channels of EEG at any time. But there is much more to this

than Reiker's crude apparatus. My system doesn't just record,"—Kalia's voice rang with pride—"it stimulates! There
are small syringes that penetrate the brain, filled with supplies
of proteins. There are tiny tubes that guide the proteins to
every important region of the brain related to behavior. Do
you understand? My radio-controlled system does not merely
record brain activity, I can manipulate it."

"My God." Jennifer let it out in a quiet voice that said
more than she intended.

Jason crossed his arms on his chest. "Push-pull perfusion?"

"Yes, Jason," Dr. Kalia smiled at his new associate's astute-
ness. "Dr. Murray is most expert. Most of the mammals are
received at the Clinical Center, implanted with the push-pull
perfusion device, and placed in the dome within a week."

"But why? What's the purpose?" Jennifer sounded both
fascinated and unnerved.

"Isn't it obvious? How else can we understand the relation
of brain activity to behavior? Look, in twenty years of observation, Jane Goodall could not predict the mood swings of
her chimpanzees, much less say what part of the brain was
responsible. This laboratory allows us to study the animal in
its natural environment—the same environment, by the way,
that nurtured the birth of *Homo sapiens*—and we can determine
precisely the effect of brain activity on social behavior."

A leopard crashed down from the rocks with a scream,
rushing into the group of apes, which scattered with screeching
cries into the branches of the nearest trees. The smallest chimp
was swinging off the ground when the yellow cat raked the
ape's foot. He escaped, but a patch of blood stained the tree
trunk. The leopard paced the bank, howling up at the apes.
A bright metal cap protruded from its skull.

Jason could hear Jennifer's heavy breathing, the only sign
she gave of reacting to the violent scene. Then she asked in
a taut voice, "What other sort of animals do you have in
there? Are all of them . . . wired up like that?"

"Well, we have quite a variety. Monkeys and apes, of course,
a number of antelopes of different species, hyenas, several
leopards, a small pride of lions, two tigers . . . there's even
a single rhinoceros. I could go on. But as to your other

question: the birds, reptiles, fish, and smallest mammals are not 'wired up,' as you call it. All of the larger ones have had the surgery."

The leopard continued to prowl the bank, its thick muscles rolling as it moved, the chimps shouting at it from the trees.

"Perhaps a demonstration would make this more clear." Kalia stepped to the electric panel, sat at a chair and began to manipulate a keyboard. "Dr. McCane," he asked, "can you tell me what area of the brain is responsible for aggression?"

Jason was rather surprised at the question. "No. It's not precisely known. Although some studies implicate the outer septal nuclei and—"

"Enough. Directed aggression is due to the release of GABA-ergic septal inhibitory pathways descending to the ventromedial hypothalamus. Please watch the apes."

The lab director turned away and spoke rapidly into a dictaphone. "This is Dr. Paul Kalia dictating a primate experiment . . ." As he spoke into the recording device, he pressed several buttons and typed instructions into a computer console. Then the scientist turned back to his visitors. "Observe, my young friends."

At first there was no sign of a change. But within a minute, the cries of the chimps became furious. Almost in concert, they dropped from the trees, baring their heavy canine teeth, pounding the ground, and screaming at the leopard. It instantly began to charge at the smallest ape, but the other three chimpanzees ran directly forward at the cat, which stopped short, leapt over the nearest ape, and sped away into the bush. It hadn't been gone a moment when the smallest chimp whirled and began viciously attacking the largest male.

"Stop it," cried Jennifer. "Stop it!"

Kalia was already tapping rapidly onto the keyboard, adjusting a radio-control. The larger ape had flung his attacker aside. The smaller animal seemed ready to renew the attack but suddenly halted. It looked around in confusion a moment, then turned and bared its hindquarters to the dominant male in a classical display of subservience.

Kalia finished his dictation and turned back to his guests.

"You see, Jason. Aggression. It is just one of the states we can produce."

The two young scientists stared across the lake in stunned silence. Finally Jason asked, "Why hasn't this work been published?"

"Ah yes, the academic plea. Well, Jason, the answer is simple: The work is incomplete. In fact, this is only phase one of a two-part project. We're moving quickly on to the second phase."

"Which is?"

Kalia hesitated a moment, then spoke, choosing his words carefully. "It's a matter of genetics. . . ."

— ■ 9 ■ —

The tires sang against the tarmac as the car moved east, back toward the urban sprawl of Washington, DC. The bright familiar rusticity of rural Virginia was comforting. A warm afternoon sun slanted through the trees, throwing crisp shadows off the weathered barns. Jason and Jennifer were quiet. Somehow, the impact of Kalia's Laboratory of Brain and Behavior was too much for words. They sat side by side, each absorbed in their own reactions to the experience, almost numb.

Jennifer was the first to speak. "Well," she said, "what do you think?"

"I'm not sure. How about you?"

"That laboratory is the most amazing thing I've seen in my life!" she declared. "And the projects! The work he's doing revolutionizes primatology, absolutely. Not to mention bio-psychology, neurophysiology, who knows what else." Her voice fairly raced with the thought of it. "It's just incredible that he hasn't capitalized on it. What do you make of that?"

"You mean, postponing publication? I don't know. He seemed sincere about not wanting to rush unfinished work into print. And he has a good point about the addition of gene transfer

95

experiments. As he said, if he could develop organisms with new behavioral traits, he could test their natural fitness right there in the laboratory. By the way, wasn't your lab in Wisconsin getting into that area?"

"Yes," she answered slowly, "a little." Jennifer turned quiet again, as if something in the question had touched a nerve. She looked out the window, and Jason sensed—with more disappointment than he would have expected—that her distance had returned. He decided not to question it. Still, through the remainder of the drive, he had the impression that she stole glances at him, looks of speculation, almost suspicion. They drove on together in uneasy silence.

—■—

Two large men approached the door to Jason's town house. The overalls they wore bore the logo of his moving company. They rang the bell, waited a polite interval, then used a key to enter. The instant the door was closed, they pulled the blinds and set to work.

The men moved through the town house with expert efficiency. They assigned each room a priority, beginning with the study, and went room by room. When they failed to find the object of their search in the first quick run-through, they began again. Every drawer was pulled out and inverted. Every document was riffled. Every piece of furniture was upended, its lining slit open and explored. The pair worked wordlessly, communicating only by hand signals. Before they began in the kitchen, they lay blankets from the linen closet on the floor to muffle the sound of falling glass and silverware. They finally abandoned the first floor and began on the second.

—■—

By the time the Land Rover turned south from the beltway, it was too late to return to NIH. Instead, Jason drove Jennifer to her apartment building, a high-rise set on a knoll just south of the Institutes.

"Jason?" The young woman twisted in her seat. "What did Dr. Kalia mean about your father? I mean, he said you should be familiar with the jungle."

He smiled. "I suppose I am. My dad was an anthropologist. We mostly lived at his dig sites, which were pretty deep in the rain forest. I guess I basically grew up in the jungle." Jason paused, looking at the young primatologist. "What about your family, Jennifer?"

Even as he asked the question, Jason could see a change come over her like a sudden cloud. "Well, I'm afraid my family background is hardly so exotic. I . . ." Her voice became unsteady.

"Yes, Jennifer?"

A tiny tear appeared at the corner of her eye. Jennifer quickly wiped it away with the back of her hand. "Jason, I'm sorry that I'm so out of it. It's just that something . . . happened recently."

Jason waited.

She lifted her eyes, searching his face as if working to decide. Deciding. "Someone close to me just . . . died. Just before I came down here from Wisconsin."

"I'm sorry, Jennifer," he said softly. "A relative?"

She swallowed, still watching his face, then her words came out in a rush, like the cracking of a dam. "Yes. My brother-in-law, my older sister's husband. He was . . . he was a researcher at the lab." She caught her breath a moment, then continued. "It was a car wreck. A terrible wreck. Only they never found the other car! Jason, he was only thirty-three." She looked up at him, biting at her lower lip, fighting back more than grief: anger. Jason reached for her hands and cradled them both in his.

She went on. "It was so strange. I mean, it just doesn't make sense! He was a safe driver, a good driver. He knew that road. He was on his way home from a meeting, coming to my folks' house for Sunday dinner. Damn . . . damn it!" A tear tracked slowly down one cheek as she squeezed his fingers.

Jason hesitated, then followed an instinct. "Jennifer, was there anything . . . anything else?"

"Yes!" She almost shouted it. "He was robbed! Oh, I'm not even sure of that; but when they found the wreck, his briefcase was gone. And it's never turned up. That's what's crazy about this. He didn't even have anything in it. Just some papers and things—data from the lab."

Jason realized he had begun squeezing back as tightly as she gripped his hands. "Jennifer, may I ask what he had been working on recently?"

She shook her head. "You know, it's odd. It was the same as you. I mean, another kind of gene mapping project." She swallowed. Her voice was shaking. "Jason, I can't believe it was an accident. But . . . why would someone want to kill him?" She looked at him, searching his face as if the answer were hidden there. He saw with surprise that her expression had turned absolutely fierce. Then she brought her cheek down to rest on their hands. The tears came. She almost hid it, the quiet tracking of wetness from her eyes, but he felt the liquid moving through their joined fingers.

"I'm sorry, Jennifer." The young doctor spoke gently. "Is there anything I can do?"

She didn't answer, but moved her head slowly back and forth. She took a deep breath, then lifted her head. "Thanks. I'll be OK." She drew the back of her wrist over her cheeks. "Really. I just have to get busy with work. The project at the Brain and Behavior Lab should keep my mind occupied pretty well." Too quickly, she gathered up her things to go.

Jason watched her closely. There was something about her rapid recovery that struck him, something about the strength she called on from some hidden reserve. It was almost as if she had been testing him. As Jennifer rose from the car, he asked her when her job at Kalia's lab would start.

"Day after tomorrow."

———■———

Jennifer entered her apartment. She dropped her keys on the coffee table and walked to the window. Standing to one side, she looked through the narrow gap between the curtains and watched Jason's Land Rover disappearing up the lane.

She walked to her kitchen table and sat down, crossed her arms before her on the tabletop, and bent forward to lay her head upon them. Her eyes were closed. An observer might have thought she was asleep, exhausted at her work, but for the tension that stiffened the muscles of her shoulders and neck. She shook her head, moving it in the cradle of her arms. For a long moment, this was her only movement. "Oh, Jason," she whispered to herself, "how could you do it?" Then at last she sat up.

She pulled the computer keyboard that sat on the table toward her. With the touch of a finger, she turned on the power and the terminal screen glowed green. She tapped several keys, pressed Enter, then tapped in a command. Letters appeared in rapid succession at the top of the screen. They said: "McCane, Jason, MD Security, Classified." She tapped once more. There was a blank space, then below it, a paragraph of type. The paragraph was headed "Case A-10178. Murder. Vict: Harkus, W., MD Ex: Palo Alto PD:"

She reached for a manila folder and opened it before her. The neat blue lines of her handwriting already filled several pages in the folder. She took a deep breath, then she followed the computer type, jotting notes as she read.

——■——

Jason drove slowly toward the Center. Thinking. Two deaths, thousands of miles apart. Perhaps, he considered, it was just the effect of his recent encounter with a speeding car that made him so suspicious. Or Red's revelation about the CIA's involvement with the Institutes. But he couldn't stop thinking about the death of Jennifer's brother-in-law. And he couldn't shake the feeling: He was disquieted somehow by what he had seen at Dr. Kalia's laboratory.

At the Center entrance, he presented his identification to the night guards, who checked him in on their computer. He ran up to his office and gathered up some papers to work on at home. As he relocked the office door, he saw Tom Sherrington down the far end of the laboratory corridor.

"Hey, Jason!" Tom grinned and waved a cheery salute with a rack of test tubes. "Good news! My laser—it's coming in tomorrow!"

"Sounds great." Jason couldn't help but smile at Tom's infectious eagerness.

"Great? It's dynamite! Man, we're going to make some interesting mice! Stop by tomorrow and I'll show it to you." He waved a farewell, and disappeared through the stairwell door.

Jason turned the other way, and trotted down to his car. In minutes, he was turning off the boulevard toward home. As he pulled into his drive, the sun disappeared entirely, leaving the woods in dusky darkness. He sat for a moment, thinking in the gathering hush. Then he left the Land Rover and walked up the flagstone path toward his town house.

"Hai!" Jason leapt into a defensive stance, his body responding reflexively as he stepped into the chaos of his front hall. He moved warily into the ravaged town house, fists raised, looking about in amazement.

The sound of a voice came from overhead.

He flattened against the wall, his eyes on the space where the stairs began. It was a male voice, speaking rapidly, the words muffled by the intervening distance. Jason stepped carefully through the chaos of overturned furniture and scattered belongings, working his way past the kitchen. Every dish lay like the tiles of a mosaic, dispersed over blankets on the floor. He moved on past the living room. A glance told him that all of his paintings had been taken down, reversed, then tipped against the wall. Jason edged toward the base of the stairs, straining to hear. Finally, he could make out the words:

"And in world affairs today . . ."

He ran up the stairs, straight to his bedroom, and flung open the door. The clock radio lay on the floor amid the wreckage of his mattress, trumpeting news. He waded through the clothing which lay about in random heaps, and bent to pull the cardboard box off the floor of the closet. He reached for the file marked Harkus—his compilation of protocols and data from the Stanford labs, with the professor's indecipherable notes and his own speculations—the data he was using to try to unravel the murder.

The file was empty.

———■———

The girl lay tied to the medical examining table, naked on her back. Her fingers clawed at the vinyl, raking it into squeaking folds, but there was no escape from the gauze restraints taped to her wrists, holding her hands above her head. She bucked in the straps, her eyes wild, biting at the towel stuffed into her mouth. Her feet were bound to the stirrups, spreading her pale legs widely up and apart, exposing her completely.

The man watched her, smiling. He was standing at the sink, fastidiously washing his hands, turning as he did to look at the struggling girl. He dried his hands with a paper towel, opened a sterile package, and snapped on a fresh pair of rubber gloves. Then he adjusted the video camera that was trained on her body, whirring silkily as it recorded her struggles.

The man began to circle the examining table. He moved around her, peering down at her bare body, silently taking in the charms of the bound girl. He stepped to the head of the table, standing out of her view, and reached out to hold her thick dark hair between his hands, fanning it out to hang freely over the edge of the table. The girl jerked her head away, shaking it back and forth to escape his touch. He stepped around to her side, brushed the hair from her face, moved his hands down and slowly, deliberately grabbed both of her breasts.

The girl's fierce struggles were useless. He kneaded her breasts with his fingers, pinching the nipples. He rubbed his hands down across her belly, then up to her shoulders, then back to her breasts. He said nothing but wore a strange grin as he started to work in a circle around her, running his hands down her legs, under her bottom, back to her breasts, toying with her body. He bent over, bringing his grinning face directly above hers and looked her in the eyes as he finally reached down.

She fought to get loose, her dark hair flying as she lifted and twisted her pelvis in a vain attempt to avoid his hand. But he held her down and did what he wished, all the while smiling into her face. She screamed, but the towel in her mouth strangled the sound to a muffled cry. At last he pulled his hand away and moved down the table to stand between her spread legs. She could hear the zipper of his trousers, feel the heat of his flesh . . .

A key twisted in the door. The man whirled to face a tall

figure who stepped briskly into the Treatment Room and quickly closed the door. "Good evening, my friend," the taller man said. "I trust I'm not intruding." His eyes bore down on the rapist with absolute contempt.

At the man's entry, a third man who was watching from the corner of the room slid off his stool and snapped off the video camera. He wore an orange jacket.

"Goddamn it!" the fat rapist swore, his face red with anger. "Just ten more minutes . . ."

"Sorry, my friend. I warned you that this was an inopportune hour. There's too much activity on the ward right now to risk it."

"But . . ."

The man's blubbering protest was ignored by the white-coated figure, who turned toward the girl. At his approach, her struggles renewed. Her hoarse cries were choked by the towel as she twisted about in the restraints.

He walked to the head of the examining table, laying a cold hand on her bare shoulder. "Ah, Cindy. The job of a Normal Volunteer is not always easy." He patted her. "But when this is over, I promise that you won't remember a thing." She fixed him with her eyes, her gaze filled with pain and terror.

The fat man said, "You're sure of that? No mistakes this time, Doctor. We don't need a repeat of that last debacle!"

"It's just a matter of dosage." The white-coated figure stepped to a cabinet, selected a small vial, and began to peel off the plastic cover. "With enough ketamine, this entire evening should just seem to her like a confused dream." He uncapped the needle on the syringe, inverted the vial, and began drawing out the yellow fluid. "And your special interest in the Institutes can remain our little secret."

"Well, you do your part," the fat man spoke, still eyeing the naked girl, "and I'll do mine."

"That's right, Senator." The tall doctor walked toward the girl, holding the syringe upright. "After all, we are men of honor." He reached for Cindy's arm.

— ■ —

The first time he passed the door, Tom Sherrington wasn't sure he had heard voices coming from the Treatment Room. However, as he passed it again, carrying his rack of blood samples off the ward, the young Fellow was more certain. He thought it was odd: There were no experiments scheduled, and no one examined patients this close to the dinner hour, unless there was an emergency. He set down his tray, slipped his key into the lock, and swung open the door.

His shout echoed in the confined space. "What the hell is going on here!"

▪ 10 ▪

Jason paced in his office at NIH. The morning sun's brilliant yellow rays did nothing to dispel his angry mood. Who had done it? Who had ripped apart his town house to find the Harkus papers? Who else? he asked himself. Red, the man he called his friend. This had to be the work of the CIA.

But why? What was it about those final papers, those indecipherable scribblings of the old professor, that was so important? What was it about that string of neuroactive chemicals, ending with the cryptic exclamation, "Check with PPP!" Who was PPP? He racked his brain as he had a hundred times before, but could not think of a single scientist with those initials.

Wait, he told himself. Why should that trio of Ps necessarily refer to a person? What about another brain protein, or a gene, or even a lab technique . . . He stopped in place. A lab technique. A technique to test the function of those neuroactive chemicals. Those *proteins,* each of which was suspected to have some role in behavior. How could you check the function of those proteins in the living animal?

Yes, that was it! Check with *push-pull perfusion!* The method Dr. Kalia had perfected. The way he injected proteins into

104

the brains of the animals in his Brain and Behavior Lab!

Could it be that Dr. Harkus had realized the incredible potential of that technology just before his death? Perhaps he even intended to launch a research project like Kalia's. But why should the CIA take such an interest in this kind of research? What was it about Dr. Kalia's project, that massive undertaking at the Laboratory of Brain and Behavior, directed by one of the nation's most respected scientists, a man who had once joined forces with his own father.

Jason spun on his heel. He reached for the phone, and went through the Center switchboard to the long-distance operator.

"Jason, my God, it's been ages! Are you in town?" a voice answered in resonant tones. The young doctor was calling Aaron Beimeyer, the noted legal scholar and now dean of the University of Chicago Law School. The executor of his father's estate.

"No, I'm calling from Washington. I'm terribly sorry to trouble you . . ."

"Not at all, not at all," the lawyer interjected. "You know I'm always delighted to hear from you. How are you doing?"

A faint high-frequency whine was audible in the background. Jason hadn't heard the sound before. He assumed it was part of the long-distance switching. "I'm well, thank you, sir. Mr. Beimeyer, I hate to say this but I need a bit of a favor."

"Anything! What can I do for you?"

"Do you still have my father's journals?"

"Why yes! Of course. Why do you ask?"

Jason paused a moment. Then he began to explain what he wanted. It didn't take long. After the brief conversation, the young doctor replaced the receiver with a very small sense of accomplishment. He wasn't sure what the call would yield, but at least he had done something. The action partly relieved his growing sense of standing by while events moved mysteriously just beyond his grasp. He had to find what was going on at the Institutes.

■

Jason was leaving the Center cafeteria when he heard his name called.

"Dr. McCane! Jason!"

He turned to see Jennifer walking quickly down the hall. Her stride was purposeful.

"Good morning, Jennifer."

"Jason, I was looking for you." She wore a look of studied control, her lips pressed into a pink line. "I want to talk to you."

He nodded.

She looked around, aware of the place, the glances from passersby in the crowded hall, the usual stares of the men.

"Coffee?" he suggested. "It might be easier to talk inside."

Without a word, she passed him and walked into the cafeteria. He had seen emotions. It was obvious that she felt strongly about something. But, captured as they were by some hidden constraint, her feelings were mysterious. The two young scientists made their way through the line. She didn't say anything until they had gotten their coffee and sat down at a small table isolated in a corner.

"Jason, what happened to Cindy?"

"Cindy? What do you mean?"

Her eyes lifted to his face, then looked quickly back down at the tabletop. He was surprised to glimpse the fierceness of her stare. She said, "You're part of the human research group, aren't you?"

"Yes. I suppose I am. But—"

"Then you would be one of the doctors who administer the experimental drugs."

"Jennifer, what did you mean about Cindy?"

Again she looked up at him. This time, her eyes lingered. She examined his face as if looking for a sign, a clue. "I mean, I ate lunch with her today. For one thing, she hardly talked to me. What she did say sounded, well, strange."

Jason frowned.

She went on, "Look, I may not be a doctor, but I know something is wrong with her. She almost seems to be delirious."

Recalling that Cindy had come to the Center to serve as a kind of guinea pig, Jason asked whether Cindy had begun a medication protocol. Jennifer shook her head. She had specifically asked Cindy last week; the volunteer wasn't due to start any experiments until next Monday. Jason mentioned that Tom Sherrington was in charge of the ward experiments and suggested that they check with him.

"I tried. Tom isn't in his lab, and his secretary hasn't seen him today. Dr. McCane, what's going on?" There was the flare of accusation in her eyes.

"Well," Jason asked hesitantly, "would Cindy use any drugs on her own?"

"Never! That girl intends to be a doctor! She even dreaded the idea of taking the drugs she expects to get here during the research. Jason, I'm . . . I'm going to have someone see her."

He looked at her green eyes, shining with concern. He didn't hesitate.

"I will. Right now."

"You? But you . . ." She swallowed. She was shaking her head as she watched him rise and progress rapidly through the cafeteria, disappearing around the corner with the last billow of his white coattails.

—■—

He found Cindy on the ward, sitting in her darkened room. She was busy at a desk, her back to the door, humming tunelessly under her breath. He stepped around the desk and saw what she was doing. Somewhere, the young Normal Volunteer had found a plastic doll. As she hummed away, oblivious to Jason, the girl was wrapping a piece of string around and around the body of the doll.

"Cindy?"

She didn't look up, but continued working at her task.

"Cindy? Are you all right?"

The girl looked up, as if Jason had just come in. "Oh, hi, Dr. McCane." She smiled up at him, her eyes not quite connecting with his, then glanced down again to her doll.

He lifted a chair and set it down beside her. "Cindy, do you know where you are?"

She continued winding the string around and around the neck of the doll, calmly, diligently. "Come on,"—she grinned up again—"you know where . . ." She stopped, leaving the thought unfinished, and smiled shyly at him for another moment before lowering her eyes again to her work.

Jason reached forward and gently disengaged her hands from the doll. She did not resist, letting him set it aside. He held her hands, feeling the sweat. "Cindy, where are you now? Are you in the hospital?"

"Yes."

"Are you at home?"

"Yes."

He felt her hands begin to fidget in his, a smile fixed on her face, her eyes looking at everything and nothing. Jason clasped her hands more firmly. "Cindy, is something wrong? What's wrong?"

"What's wrong?" she echoed him. "What's wrong? I don't know. . . ." The girl looked down at where their hands met, blinking, as if wondering at the sight, then looked out the window opposite. "Are we going to have more experiments today?" Her eyes flashed anxiously toward Jason for a moment, then turned again to stare out the window.

He looked at her carefully. "What do you mean, experiments, Cindy?"

"You know. . . ." She swallowed as her words trailed off, and she hugged herself, starting to shiver.

"Cindy, have you had any drugs?"

"Drugs . . . No . . . Please. No drugs. I don't want any needles! Oh, Dr. McCane, I don't want it!" She suddenly broke out in piteous sobs, burying her head against his chest. Jason embraced her, rocking her gently. "Dr. McCane, I can't think! It's all wrong! I've had such terrible dreams!" She continued crying, holding him tightly, soaking the front of his lab coat with her tears.

"OK," he said, "OK, Cindy. It will be all right." The crying went on as the girl clung to him like a terrified child. He rocked her, soothing her, saying it over and over again, "It's all right. You're safe now. It's all right. . . ." Finally, she turned her tear-streaked face toward his, still sobbing, but looking at him with the beginning of recognition.

"Cindy," he asked quietly, "what is it? What are you afraid of?"

The girl slowly shook her head, continuing to look at him,

her eyes staring forward with confusion and pain. Then she spoke, just a hoarse whisper, "Take me away from here, Dr. McCane. I don't want to be here anymore. Please . . ." She looked at him as if he were her last hope on earth.

"Cindy," he asked, "would you like to go for a walk?"

The girl nodded, her eyes fixed on his face as if afraid to look away, her face precariously at the edge of tears. Jason helped her to her feet and walked her to the door, supporting her with an arm wrapped around her waist. They stepped into the carpeted hall where a nurse was hovering with a look of concern, and Jason signaled to her that he would take care of the girl.

The two of them moved slowly down the pastel hall toward the ward exit. Cindy was slumped against the young doctor, exhausted, clinging to him like a survivor to a life raft. She said nothing, but continued to look up at him silently. Then, as they neared the door to the Treatment Room, the girl gave out a strangled gasp and began to moan, "No, no . . ." staring at the door. Suddenly, she started thrashing wildly in his arms.

"Cindy! Cindy, what is it?"

Jason felt a sledgehammer blow slam into his back and he flew to the floor. In a quick roll, he shot back to his feet, facing down the hall in a crouch.

"You stay away from her!" Tony shouted. The huge weight lifter was standing in the hall, glaring viciously at the doctor, clasping and unclasping his meaty fists. "You keep away! You're just trying to turn her against me! She's my girl!"

Jason straightened, keeping his distance. "Tony, she's sick, can't you see that? She needs help!"

"Like hell she does! If I see you with her again, I'll kill you!"

The charge nurse came bustling down the hall. She stooped to help Cindy from the floor, holding the crying girl like a baby. "Tony," she demanded, "what's going on here? Control yourself!"

"You go to hell!" He turned to face the nurse, then back to Jason. "You all go to hell!" Tony whirled and stalked heavily down the hall. He entered his room, and they could hear the banging of cabinets and the screech of drawers.

"It sounds like we're about to lose a Normal Volunteer," the nurse said anxiously to Jason. "I have to notify the Human Experimentation Committee at once." The matronly figure put her arm around Cindy, who was still staring blankly at the door to the Treatment Room, shaking her head slowly back and forth. The two moved together down the hall toward the nurses' station.

Jason straightened completely, wincing from the contusion between his shoulder blades. He turned to face the Treatment Room. Finding the key among the bunch on his ring, he unlocked the door and stepped inside. The room looked perfectly normal. He checked the drug cabinets and saw that they were all locked. He searched the drawers and found the usual array of instruments. He ignored the brown stains of dried blood on the floor—a common sight in a room used for blood drawing. As an afterthought, he checked the trash can. All he found was a random collection of hospital trash, tubing and bandage wrappers and paper towels. Except for the bottom of the can, where he found several long lengths of unrolled gauze taped into mashed wads of sweat-stained cotton, in the typical form of padded restraints.

—■—

Dr. Murray was just leaving the laboratory wing when he encountered Jason as he was coming down the corridor. "Well, Jason—"

"Dr. Murray," Jason interjected, "have you seen Tom?" The branch chief pulled a face at Jason's abruptness. Jason said, "Forgive me, but something has come up with one of the Normal Volunteers." As he spoke, Jason arched his shoulders back, trying to control the stabbing pain between his shoulder blades. "Tom's not in his lab or his office. I even tried his home."

"Jason," Murray began, smiling tightly. His tone conveyed a reproof, "I hardly think we need concern ourselves with Dr. Sherrington's whereabouts. He's probably decided to make a long weekend of it. Now, what's this about a Normal Volunteer?"

Jason described how he had found Cindy.

The chief's face drew into a frown. "A medication effect, I suppose."

Jason shook his head. "To my knowledge she wasn't due for any medication experiments this week."

"Have you checked the computer?"

"No, I—"

"Have you run a full tox screen?"

"No," Jason answered. "But that's certainly a good idea. I'll—"

"Jason,"—Murray folded his arms and faced his young colleague with something akin to a glare—"look here. As the head of human experimentation, I am responsible for those volunteers. Don't trouble yourself any further with this matter. I'll take care of Cindy. Personally."

———■———

"Jason, what is it? You look beat." Jennifer found him standing outside his office in the third-floor hall, reaching to massage his spine.

He half chuckled. "That's the word for it." He told her the story of his visit to the ward, both of his encounter with Cindy and his run-in with the menacing Tony.

Her only response was a quiet "My God."

"I've just finished talking to Dr. Murray now. He had no idea what could have happened to her . . . except for the possibility that she'd been on a drug protocol. Then he suggested we check the computer experiment log."

"And?"

Jason explained that the computer files showed no record of any drug given to the young volunteer. Just to be sure, he planned to run a complete toxicology screen, blood and urine. "Unfortunately, until Tony is off the ward, it would probably only compound the problem if I do it. Dr. Murray promised to take care of Cindy himself."

"Do you think she'll be all right?"

He continued moving his fist in slow circles along his back. "I wish I could say. If I didn't know better, I'd suspect this was a psychotic break. Or a drug intoxication. Frankly, I can't make a diagnosis at this point. But I'll say one thing: That girl is terrified." He winced a little as the pain shot up to his neck and rubbed more vigorously.

"Oh, my poor Jason." Jennifer came closer. She reached behind him, gently pushing his hand away, and expertly began to work her fingers into the muscles along his spine.

He looked at her with surprise, but he couldn't catch her eyes. She was solemnly concentrating on his back, digging with a soft diligent pressure into the muscle, rubbing away the pain.

He grunted, then faced the wall, leaning with his hands flat against it. "Oh yes, just like that. Where did you learn to do this?"

Jennifer didn't answer his question. She continued kneading his back, and then resolutely declared, "It's my fault."

"Jennifer . . ."

She dismissed his protest. "No, you only went up there because of me. How can I make it up to you?"

"You are." He shifted his back under her expert fingers.

Jennifer thought a moment. She took in one deep breath. Then she spoke, "Dinner at my place, seven-thirty?"

Jason turned slowly from the wall to face her. He smiled. "I'll bring the wine."

———■———

"Eighty-four, eighty-five . . ." Red whispered the count to himself as he strained at his push-ups. All around him in the Research Oversight Directorate data center, his CIA colleagues bent over their computer terminals. They stared at their glowing screens, tapped quickly at their keyboards, activated their printers. "Eighty-eight . . ." They ignored the big agent as he exercised in the middle of the floor—a familiar sight. Red could not bear to wait as his computer followed his instructions, searching through a list of donors to the NIH, analyzing, testing hypotheses, looking for any hint of a pattern. A week of data crunching had yielded nothing. They were running out of tricks. He took out his frustration on his triceps. "Ninety-three . . ."

A sudden beep brought him to a halt. He rose from the

floor to see the screen of his terminal fill with symbols. An instant later, his printer clattered to life.

"Ah hah!" he exclaimed. Jimmy, his young assistant, swung out of his seat. Mrs. B., the senior data analyst, scurried over. The three of them looked together at the printout.

Four names appeared. Each was a private foundation that had sprung into existence in the last two years. Each gave away more than one hundred million dollars a year. Each had a single benefactor: the National Institutes of Health.

"Fronts!" Red nearly shouted. "They're all just fronts to feed money into NIH. Mrs. B.,"—he turned toward the woman—"where the hell is that money coming from?"

The buxom analyst grinned. She loved the chase. She plopped herself down at Red's computer and went to work. As Red and Jimmy looked on, awed by the speed of her fingers, she used the CIA's remarkable computer network to stalk the financial histories of those four foundations. In a matter of minutes, she cleared the screen and pressed the Print key. She giggled aloud. A twelve-digit number appeared in the center of a single sheet.

"What is it?" Red ripped off the sheet and stared at the number. The woman was still giggling. "OK, Mrs. B., don't torture me!"

Her eyes twinkled as she responded, "Swiss bank account."

"You mean . . . ?"

"Yep. All four of those foundations move their money through the same account. And that's not all: I can tell you that this account is controlled through Washington DC!"

Red bent and kissed her soundly on the cheek. "I love you!"

Mrs. B. histrionically wiped her cheek. "Red, we have simply got to find you a younger woman."

The big agent just smiled. "Now, just tell me two things: First, who controls this account? Second, what the hell is NIH doing with all that money?"

The woman made a face. She said she could work on the first problem, but it would take time. In regard to the second question, she told Red that accounting within the Institutes was incredibly tough to track.

"Great," he said. "We don't know where the money comes from, or where it's going! Isn't there a congressional committee that oversees the Institutes' spending? Who's in charge of that?"

"Senator Bowie," she responded.

Just then, the phone rang. Red grabbed it. "What? Sonofabitch, why didn't you tell me his apartment was broken into last night! No, it wasn't my team. So who the hell was it?"

―∎11∎―

O h, this is just delicious!" Jennifer took another sip of the
Bordeaux and rolled the glass between her hands, bending
her head forward to savor the bouquet, her eyes closed,
her lips in a slight smile. They had moved to the living room
to finish the wine after dinner. She was stretched out in an
overstuffed velvet chair, with her bare feet propped on a
hassock. "Where did you say it's from?"

Jason lay on his back on the thick rug, listening to the
chamber music she had selected. "Cos d'Estournel? Well, they
share a border with Château Lafite, just across a little stream.
I suppose it tastes something like its famous neighbor, but I
can almost afford it."

Jennifer smiled a little wistfully and looked down at the
swirling claret in her glass. "I guess you've been just about
every place."

He shook his head, facing the ceiling. "No. A few places.
Enough to feel like I've got a lot to see." He rolled onto his
side to smile up at her. From the floor, he had a disturbingly
good view of her legs. "How about you?"

Jennifer looked down at him, her startling blue-green eyes
meeting Jason's for a moment, then looked back into her

glass. She slowly moved the tip of a finger around the rim. "I guess I'm basically a Midwest girl. In fact, I was born about three streets away from the place where I've been living in Madison. My father's on the English faculty at the university."

"Then, the East Coast is a new experience for you?"

She shook her head. "I came out east to Radcliffe, but I went straight back after grad school. To tell the truth, the East Coast seemed a bit stuffy. A little too much . . . posturing. Do you know what I mean? Academics in place of scholarship, scholarship in place of thought, something like that." Jennifer took another sip of the wine, still looking contemplative, as her tongue caught a ruby drop and lightly traced the outline of her pink lips. "I guess the only other place I've been was my senior year in Japan. That's where I learned to do massage." She smiled at him. "Shiatsu, they call it."

Jason nodded, turning onto his back again. "Ah, that was wonderful." He shifted his back against the carpet.

Jennifer watched him a moment, hesitating. Her grip on the stem of the glass became so tight that the red surface broke in tremulous ripples. She set down her glass and moved to kneel beside him on the rug. "You haven't gotten the full effect. It's really much better if I can work directly on your skin." She reached forward and started unbuttoning his shirt.

Jason looked up at her speculatively. The light from the wicker lamp shone warmly off her swinging hair. She worked at the buttons with a calm diligence that was at the verge of being something else. As she started to pull his shirttails out, he reached for her hands, gently holding them in his. She held very still. He looked up into her face, trying to capture her gaze with his.

"Jennifer?" he asked softly.

For a moment more they searched each other's faces. Then she quickly bent her head down to him, and they kissed. Their mouths joined hungrily, the tongues meeting. He rolled them over, his lips moving down to her neck, his hands touching her gently, exploring. She lifted her hands up to him, pulling off his shirt, then she caressed his chest as he was caressing hers.

"You haven't gotten the full effect," Jason said, smiling

between kisses. "It's really much better if I can work directly on your skin."

"Oh! You plagiarist! I've been practicing that line all afternoon!" She pretended outrage for a moment, then stretched her arms overhead.

He pulled her blouse off over her head. Then he unhooked her bra and her breasts were bare, swinging gently, her tan blending into their pinkness. A furious blush lit her cheeks. He kissed her mouth again, and he licked the tips of two fingers. Barely touching, he ran his hand over one breast, found her nipple, and began to roll it lightly between his wet fingertips. He returned his mouth to hers.

She moaned and pulled her mouth away from his lips. "Wait," she said softly. She stopped him, lightly placing her hand atop his. She licked his neck beneath his beard and kissed the wet place that her tongue had been. "Wait, just a moment." She had begun to tremble again, a trembling that contradicted the heat he could feel in her. She ran her hand over his face, tracing his lips with her agile fingertips. "I'd better take care of . . ." She shrugged, glancing away.

He lifted himself onto his arm. She gripped his shoulder as if to get up. He felt a shiver cascade from her hand to his shoulder. She slipped from beneath him and walked quickly across the room, half-nude. Her hand went around the corner, and the light went on in the bathroom. She stepped inside, out of his sight.

When Jennifer stepped out again, she was holding a revolver. He leapt to his feet.

"No!" she shouted. "Stay where you are!" Her eyes were like fire. She was crouched, clasping the gun in both hands, pointing it at his head.

"Jennifer, what in hell is going on?" he said in a clipped low voice.

"You . . ." She shook her head, sweeping her mane of hair as if trying to clear a thought. "You're going to tell me exactly that."

She reached one hand behind her into the bathroom and pulled out a length of rope. Without deflecting the aim of the gun a moment, she tossed the rope at his feet. "You're going to give me some information. We're going to stay here until you do. Tie your feet together." She was breathing deeply, and her shoulders were shaking. The muzzle of the gun shook too, but she kept it sighted on his forehead.

Jason stood perfectly still. He ignored the rope. His feet had automatically spaced themselves at the width of his shoulders. He rested his hands lightly on his thighs. "Jennifer, I don't know why you're doing this. Put down the gun."

"Oh, no! Don't even imagine you can talk me out of this. Tie them." She pointed at the rope with one hand.

"Now, look here," he said as he took a step closer.

"Don't!" She returned her hand to the gun and thrust it out, her finger trembling on the trigger.

Jason's eyes had narrowed. His gaze centered on the gun. He was taking slow even breaths. "I don't like guns," he said quietly. His jaw tightened. The muscles of his abdomen bunched into a nobby sheet. His arms didn't move but tensed like cables of braided copper. "Now I'm going to take yours away."

She looked at his transformation with confusion. Then she screamed.

Jason launched himself across the room, whirling in the air, spinning the heel of his foot up, slamming it from beneath into the butt of the gun, which soared into the wall. His hands pinned Jennifer's body to the floor, her arms behind her back.

"No!" she screamed. She struggled, kicking with her feet, twisting her body to escape him. He shot one hand behind her knees, the other clamping her wrists together, and held her facedown on the carpet, immobilized, helpless, with all her limbs locked behind her waist. "No, no, no!" Her voice became a sob, stifled by the carpet.

"Who are you working for, Jennifer?" His voice was calm. "The CIA? The Department of Defense? Who?"

"Let me go, goddamn you to hell!" She wriggled furiously, hardly moving on the floor.

"Who, Jennifer? Are you one of Red's spies? An agent of our noble government? The Research Oversight Directorate?"

"Let go!" She continued to fight, tugging with her wrists, lifting her body off the floor with the arching of her back, then slamming her pelvis back onto the carpet. She wrenched herself from side to side. Her face went red. Her eyes filled with tears. "Damn you, you won't get away with this!"

He nodded. "Perhaps you're right. But I'll probably be wiser for it. Who are you working for, Jennifer?"

"You bastard! What are you going to do with me? Pump me full of drugs like Cindy? Run me off the road like my brother-in-law? Or just break my skull like your dear Professor Harkus?"

"What? What in God's name are you talking about?"

"Don't you give me that. You can't get away with it! The evidence is there! You can kill me, but you won't ever get away with it!"

Jason looked at the crying girl he was holding on the floor. Wet tangles of her tawny hair spilled across her face. Her eyes were rimmed with red. A pink burn spread across her breasts from rubbing on the carpet.

He let go of her arms and sat back beside her cross-legged, his hands on his knees.

Jennifer didn't move for a moment. The sudden release of her limbs surprised her. Slowly, looking up at him as if she expected him to overpower her again at any moment, she straightened her legs. She drew her hands from behind her back and pushed herself off the floor. On her hands and knees, she eyed the revolver, several feet in front of her on the carpet.

"Go ahead," Jason said.

She reached a hand to her face, pulling her hair away from her eyes and dragging the wet strands out of her mouth. She turned her head to look at him. Freed from the constraints of her acting, the wariness of her look was vivid.

"Go ahead," Jason repeated.

She shook her head slowly, as if all of the energy had seeped from her with her tears. A shrug of defeat.

Then, like a cat, she sprang across the floor. Her hands closed on the revolver. She threw her back against the wall and sat, centering the barrel on his chest.

Jason didn't move. His arms were loose, his hands hung in a relaxed way over his knees. "Your finger is outside the trigger guard," he said, nodding toward the gun.

"Oh!" She looked at her hands and realized that he was right. She put her index finger carefully onto the trigger and looked up at him again. Her hair had fallen over one eye and she was sitting with her legs exposed, her skirt bunched at her waist.

"Now," Jason said quietly. "Tell me why you think I am responsible for these things."

"I . . ." Jennifer shook her head. She glanced down at herself. Self-consciously, she dropped her hand and pulled her skirt down between her legs.

"Yes?" he encouraged.

She pursed her lips, closing them so tightly they turned white. Then she spoke. Her words came out in a rapid eruption. "First of all, I know about Harkus. You were one of the last people to see him alive. You had access to the labs. You 'found' his body. You were the first listed suspect of the Stanford police."

"Palo Alto," he corrected. "Go on."

"Palo Alto," she concurred. She seemed to realize her bareness and laid one arm across her breasts while continuing her angry soliloquy: "Second, you have an article by Steven Shay that has never been published. It was one of the papers stolen from his car when he was killed on his way home. He was coming from the Chicago neuroscience meetings. You were at those meetings!"

"Steven Shay! You mean, he was . . ."

"Yes. He is . . . was my brother-in-law." Her eyes filled for a moment. "Third," she continued, "you entered the Center last night at seven forty-eight P.M. and left soon after. I checked on the drug screen this afternoon; the pharmacologist estimates that Cindy was given an injection of ketamine at almost exactly that time last night." She glared at him with undisguised hate. "What's going on, Dr. Jason McCane?"

Jason's posture hadn't changed. He sat as if he were meditating, except that his eyes were resting on Jennifer's face. "Jennifer," he responded, "may I ask how it is that you gathered this information?"

"The computer." There might have been a note of pride in her voice, if it weren't for the evident rage. She told him how she had investigated him: using a link to the FBI computers to verify his identity with a fingerprint, discovering that the FBI had listed him as a possible suspect in the Harkus murder, checking his comings and goings at the Center through the computer records entered by the guards. "Steven's article,"—she took a breath, and let it out—"of course, I know about on my own."

He nodded, closing his eyes.

"Jason," she said, her voice ringing with anger, "explain what you've done! Why did you kill Professor Harkus?"

"I didn't."

"Why did you drug Cindy?"

"I didn't."

"Then what . . . how did you get Steven's article?"

"I told you, Dr. Murray gave it to me."

"That's not true!" She was emphatic. "I worked with Steven. I know he didn't send it to NIH!"

"Murray pulled the article out of his file. He didn't say how he'd gotten it."

Her arms were shaking. At first he thought it was the weight of the gun. Then he saw that her entire upper body was shivering. "What about last night? Explain why you were at the Center."

"I went to get some papers to work on at home. I was in the building less than fifteen minutes! Tom Sherrington saw me. You can ask him."

"Dr. Sherrington never showed up at work today."

Jason frowned.

"What about Dr. Harkus?" Jennifer sniffed and drew her hand across her nose, then reaimed the gun at Jason. "How do you explain the fact that the FBI listed you as a suspect?"

Jason stroked his thumb down his cheek. He saw Jennifer start at the gesture, and he returned his hand slowly to his knee. "If the FBI has the case, why don't you ask them?"

"I have. They . . . don't have any evidence that you were the murderer." She appeared reluctant to say it.

"You don't work for them?"

"Of course not!"

"Or for the CIA?"

"No! . . . Jason?" She was still shaking. She wrapped her other arm around, hugging herself, pointing the gun behind her as if she had forgotten it. "What are you talking about? The CIA? Oh, goddamn it, what's going on?"

"No." He exhaled slowly. "Perhaps you're not one of Red's. You are an extraordinary actress, but why act with a blown cover and a gun in your hand?" He shook his head back and forth. "Speaking of which, if you're not with the Company, what are you doing with a police special?"

"A what?"

"Your thirty-eight. That metal object you're holding."

She looked at the gun as if he'd just announced it had magical properties. "It's . . . My father made me bring it. Country girl goes to the big city and all that." She almost smiled before the anger saved her. "It's a good thing he did."

Jason looked at the young woman, her back against the wall, shivering and awkwardly trying to cover her breasts. The doctor let out a breath. He reached across the floor with one hand, retrieving her blouse. He rose and brought it over to her. She swung the revolver to follow him. He held out the blouse, keeping his distance.

"Drop it," she told him.

He did so and returned to his place on the floor, crossing his legs.

She hesitated. Then, with quick motions she placed the revolver beside her on the floor, lifted the blouse, pulled it over her head, and grabbed up the gun again. Jason hadn't moved.

"Jennifer," he said, "it seems we have something in common."

"What do you mean?"

"Just before each of us arrived here, someone at each of our labs was apparently murdered. I agree with you that something's going on, and I want to know what it is just as badly as you do."

"I'm sure."

He closed his eyes a moment, as if lost in thought, or tired of thought. When he opened them, he looked straight into her eyes and spoke very softly. "Jennifer, this is very important:

I did not kill Dr. Harkus. And I did not kill your brother-in-law."

She tightened her chin. The gun was still pointed at him. "Please believe me."

She didn't move. The expression she wore was filled with fury and suspicion, a persistence, a wall. The gun remained aimed at his chest.

He stood up and began to pull on his shirt. He tucked it in, not bothering with the buttons.

"Damn you!" she cried. "You . . . you're so damned cool! So fucking unmovable! Nothing matters to you! Nothing touches you! You've got a heart like a goddamned stone!"

"I've been told."

"Goddamn you to hell! Jason McCane, you don't know what it's like! You have no idea what it means to lose someone you love!"

He stopped. For a minute he just stood quite still, looking at her. Even as she held the gun on him, she felt afraid, looking into those eyes. She saw something there she couldn't name, something that made her suck in a breath and bring her hand to her mouth.

"Good night, Jennifer." He said it gently. He threw his jacket over his shoulder and left.

———■———

The Orion Club stood just off Embassy Row, west of Dupont Circle, in a neighborhood of stately four-story mansions, town homes of the diplomatic elite. The club exuded the ambience of a private bank, an unblushing bastion of certain kind of privilege. Traffic pulled to its steps up a banked cobble drive, moving in a single direction following the injunctions In and Out carved deeply into the two widely spaced marble gateways.

A long Mercedes purred up to the doors and disgorged its passenger, then sped around the drive to search for parking.

"Good evening, Senator." The liveried doorman bowed him through the door, and the man passed with a nod, working at the buttons of his vicuña coat. He deposited it at the cloak room and followed the hall toward the man stationed at the tall escritoire outside the dining room.

"Ah, Senator Bowie! A late dinner, sir?" the man greeted him. The maître d' searched the room with his eyes, then turned back. "I believe your usual table is available." He bowed to the senator, then jauntily led the way through the other diners to a small corner table, draped in white Irish linen, set with silver and crystal.

Though the crowd was sparse, it was studded with elegantly dressed older men—politicians, luminaries of the Washington social scene, or beyond-the-scenes power brokers, in many cases accompanied by pretty young women half their age. Tables were set discreetly apart, and though a hum of conversation filled the room, the talk was private. The diners huddled over their drinks, some with heads bent in close discussion, some exchanging only freighted glances across the room, all taking for granted the aura of quiet luxury.

The maître d' pulled back a chair, bowed again, and left to make his way back to his station. Senator Bowie was seated facing the harpist, who strummed a melodic air for the distinguished diners.

A black-suited waiter appeared at his side. "Good evening, sir. May I present the selections?" He passed a gilt-edged card to the senator, along with a pencil.

"Thank you, Alfred," the rotund man said as he accepted the card.

"May I suggest the Rockfish en croute, sir? I believe the recipe was extorted from the personnel at Le Lion d'Or."

The senator laughed. "Very good! We shall see."

The waiter left him to peruse the menu. Bowie scanned quickly down the card, checking off his choices with the pencil, then laid them both aside. Leaning forward onto his soft thick forearms, he turned his attention to the young harpist. She was quite young, with a thin waist under the long black dress. Probably a conservatory student, he guessed. He tried to imagine her without the dress, her pale limbs taut with sexual energy and fear. He made a mental note to initiate inquiries.

The waiter returned and accepted the card from the politician. "Yes, sir," he said, "and about a wine?"

Bowie looked thoughtful. "Actually, Alfred, I believe I shall make my own selection tonight."

"Shall I ask the sommelier to bring a key to the cellar?"

"Thank you, no. I believe I have my own."

"Very good, sir." The waiter bowed and moved off toward the kitchen.

The senator waited only a minute, casually surveying the crowd, then he rose from his seat and made his way back toward the entrance to the dining room. However, as he passed through the vestibule, he turned sharply into a narrow companionway, around a corner, then down a steep winding staircase. Stepping across the basement hall, he produced a key and approached a paneled door of split veneer.

He worked the key into the lock and swung open the wine cellar door. Then he reached out, fumbling for the light chain.

"Greetings, Senator."

The light flashed on suddenly. A square-jawed man sat directly before him on stacked cases of champagne, holding the end of the light chain with the tips of his fingers.

Bowie recovered his composure. "Hello, 'Mr. Williams.' " He said the name ironically. The politician closed the door, and barely acknowledged the other man's presence. He turned instead to search among the wines laid down in tall racks.

"Senator,"—the man shifted slightly on his perch, fingering the mole under his left eye—"I believe we have a problem."

"Oh?" Bowie unracked an old St. Emilion, brushing the dust off the vintage label.

"Yes. As you know, we liberated the Harkus papers from the young doctor, hoping to stop him from uncovering the Agency's role in the murder. However, the Director is concerned that the Agency is facing another risk."

"The Agency is facing a risk?" The fat senator replaced the bottle with a clatter and turned to face the other man. "The *Agency* is facing a risk? What the hell do you think *I'm* facing! I've got the goddamned CIA asking for my NIH financial records!"

"Senator, the Research Oversight Directorate has no idea what we are doing at the Institutes, I can assure you—"

"You can assure me like hell!" the politician exploded. "Your Director sends his men all over the damned country, blowing people away just to get research data to speed up the project!

Then he moves into my own backyard, trying to run down experts that it's taken us years to locate!" His face went red with anger. "And now I'm the one who has to hide the project from the CIA!"

"Mr. Bowie, we don't enjoy these complications any more than you do! But circumstances have forced us to change our plan."

"Cut the bullshit."

The other man controlled a tremor at the angle of his jaw. "As you wish. Dr. McCane has not confined himself to investigating the murder of Dr. Harkus. We have evidence that he has become suspicious of activities at the Institutes."

"What! But Layla didn't tell me."

"Ah, so you were using Dr. Kalia's daughter to watch Dr. McCane! Very clever, Senator. But she clearly was distracted from obtaining this information, or we might have known this sooner."

"What is the evidence?" Bowie snapped.

"Oh, a telephone call here, a recorded conversation there. It falls into a pattern. We cannot let him discover our involvement in the Institutes."

"But we haven't even gotten his input on the automatic gene sequen—"

The man raised his hand. "I'm afraid there's more. The young lady. Her suspicions also seem to be aroused, and—"

The senator interrupted, speaking through clenched teeth, "And just what in hell do you plan to do about it?"

The man called Williams dropped his hands onto his knees. He tilted his head up to face the senator. "Tell your team to get whatever research help they can from Doctors McCane and Darien immediately. Then,"—he sighed heavily—"your friends at the Institutes can take care of them."

"Goddamnit!" the fat senator exploded. He waddled toward the other man, his face as red as a beet. "Do you know what we go through to recruit these people? Do you know the risks I've taken for you bloodthirsty bastards? That's it! I've had enough! I want out."

The square-jawed man leapt off the stack of boxes with surprising agility, grabbed the fat man by his lapels, and slammed him back against the racks of wine. "You want out, do you? You don't like risks? Well, how about those risks you take in the Treatment Room? How about those videotapes of yours, the ones that so vividly document your adventures with those lovely Normal Volunteers? How would you like us to send copies straight to the TV networks?"

The fat politician's face became grotesquely pale. "You wouldn't . . ." he whispered. But he saw from Williams's face that he would.

The man who called himself Williams dropped the senator and stepped back. "You'll cooperate, Mr. Bowie. You'll do what you're told in regard to the two young scientists." Then, as if he was remembering something, a smile began to curl the edge of one thin lip. "Perhaps this will make up for your trouble." He drew a small envelope from his jacket, and held it out to the senator.

Bowie straightened his jacket, struggling to regain his dignity. He reached for the envelope, ripped it open, and withdrew two photographs. Terror gradually left his face. It was replaced with another kind of heat. "This is the girl?"

"You didn't know? They say she is quite beautiful." He wore an expression that verged toward a sneer.

The politician swallowed. He spoke, almost to himself, "I had no idea . . ." He continued to look at the picture, running his tongue unconsciously back and forth behind his heavy lips. Then he looked up, pocketing the photos. "I'll let the doctor know in the morning."

—■—

Bowie sat back contentedly from the remains of his fish, tilting the Chambertin back and forth in his glass. After gulping down the last of the wine, he accepted a slender cheroot from a wooden box brought by the waiter. He snipped off the end and let the waiter light it with a long match. He watched the waiter move away across the room.

Discreetly, he slipped a photograph from his pocket, cupping it in his hand. The young harpist was forgotten. Bowie sucked in the smoke, then blew it out in a dense blue cloud, holding the cigar to one side, looking at the picture.

One of his fellow senators entered the dining room. The man hailed him with a hearty hello from the door. Heads turned all around the room. Bowie's eyes didn't move. They were fixed on the photo, arrested by the small black and white image of a young primatologist from Wisconsin.

— ■ 12 ■ —

rickets were singing in the grass. Their gentle music rose and fell on the midnight wind. Only the crickets, the wind, and the rhythmic landings of his feet broke the silence of the night as Jason returned from his run.

He had needed the run. He had needed to use his body, to harness his energy into an action that would rescue him from thought. The run had been a good one, quick, hard, a willful floating through the oblivion of midnight. But he knew just why he'd run and why the run had failed. Jennifer. Her image burned as bright as ever in his mind.

He slowed to a trot, leapt the boxwood hedge, and crossed the lawn, lifting his knees to his chest, like a stallion in traces, stretching the tendons, shaking out the muscles. He didn't see the figure in the shadows until he was yards away.

He stopped. His entire body tensed. His heart thudded a crescendo. His eyes shifted quickly, scanning the vicinity. He saw no one else.

The figure didn't move. It was sitting on the top of the darkened steps, just a black form barely seen against the blackness of the night.

"Jason?" The voice was hesitant.

He stepped forward, peering into the shadows. "Jennifer?"

She was hugging herself, her arms wrapped around her knees to draw them to her chest. As he approached the steps, she unfolded her arms and held them out to him, palms up. In another setting, the gesture might have been an invitation to embrace. He knew she was simply showing him that she had no weapon.

He stood at the bottom of the stairs, several feet below her, and waited.

"Jason,"—her voice sounded strained—"may I ask you a question?"

"What is it, Jennifer?" Damn her, he thought. Damn her. Even in the stark shadows of the night, the pale moonlight sculpting her in unforgiving marble, she was so beautiful.

"Jason." She swallowed once, "I . . . You let me get the gun back, didn't you?"

He nodded.

"Why?"

He was silent for a moment. When he spoke again he was looking away from her, looking into space. "When I was young, I spent a year with a teacher named Ie Ming. He had a saying: There is only one thing more dangerous than not recognizing an enemy—that is not recognizing a friend."

Jennifer swallowed. "Jason . . . I thought about what you said. About the timing of your visit to the Center last night, about Steven's paper, about . . . Jason, I was wrong." Her eyes sought his. He knew it. He had to meet them. A silver tear caught the moonlight, running slowly over her cheek. She ignored it, she didn't wipe the tear, she just locked her gaze unblinking on his face and said with her eyes what she had come to say. "Jason . . . I didn't know . . . I went back to the computer tonight, I mean, your parents . . ."

"Do you want to walk a little?"

"Jason, I'm so sorry . . ."

"Come on. Let's walk."

She was up. She came down the stairs in a rush, then stood before him, as if perched at the edge of a body of water. He drew a breath. Then he opened his arms. She was in them in an instant. "Oh, Jason, I didn't mean . . ."

"Hey . . ." he held her and stroked a hand down the back of her head. "Hey, Jennifer! Don't . . . it doesn't matter."

"It does! Oh, I was such a fool! Why didn't I trust—"

"Shh, come on. You had no reason to trust me."

"Not you—myself! Jason,"—she tilted her head back from his chest to look up into his face—"I had an instinct, a feeling. About you, I mean. I ignored it. I was so bent on finding out. . . . Oh, hell."

"From what I understand, you had every reason for what you did. You were very brave. Come on," he said gently.

She shook her head. He could feel her moving it under his hand. Then she was still. She just held him, her breast rising and falling, her body pressing into his. He could feel her form in that heat, the firm swell of her breasts, the wetness of her cheek warm against his neck.

Jason stepped back. She looked up with confusion. He crooked his arm, offering it to her. Silently, she pulled her shawl around her shoulders and linked her arm in his. They walked together across the drive and the lawn to the rear of the town house. A path began there, entering the woods.

"Are your shoes all right for this?"

"Sure." She nodded.

They started down the path. It was floored with leaves and fallen pine needles, broad enough to walk side by side. They didn't talk. They just walked, slowly and steadily. Their footsteps made a sound that blended with the rustlings of the night. The path cut through a clearing, where moonlight spilled on the meadow grass, lighting it into thousands of luminous fingers.

Jason was the first to speak. "So, it appears that we are both facing the same problem. Dr. Harkus and Dr. Shay were both killed, and both of them were robbed of data." He paused, then went on. "Part of the data we lost at Stanford related to my own project—gene mapping of manic-depressive illness. Let's say there is a connection between the two murders. . . ."

"Then," she offered, "the link may be the same subject that we're working on at the Institutes: the genetics of behavior."

Jason nodded and walked on silently. He lifted a branch with his hand and held it for her to cross beneath. Finally, he said, "Jennifer . . . this may sound slightly wild but has anyone from the CIA contacted you since you came out here?"

"The CIA . . . no! You mentioned them before. Why do you ask that?"

"You remember my friend Red?" He slowed his steps and turned to face her. "Jennifer, Red is with the CIA."

"Oh?" She looked up at him.

"He's part of a division that . . . works with scientists. He called it the Research Oversight Directorate. The Defense Department apparently has a similar division. Red says the CIA is operating at the National Institutes."

"Why?" She said it quietly, a shaken look on her face. "Why would they?"

He described the CIA's mission as Red had: to keep American research out of the hands of the communists and to 'guide' the research toward discoveries that might produce some kind of strategic superiority.

"Oh, Christ. Those fools!" She stopped still. "What do they think medical research is for!"

"I know. I know," he agreed. "That was my reaction exactly. But it made me wonder: Could this have something to do with the murders?" She stared at him. He encircled her with his arm and continued with her down the forest path. Their feet kicked through a crackling pile of dry leaves, then the dark quiet of the woods surrounded them again.

"Jason?" She paused, then said it. "What's happening at the Institutes?"

Jason drew her closer into the crook of his arm. "You mean, what happened to Cindy? Or this damned CIA business?"

"Yes. Well, not just that. I get the feeling that something's going on there, something . . ." Jennifer paused. "I mean, where do you think Dr. Kalia's research is leading?"

He shrugged. "Well, if the genetics work pans out, toward an understanding of how genes produce behaviors."

Jennifer was very quiet, stepping through the dark woods with her arm around his waist. "But I've been thinking. It's almost as if . . . as if he were trying to influence the development of the primate brain."

"Build a better monkey?" He smiled.

"Right. Something like that." She looked up at him. "I mean, really? Could it be done?"

He looked down again and met her eyes. She was watching him, asking a simple question. The autumn wheat of her hair caught the glow of the moonlight, casting reflected beams. She went on, "I mean, Jason, just theoretically. Let's say you did set out to build a better monkey. What would it take?"

"Well," he spoke carefully, "even in the simplest case, you'd need quite an array of talent: biochemists, molecular biologists, geneticists, zoologists . . . not to mention the laboratory equipment, the computers. You're talking about an enormous collection of resources, a multimillion-dollar budget."

"Like the Institutes?" She said it quietly.

Jason didn't answer immediately. He felt his heart beating faster and wondered, with some part of his consciousness, if Jennifer could sense it. "No," he said, frowning. "At least, not yet. There are just too many things to sort out first. Like the question of gene mapping. Which piece of DNA does what? It's critical—"

"But isn't that exactly what they brought you here to work on?"

Jason stopped still. He stared straight ahead, fixing the black woods before them with an unblinking gaze. For almost a minute, he didn't move. All he had was a group of disjointed events, an impression that all was not right, a sense of threat. And the revelation of his erstwhile friend, Red. No . . . even at the Institutes, even for the CIA, it was simply too much to believe.

Finally, he spoke. "A brave new world?" He shook his head. "No, Jennifer. Even if you did build your better monkey, you'd simply run straight up against the wild type."

"Wild type?" Jennifer asked. "What's that?"

"Well," he answered, "in genetics, the wild type is the true wild animal, the animal as it occurs in nature—as opposed to any mutants that might appear."

"So, why is that a problem?"

Jason began to walk with her again. "Because there's something very special about the wild type. He's robust as hell."

"What do you mean?"

"Well, if you breed mutants with wild types, the wild type usually wipes out the mutation and carries on. The wild type is tough to beat."

Jennifer smiled. "Good. I think I like this wild type."

They came to a log. He vaulted it and held out his hands for her. She quickly drew her skirt above her knees, took his hands, and let herself be pulled up. She jumped from the top of the log and nearly lost her balance. He caught her in his arms. There was an instant of intimate contact between their bodies. Then it was over. She tugged her woven shawl back around her and took his arm again, as if nothing had occurred.

The path at last let out where it began. They left the trees and walked across the uncut summer grass. They reached the flagstone walk. Whether from their private thoughts or the place, his home, their pace slowed. Jennifer still held his arm.

The breeze had freshened again. She felt a shiver rush down his arm and disappear.

"You must be freezing!" She released her grip and stood before him at the base of the steps.

"I'm all right."

"Nonsense. Just look at you! Goosebumps everywhere." Her hand want to his shoulder. She touched the bumpy skin, then rapidly withdrew her fingers, as if his bare skin were not cold but hot. "Do you often run in the middle of the night?"

"Sometimes," he said.

"Me too."

"Oh?"

"Sometimes," she said. "When I have something to think about." She drew her cheeks into a shy smile.

"I see." He looked at her, meeting her eyes where she stood before him. He shivered again. The shiver seemed to begin where she had touched. He crossed his arms and raced his hands up and down his triceps.

"Jason, you're going to freeze to death."

"I was planning to make some tea."

"Oh."

He halted the rubbing of his hands. His arms remained locked around his chest, as she held her shawl around hers. They stood still, enveloped and solemn. It was an odd sensation, he thought, that both drew his eyes to hers and made him want to look away. But he didn't break the gaze. He cleared his throat. "Would you like some tea?"

"Yes."

—■—

Once they were inside, it took him only a minute to boil the water and start steeping the tea. In each operation, he felt her presence, seated at the table watching him, though it wasn't the watching so much as her womanly presence itself. Despite the T-shirt he'd pulled on, he still felt the chill of the night. He set the pot between them on the kitchen table and surrounded it with his hands, drawing its heat into him. Neither of them spoke. He poured the tea into mismatched pottery mugs, giving her the fuller of the two.

Her hands came out between the folds of her shawl to reach her cup. She lifted it and immediately smelled the rich exotic tang. "What kind of tea is it?" She brought her cup to her lips, forming them to blow swells across the surface.

"Bandrek. It's a sort of ginger tea."

"Bandrek?"

He nodded. Her pronunciation was exact. "My family lived on Java for some time. I discovered it there. You may find it a little unusual."

She sipped. Her eyes closed as she swallowed down the strong, strangely sweet liquid. "Oh," she said as she opened her eyes, "it's delicious! Aren't you going to have yours?"

He had stood up. "In just a minute. I'm going to find some decent clothing."

She smiled as she watched him disappear around the corner in his running shorts. She listened to the muffled creaks of the stairs, then his steps overhead. Her lips returned to her tea. She sipped again. Her tongue felt immediately at home with the very foreign taste, like a child's tongue exposed at last to a flavor it has been awaiting without knowing it. Jennifer glanced about the kitchen. It barely showed signs of habitation.

She saw the doorway to another room. She rose.

When Jason returned in jeans and a sweatshirt, he found Jennifer in the living room. She'd taken off her shawl and kicked off her shoes. She was facing the wall opposite the big window. Her eyes were fixed intently on one of the paintings that covered the wall. She was very still. Then she bent forward to look closely at the rough-daubed plane of paint.

"J.M.," she read aloud the initials in the lower right corner, and turned to him. "These are yours!"

He nodded.

"I had no idea . . . They are so . . . fantastic! I mean, Jason, I didn't know you painted."

"I don't." He shrugged. "I haven't in years."

Something about his tone stopped her asking why. "But, I've never seen anything like this. These colors! What are these?" She pointed at the figures that danced across his pictures. They were tall and remarkably thin, with limbs bent in crazy postures at every joint and faces that were grotesque but somehow friendly.

"They're puppets," he explained. "Indonesian shadow puppets. They're taking part in a play."

"You mean, like a puppet theater?"

"Exactly," he said. He told her how the puppets were moved behind a screen, illuminated by a fire, as the entire village gathered to watch from the front.

"It sounds just beautiful!" she said.

"It was. Very beautiful." Jason folded his arms and stood still. He tried not to stare, but he realized how much he wanted to look at her, just to watch her, pacing barefoot along the wall of paintings, one hand holding her tea, the other smoothing the thin gauze of her skirt. She was so different from before, so free and unself-conscious, as if her tears had dissolved the mask of aloofness and freed her spirit. Watching her, he felt something happening to him. He wasn't often frightened. He was almost frightened now.

"Jason?" She turned to him. "Do your . . . I mean, did your parents like theater a great deal?"

"We used to put on plays."

"You did! How?"

Jason grinned. "We'd huddle around the fire in the evenings with three chewed-up copies of Shakespeare, and each of us would take a handful of parts. I'm sure we were quite terrible."

"Oh, Jason, that's wonderful! How I wish I could have done it!"

He looked at her uncertainly. "Read them?"

"Acted them! God, how I wanted to. All I wanted, all I ever wanted as a little girl was to be an actress!"

"Jennifer," he spoke quietly, "you know, you are really quite good. Have you ever acted professionally?"

Her smooth cheeks went flame red. The young woman was suddenly quiet. She dropped her gaze to the floor, watching her toe as she swept her bare foot over the carpet. "Jason, I haven't acted since high school. Except . . . what I was doing ever since I met you."

"You were very"—he paused, looking at her seriously—"convincing."

She walked quickly across the distance between them. "Jason . . ." She touched him lightly on the arm. "Please, it wasn't all acting. Not when I . . ."

Jason found his eyes locked on hers. He didn't move a muscle, but he could feel the slam of his heart in his chest.

Jennifer spoke with gentle urgency, "Jason, you asked me to believe you. Now I'm asking you. Please . . ."—she looked up into his face with shining eyes—"believe me."

Jason extended his hands for hers. He silently drew her down until they faced each other, kneeling on the carpet. He said nothing, but lifted his hands and gently brushed her red and golden hair back from her face. She lifted her hands to his face as well, her fingers barely touching him. For a minute, they did nothing more than this gentle caressing, nearly shivering at each other's touch. Finally, tenderly, their lips met in a kiss.

"Jason," she said, as his mouth moved to her cheeks. He kissed her neck. "Oh, Jason." He pulled her blouse to one side and kissed his way gently across the hollow of her shoulder. Her hands circled him as she lay back onto the carpet, pulling at his weight. She moved her head from side to side, meeting his mouth and parting from it, only to meet it again. "Yes,

Jason." He kissed every part of her face, her cheeks, her eyes, until he met her mouth once more and they locked into a fiery kiss. Their tongues explored, their bodies writhed together, as if trying to meet everywhere at once.

He lifted his torso and moved his hands down to her waist and gathered the soft fabric of her blouse in his fingers. She lifted her hands over her head. With a single motion, he pulled her blouse up and off. Her breasts danced bare and free, moving their separate ways, colored with the roseate flush that was spreading down from her neck. He kissed her neck, then dipped his mouth to find one red and filling nipple. "Yes!" she said. She closed her eyes and arched her back to lift herself to meet his mouth. He surrounded the tense nipple with his lips, licking her, rushing his wet tongue over the tip. She tangled her fingers in his hair, and answered his moving tongue with a quiet moan. As he licked her, his hands stroked down the length of her body, his fingers found the button of her skirt, and loosed it, and pulled the zipper down. He gave her breast one last quick kiss, then he reached down to her skirt. She lifted her bottom into the air to help him pull it off. He repeated the motion with her little pants.

She blushed furiously, seeing his eyes take her in so completely. A rising array of tiny goosebumps spread over her shoulders and down her arms and sides. Her slender body was even more beautiful than he had guessed, taut and perfect as a young girl's. He pulled his sweatshirt over his head and tossed it away. She ran her hands over the bars of muscle along his abdomen and chest, exploring their hard contours as he completed undressing. Then he circled her with his arms, bare skin to skin, kissing her as he lay her back down onto the thick carpet.

He began gently. He used his mouth and his big hands. They were the agents of his will, to lift her senses beyond their limits. And quickly, she gave in, raising her arms over her head, unable to do anything but surrender to the power of his hands, his lips and tongue and teeth that mastered her skin and her nerves and made her feel both terribly embarrassed and terribly ready to let him do anything that he wanted to her. She arched herself, lifting her own pelvis, presenting herself to him, a gift, and was rewarded in turn. For a minute, he balanced her at that plateau of pleasure, using her breathing and the red flush of her skin as measures of her sweet agony, to guide his actions, to keep her at the height of anticipation.

Then he entered her.

"Jason!" She let out a little cry and her eyes flashed open. Their eyes met, sharing that moment of absolute intimacy, reveling in the completeness of their touching.

And then they were moving. Moving as one, moving with rising heat and uninhibited passion. "Oh!" she moaned, "Oh, yes, yes . . ." She gave herself to his rhythm, until with each thrust of his body her own was at the peak of its openness and her lips were drawn back in abandonment to utter pleasure.

"Oh, yes!" she cried. She wrapped her arms and legs around him as if holding on to a galloping beast. A raging pink flush began to spread over her breasts, up to her neck, onto her cheeks. She cried in time with each collision of their flesh, "Yes—yes—Jason—please—yes—more!" He responded by quickening his pace, pounding into her nakedness. Her words trailed off as her body started to tremble under his rhythmic charge. Her head was thrown back, her mouth open, and her moaning and her tremor went on and on and on. And he reached down with his big hands and he held her moving pelvis tight and thrust deep into her center.

"Ah!" She shook as a wild climax suddenly arrived and wave upon wave of pleasure rushed through her naked body, and she moved uncontrollably, clutching him to her breast, moaning, trembling, until her tremor became a wild shaking and a final gasp of sweet ecstasy escaped her.

Gradually, the tension drained from her arms, and the arch left her back, and her neck, and her crimson face, and she lay beneath him, still moving, running her hands from his shoulders to his buttocks, still touching everything, still feeling his body in hers, softly, gently.

Slowly, slowly, they came to a rest. He sank down onto her. His eyes were closed. He cradled her in his arms. He gently kissed her soft pink cheek. Her face was suffused with a look of unutterable peace. She held him, one hand barely moving at the back of his neck. She whispered his name, "Jason," once, and again, "Jason." He lay his head on her breast, and he listened to her heart, and he closed his own eyes. Remembering . . . forgetting . . .

———■———

Much later, he raised the cotton sheet and kissed her shoulder. She shifted beside him. She opened her eyes and lifted her mouth to meet his in a long deliberate kiss.

He drew her into the circle of his arm, reaching a hand around to stroke her back. His fingers found the space where her muscles dipped to meet the long curve of her spine, and he softly rubbed the length of it. "Jennifer?"

"Yes, Jason?"

He said nothing for a moment, but continued stroking his hand gently along her back. His eyes were lost in the blank of the ceiling. Tenderly, she lay her hand on his chest. She pressed her palm flat, touching the tanned skin of him, the muscle underneath. "What is it, Jason?"

Jason sighed. Then he pulled her closer, deeper into the safety of his body. "Jennifer, there's something I didn't say yesterday. I didn't want to intrude, I suppose. But now I . . . Look, Jennifer, when you're out at Dr. Kalia's lab, just please be careful."

"Me? Jason, it's you who will be working with Dr. Murray. If there's anyone—"

"I know," he stopped her. "But there's something about that lab . . ."

"There sure is. Her name's Layla."

He smiled at her tone. "Oh, come on."

"Come on! I saw the way she looked at you. She'd just as soon jump out of her pants as shake your hand."

"I'm sure you're exaggerating."

"Like hell I am!" Jennifer lifted herself up on her elbow. "You two were quite obvious. You've got a date with her."

"That"—he attempted to control his grin—"is purely for professional purposes."

"Like what? This I have to hear."

He laughed. "She just wants to learn some of the operating

details of the automatic gene sequencer. For her rice project."

"Your . . . I know what kind of gene exchange she has in mind for you."

He couldn't help the smile. "Jennifer—"

"Don't you Jennifer me, Jason McCane!"

Jason was silent.

"You think I'm just jealous, don't you?"

He remained silent.

"Why you . . . you morally degenerate, self-aggrandizing, testicle-driven male! You think you know everything just because—"

"You're not jealous?"

"That has nothing to do with this!"

"Oh." He cleared his throat. "I see."

"You!" She pulled the pillow from beneath his head and swung it down on him. "You!"

"Jennifer!" He laughed, covering his head with his arms. "Jennifer, wait, wait, my love, I give up!"

She stopped. "What did you call me?"

Jason was suddenly still, the lines of his smile subsiding. "I called you Jennifer."

"Jason . . . you know what I mean."

He shrugged. "A slip of the tongue. Think nothing."

"I'm sure." Jennifer crawled on top of him. She closed her eyes and brought her lips close to his. Gently, with infinite patience, she brought her moist lips down against his mouth, pressing so gradually that they could each feel the sweet inevitable progress of the kiss. At last she lifted her head. Her voice was solemn and quiet and clear: "Jason, I know that . . . your heart is somewhere far away. But I . . ." She stopped her voice and spoke with her bright eyes what no words could say.

He looked straight up into her face. His brow was tensed in a quiet agony. He took a breath that lifted her on his chest. He whispered her name, "Jennifer." He swallowed, and said no more. He laid his hands gently on her head, hardly touching, just a brush at the veil of her hair, and drew her mouth down to his. They kissed.

She shifted to the side, so that half of her lay on him,

curling into him with her legs and belly and the hard press of her pubis against his thigh and the soft press of her breasts against his ribs. They molded into one another, becoming one. She closed her eyes. Her face relaxed into a transcendent quiet. Her mouth formed a tiny grin, just a lifting at the corners of her lips, almost invisible.

"Jennifer?" He said it quietly.

She shifted her head on his chest and slowly opened her eyes. "Yes, Jason?"

"About the lab . . ." His chest rose and fell once more, lifting her hand, letting it down. "Just, please . . . be careful."

Jennifer stretched herself up to kiss his cheek. "If I'm not back by sundown, send in the marines." She smiled, just a tiny sleepy grin, and began to yawn. She snuggled down against him, her ear to his heart, her hand lying on the muscles of his arm as gently as a sleeping bird. Her voice was languid, slow with the hour of the night. "Don't worry, my Jason. I plan to spend tomorrow night just like tonight. In this bed with you." Her hair spread like a golden fan over his chest. She closed her eyes. "I'll be fine," she murmured. "Just fine."

Jason remained very still, encircling Jennifer with one arm, listening to her breathing become quiet and even. He reached out his other arm and switched off the bedside lamp. Then he lay back, holding her. Just holding her.

He realized, with surprise, that he was staring into the darkness. He grew aware of the tension in his arms, holding her close, waiting for her to sleep, feeling the warmth of her and feeling his heart beat and a wetness form in the corners of his eyes, making him blink. He didn't understand it for a moment. It was an odd sensation, that gathering of wetness that filled his lids with salty liquid that blurred his sight and overflowed and made its way down the side of his head. Then he realized what it was. Tears. He hadn't remembered what they felt like. It had been so many years. It had been so very long.

Time passed in the dark silence, marked by Jennifer's even breaths. His body relaxed, slowly. His own breathing evened. He turned his head toward her, and kissed her sleeping head, and closed his eyes. Finally, finally, he slept.

— ▪ 13 ▪—

Busy?"

"Layla!"

She stood at the door to Jason's office with her arms crossed, smiling and leaning against the doorjamb. She wore a white lab coat, open over a dress that mercilessly followed the long curves of her body.

"Wasn't our date for tomorrow?" he asked.

"I couldn't wait. Am I welcome?" As he rose from his chair, she came straight to him and kissed him quickly on the mouth. "Mmm, I remember that flavor."

"Young lady, I thought this meeting was purely for scientific purposes."

"Well! If you want to be that way about it . . . would you care for a little experiment?" She pressed herself against him, slipping her fingers up under his collar and starting them around his neck.

He gently disengaged her arms before she could kiss him again, and held her hands together between his. "Miss Kalia," he said as he leveled his eyes at hers, adopting a stern tone, "if you start that, I can quite guarantee that we'll never get our work done. The gods of science are watching."

She laughed and drew back from him. "What willpower, Dr. McCane! You surprise me."

"I surprise myself. Now"—he gestured with a bow toward the spare chair—"what would you like to know?"

"Everything," she said, gracefully taking her seat.

"Everything?"

"Everything you can tell me about automatic gene sequencing. Anything that would help put our sequencer together here."

"You know," he said, laying the edge of his hand on the arm of his chair, "I'm happy to do it, but isn't this information available in the journals?"

"It is," she agreed. "But there's something missing. Even though I follow the published methods, we . . . I'm just not getting consistent results. I was hoping that going over the basics with you would shed some light."

"OK," he nodded. "The basics."

Jason pulled a blank tablet of paper from the confusion of the desk and set it on his lap. As he began to explain the design of the automated gene sequencer, he made a simple diagram. Layla lifted one foot up onto the corner of the desk drawer, and leaned forward to see better. Her skirt divided.

"Here's where the action begins," Jason said. He wondered if she was aware of her generous show of leg. "The gene fragments line up,"—he drew a picture—"the laser excites the dyes, the computer reads off the color code, and you have . . . the sequence. There."

Layla accepted the sheet and pored over it intently. She swung her hair in a dark arc as she shook her head. "I just don't get it."

"What?"

"I'm using the same technique, but I'm getting lousy results, time after time."

"Well," he said, "there are at least two factors I can think of that might explain your problems. One is too-long incubation time."

She wrote quickly. "And the other?"

"Well, look at this!" Dr. Murray was leaning into the door.

"Dr. Murray!" Layla dropped her foot from the desk drawer and smoothed her skirt into place.

"Layla, it's good to see you." The branch chief grinned. "I'm glad to see you two are getting, I mean, are working together."

"Jason was just giving me a hand with the sequencer. He's really quite . . ." She smiled at the young doctor, lifting her shoulders in a motion that finished the compliment.

"Good." Murray nodded. "Good. Jason, shall I assume that this means that you're interested in tackling our larger genetics project?"

"Ah, I—"

"Excuse me, Dr. Murray," the young woman interrupted. She gave the older man a look that appeared to Jason to be half a command. "We were almost done."

Murray cleared his throat and said, "Certainly, my dear."

"And the other?" Layla turned back to Jason. "The other factor you were going to mention?"

Layla's look to his branch chief gave him pause. "Yes. The dye stability. Your dye may be degrading at the center of your gels."

"That explains it!" Layla wrote rapidly.

"But, Layla," the young doctor said, frowning, "I have to caution you: This technique was developed for animal chromosomes. I'm not sure how well it will work with your plants."

"That's all right; I'm sure we can put it to good use." She finished writing with a jab of the pen and lifted her head. "Jason, you're wonderful! Dr. Murray, I'm sorry for holding you up. I have to admit that I am also interested in Jason's answer."

The chief nodded. "Well, what about it, Jason? Thought about joining our project?"

Jason tilted back in his chair, eliciting the little wail of strangled steel. None of them paid heed. "Yes," he said at last. "I have thought about it."

"And?"

"And?" Layla echoed the branch chief.

Then Jason remembered. "Dr. Murray, excuse me, but what about Cindy, the Normal Volunteer?"

The branch chief lifted his eyebrows. "Hmph. Awkward business, that. I suppose it's out of our hands now." He told them that both Cindy and Tony had apparently left the Center; they hadn't been seen since the previous night.

"Cindy and Tony are both gone? Did they leave together? Does anyone know where they are?"

"Jason, calm down a bit. They probably more or less 'eloped.' I've seen it happen before: two young volunteers . . ."

Jason was about to speak when they heard the scream.

He leapt to his feet and ran out the door, followed closely by Dr. Murray. The scream came again. A woman's voice, coming from around the corner. Jason sprinted down the corridor and turned into the laboratory wing. Heads were appearing in the doors lining the hall, as the terrified cry startled the scientists from their work. Two of the orange-jacketed security men were already running down the hall ahead of Jason. Another appeared from the stairwell, reaching for his hidden holster.

A blond figure hurtled through the doors at the far end of the corridor. It was Linda, the lab service director, her face white with horror.

"What is it, Linda?" Jason met her at midhall. The security men crashed through the double doors, their guns drawn. She pointed frantically down the hall and then, seeing Murray, ran on past Jason and into the arms of the branch chief. The young scientist followed the orange figures through the doors, into the dim tunnel of the maintenance area.

They were standing at the open bulkhead of a massive storage freezer. Clouds of condensation fogged the stairwell, billowing up from the eighty-below-zero interior of the big steel box. Jason stepped between the men, who were already holstering their revolvers. For a moment, he couldn't see through the dense white fog. Then he saw the ice-covered form, lying on its side, tightly curled in a fetal crouch.

Looking down into the freezer, he recognized through a solid white shell the slender features of his colleague, Dr. Tom Sherrington.

———■———

"Why, Jennifer." Kalia looked up from the expanse of his desk as she entered. "It's good to see you again." He raised his bushy white eyebrows and nodded toward a chair. "Won't you take a seat?"

She dropped her bag beside the chair and sat down, smoothing her dress over her knees. "I'm sorry I'm late, Dr. Kalia. I had a time of it getting my car down your access road."

"Not at all, not at all," he assured her. "It is I who should apologize. But I'm afraid the entrance road will remain an obstacle. Discourages the curious." The scientist smiled benignly at his new assistant. "Well, are you ready for your first day?"

"I suppose." She exhaled, still recovering from the drive.

"Fine. Then let's get started, shall we?" He rose smoothly and came around the desk, his hand extended toward the door. Jennifer returned to her feet and gathered her satchel, while he lifted a small pile of documents off his desk. They followed the corridor to the elevator where he addressed the voicelock, "This is Dr. Paul Kalia," and the door slid open at his command.

As they descended into the depths of the lab, Jennifer asked, "No black suits this time?"

"No, that won't be necessary. You'll be working down in the computer room, of course, not in the dome." He turned to face her. "As a matter of fact, I must absolutely insist that you confine yourself to the peripheral labs. We wouldn't want to jeopardize the animal studies by appearing visibly outside the dome wall. Do you understand?"

"Naturally," she agreed.

The elevator stopped and they quickly made their way down the hall and through the biochemistry and tissue culture labs. In the tissue room one of Kalia's black-garbed assistants was working at a laminar flow hood. The man turned to eye Jennifer, then caught a glance from Kalia and turned back to his work. Kalia continued leading the way until they arrived at the door to the computer room. He opened the door for her.

"Oh, how lovely!" Stepping into the white-walled room, the first thing Jennifer noticed was a brilliant red orchid in a crystal vase on the work desk. She walked to the terminal area and lifted the vase, sampling the fragrance.

"I thought you might appreciate a touch of color in here. Just to welcome you to the laboratory."

"Why, thank you Dr. Kalia." Jennifer grinned.

The laboratory director smiled back and bowed slightly to her. Then he sat and began organizing files and charts on the table. "Well, shall we get underway?" There was only a hint of impatience.

"Oh, yes. Of course." She quickly returned the flower to its place and moved to sit beside him at the table.

Dr. Kalia flipped open his files. "As you know, the key to group behavior in an ape colony is dominance. One ape is usually the leader. He is often found sitting at the center of the group, surrounded by females, with subordinate males out at the periphery." Kalia pointed to computer-generated drawings that showed the distribution of apes in a typical colony. "He is the ruler, the defender, the one who settles disputes and hands out favors. And—with all due respect to women— it is always a dominant male."

Jennifer smiled. "Not so, Dr. Kalia. What about the patas monkey? For them it may be the females who run things."

Kalia shot her a look. "Yes, but we're talking about great apes, not Old World monkeys."

"Of course," she said. She shifted to see better as he laid his papers out across the desk.

Kalia continued. "We actually have gathered some very good data that predict behavior within the group, once we have established the dominance hierarchy." He laid several sheets in front of her on the desk. "However, we want to go beyond the question of behavior within the group. Instead, imagine two separate colonies of apes. Which group will become dominant over the other group?"

Jennifer looked puzzled. "Dr. Kalia, there's very little known about group rivalries in chimpanzees. I mean, in the wild, each group has its own territory. If another group moves in, it's not like there's a battle for dominance or anything. The two groups just share the resources."

"It's not that simple, Dr. Darien." He pointed out that many chimpanzee encounters were seen in Tanzania that look exactly like a battle. The males attack as a group, they gang up to bite their enemies, they even rescue their wounded. "What would you call that, if not a battle? And I'm sure you know that chimpanzees from one group will sometimes capture, kill, and eat babies from another group."

"Yes, but—"

"Let me finish." He held up his hand. "As to your comment about sharing resources, what if the resources are limited? What if there's only enough food to supply one of the groups? Which one will prevail? How can we predict the winner? What sort of behavioral traits will determine the victor? And how will they establish their rule over the other colony? These are the questions I want you to work on."

"But Dr. Kalia, why are you specifically interested in—"

A buzzer interrupted them. Kalia pressed a button on the intercom panel built into the computer console. "Dr. Kalia, I have an important call for you," the secretary's voice came nasally over the small speaker.

"Who is it?"

"It's Senator Bowie. He says he must speak with you."

The scientist's bushy eyebrows rose. "Very well, I'll take it in my office." He flicked off the intercom and got up, grinning at Jennifer. "Forgive me. The good senator is rather important to me. He is principally responsible for congressional support of the laboratory, so we try to keep him happy." He winked at her.

"Yes, I understand. Thank you . . ." Her words trailed off as he turned quickly and strode out the door. She watched his back retreating up the hall until the brushed steel door swung into place with a click. She was left alone in the stark white room. Jennifer sat back, holding one of his papers for predicting ape behavior but gazing idly about the room. Her eyes followed the crisp bare lines of the work space out toward the blank white walls, a study in perspective. She looked up to the towering computer console, flickering with subdued lights. Her eye was attracted, as to a sun in the dawning sky, by the brilliant red of the orchid. She gazed at it for a silent moment.

Sighing, Jennifer turned to her work.

———■———

In the data center of the CIA's Research Oversight Directorate, Mrs. B. set down her coffee. She was watching the screen of her computer. She couldn't believe what she saw. The word *Classified* blinked in the center of her screen like a guardian spirit, barring her way to the data she sought. It could mean only one thing: Some agency of the government itself had restricted access to the data.

She wasn't going to let that stop her. In the hierarchy of security classification, her high-level CIA status gave her access to almost any government information. She activated the codes that declassified most programs. A red light came on. She placed the tips of her fingers briefly on the fingerprint log-on device. The light turned green. She asked the question again: Who controlled that Swiss bank account? Even if every transaction could be run via an untraceable computer link, there was always a human hand that signed the account into existence. Who controlled that account?

The word appeared again: *Classified.*

"Damn you," she swore at the computer with an uncharacteristic show of umbrage, "you can't stop me!" Years of tenure at the Company had taught her a trick or two. She bent to pull her handbag from under the desk. A brief search yielded the scarred little notebook that she kept against all regulations. She ran through a coding program she had invented herself, then entered the personal declassification code of her boss, the deputy director for Science and Technology. She asked the question again.

Her eyes went wide.

She was on the telephone in an instant. "Red, could you come up here, please? Yes, right now. There's something I have to show you."

———■———

The chief of NIH Security Services had assembled them all in the branch office. Dr. Murray and the Fellow Larry sat on a workbench, Linda was seated to the side, the secretaries still occupied their typing seats, and Jason had found a place on a low filing cabinet. Two of the orange jackets stood at the door, arms folded imperiously on their chests, while the security chief addressed them. Dr. Murray was watching the others with deliberate and undisguised interest. Jason noted his studious avoidance of Linda's reddened eyes. Layla had been allowed to leave.

Jason was fast becoming impatient. Early in the discussion, he had asked why the police were not being notified and had received the clipped reply, "We are the police here, Dr. McCane." Since that time, he had regarded the gnomelike detective with wary annoyance. The questions seemed perfunctory. In his terse way, the security man had collected what he called the facts of the matter, a bare congeries of negatives, scribbled briskly onto the appropriate spaces of his standard yellow form: No one had seen Tom for at least a day. No one could pinpoint the time of his disappearance. No one recalled any suspicious persons on the floor in the last week. No one could offer anything, any clue or observation or theory that could expand the obvious "facts of the matter." Jason felt himself burning at the single incontrovertible fact, the fact beyond all bearing: the death. The murder.

"Then," the security director finally asked, "just who did see Dr. Sherrington last?"

The group looked at each other.

"I . . ." Linda lifted her hand hesitantly. "I was helping him with an assay the day before yesterday."

"What time?"

She spread her palms, "Maybe two o'clock?"

"Maybe? Do you realize—"

Jason interrupted. "I saw Tom in the hall outside his lab at seven-thirty, night before last."

The eyes of the group swung to him.

The detective rose. "And just what were you doing at the Center after hours?" He pointed at the doctor's face with his pencil.

"I was picking up several articles to look at at home. Tom was down the hall, carrying some lab equipment."

"And what did he say to you?"

"He told me his new laser was coming. He invited me to see it."

"That's all?" The doubt was evident.

"That's all. He was carrying some test tubes. I believe he was on his way to the ward."

"Dr. McCane,"—the man continued to aim his pencil— "was anyone else present? Can anyone confirm your story?"

"No."

"And have any of you seen Dr. Sherrington since then?" The researchers and secretaries shifted uncomfortably. None of them spoke.

The security man turned back to Jason. "Then you were the last one to see Dr. Thomas Sherrington alive."

The phone rang. No one paid attention. A secretary answered, informing the caller that the doctors couldn't be disturbed. However, as she listened, her face took on a worried look. She interrupted the detective in the middle of a question. "Excuse me, Dr. McCane. It's for you. Someone called Red."

Jason frowned. "Could you please take a message?"

"He insists, Dr. McCane. He says it's urgent."

The interest of the room was centered on the young scientist. Jason could sense their attentive postures. He turned to Dr. Murray. "Ben, I'll take the call in your office, if that's all right."

The branch chief balked a moment, then nodded once. After the secretary clicked the phone onto Hold, Jason rose and stepped through the storage area into Murray's office. He shut the glass-paneled door behind him.

He stood looking down at the phone. Why was Red calling now? All the tension of that awkward parting at Red's athletic club came back to him—the feeling of betrayal, the accumulated suspicions, the loss, the anger. He laid his hand on the phone. Then, with decision, he lifted the receiver.

Jason didn't bring it to his ear. He held it an inch above the cradle, then brought it down. The light went out. He didn't want to talk to Red. He didn't want to talk to the CIA. Not yet.

He sat back in Dr. Murray's chair, exhaling slowly. He thought. Why was Tom killed? His work? Something he discovered? Something to do with Cindy? Or just an act of deranged passion, the kind of sudden rage that ignited the big volunteer, Tony? Why? He turned his head, looking randomly about the office, as if he might find the solution to the senseless puzzle in that cluttered collage of files and articles, jumbled into cabinets and labeled with words like . . .

Classified. He almost missed it. Shooting his eyes back down under the desk, he saw the label, an orange sticker pasted onto the flecked gray plating of a steel safe. It was slung beneath the desk, apparently welded in place, fitted between two legs. The knurled dial of a combination lock was its only feature, other than the stark orange label lettered in black: Classified. Order of NIH Security.

He leaned down, examining the small vault more carefully. The door was square, about eight inches on a side. He tapped it with a knuckle, and it sounded as dull and thick as a solid block of steel. In the narrow space between the door edge and the frame, he thought he could see an exposed half millimeter of two thick bolts.

Jason heard the scrape of chairs in the outer office. He got up quickly and walked through the file room, entering the outer office as inconspicuously as he could. The meeting was adjourning, with the group rising from their chairs. He headed for the door to the hallway.

"Jason." Dr. Murray was tamping his pipe again. He looked up at the younger man. "What was that all about, may I ask?"

Jason stopped, and half turned toward Dr. Murray. "Actually," he demurred, "nothing terribly important."

"Come now, it was important enough to interrupt this discussion. What did this fellow Red have to say that was so urgent?"

Again the assembly began to focus on him, regarding him expectantly. The security man had stopped stacking his yellow sheets to eye him with suspicious interest.

Jason looked up, then shifted his eyes down to the floor, rubbing his neck. "Well." He cleared his throat. "It was Port-of-Call in the fifth race by a length."

There was a moment of silence. Nancy was the first to end it, breaking into a high nervous giggle. Then the others joined in, laughing, relieved by the break in the tension. Even the security men were grinning. The young doctor half smiled in embarrassment.

Dr. Murray's eyes remained fixed on Jason in a humorless gaze.

—■14■—

Jason left the Center, moving into the silken heat of the summer afternoon. The large pool west of the building reflected a shifting patchwork of clouds scudding fitfully across the sky. Leaves on the trees seemed to hang exhausted in the humidity. The air was ripe with moisture. He glanced up at the sky, estimating the chance of rain.

He angled across the rolling lawns and left the campus by the western entrance. After several minutes he had passed the final boundary of the Institutes, leaving the big research complex behind as he approached Bethesda proper. He covered a mile with long strides and soon arrived at the commercial district.

His first stop was at a hardware store. He scanned the aisles until he located a sheet of galvanized tin. Then he picked up a short-handled five-pound sledgehammer and several thin-bladed cold chisels. Finally, he added a heavy pair of metal shears. He paid for the purchases and stepped back onto the sidewalk. He walked south, searching, until he found what he was looking for two blocks down: BARON SONS, HEATING AND COOLING.

Jason entered the office, found a supervisor, and quickly

explained what he needed. It took only a few minutes to complete the transaction. Then he returned again to the street.

The clouds had aggregated into a pale gray overcast, and rolls of thunder sounded softly in the distance. The young scientist checked his watch. It was almost 5:00 P.M. Too early, he thought. As he walked into the residential area, a fine mist began to float down, interspersed with droplets that patted onto the leaves. Quickly, the mist became a drizzle, then a light rain progressing to a steady shower.

Clutching the heavy sack close to his body, Jason converted his stride to an easy lope. The sky rapidly darkened to heavy charcoal, and most cars had turned on their headlights. He ran steadily, the water wetting him to the skin as his legs pumped along the winding blacktop streets. Splashing through shallow puddles, Jason kept running, letting the rain sweep across his face, his eyes squeezed halfway shut against the stinging drops. He reached the boulevard leading home and trotted down the central tree lawn, which was already beginning to mat down from the deluge. Finally, he turned into his cul-de-sac, vaulted the hedge, and climbed the flagstone steps to his town house.

He stood under the awning, still clutching the heavy parcel at his side, and looked out at the storm. Wind lashed the rain against the trees, whose branches whipped their greenery in the gathering dusk. The temperature was falling fast.

Jason's eyes looked out into the night, but his mind was elsewhere. He felt the weight of his package, the hard press of metal at his side. Could he do it? he thought. Could he set aside the rules, the lessons of a lifetime, and take the law into his own hands? A corner of his mind began remembering . . .

—■—

"Jason."

The boy looked up at his father. He felt tears moving to the corners of his eyes but squeezed them back with ten-year-old pride.

"Did you steal the cook's knife?"

He felt as if his throat was lined with sand. "Yes, I did.

But, Dad, the cook traded it with Lo-pei for some rice, but he gave her short weight and when she checked it he wouldn't trade back. They need it, Dad."

"Jason, what would we do without laws? What did that fellow Hobbes say about man's life in the state of nature?"

Young Jason's voice shook as he responded, "Nasty."

"That's right. Nasty, brutish, and short. Should you have taken the knife?"

The boy clenched his hands. "I don't know."

His father eyed him sternly. The two faced each other across the stretch of sand. Then Lowell McCane just shook his head. He sat down next to his son on a log, sighing, and laid a big arm across the boy. He pulled Jason close, tousling his hair. "I don't know either."

The memory of that moment with his father had stuck with him. Sometimes, the rules didn't work. Jason didn't know what was right. But he had seen enough. It was time to act.

He went inside, stripped and dried, then changed into jeans and a ragged navy sweater. He worked the tin sheeting into the shape he wanted with the metal shears. Finally he transferred the tools into his gym bag, threw on a dark slicker, and walked out through the rain to his Land Rover.

— ■ —

Jennifer set down her pen and sat back, stretching her arms over her head. She rolled her head in circles, relaxing her neck after hours of work. Then she checked her watch. It was almost 5:00 P.M. She hadn't even stopped for lunch.

For a moment, she glanced at the terminal. Her preliminary calculations glowed on the screen, neat lines of computer type. Contemplating the immense job, she almost hated to stop working, but she knew it was nearly time to head home.

She turned off the monitor and sat back in her chair. Her gaze was lost in the featureless white room. She thought about the project. Whatever her earlier reservations about the dominance theory had been, they were laid to rest by Kalia's observations of the animals in his huge enclosed jungle.

The studies of animals without brain stimulation were enough to confirm other reports of warlike primate behavior. However, when added to the information they got when the animals' brains were stimulated, the data was nearly overwhelming. Kalia could elicit almost any emotion in the animals, just by his radio-controlled brain perfusers. Hunger, satisfaction, reward, fear, rage, pain, or even sexual pleasure were just electrochemical events in the brain which he manipulated at will. What emerged from this was a growing body of information about the interaction of brain, behavior, and the dominance hierarchy. It was hard to take it all in. It was more than a little frightening.

Jennifer thought about the jungle. It still seemed incredible that such a place could exist in rural Virginia. Just beyond these walls, she thought, was a jungle—as wild as any place on earth. However, unlike any other wild place, it had been deliberately built for the purposes of science.

She got up and began to pace. Beside her, the tape drives of the mainframe whispered in their housings, taking in data from the jungle, analyzing, memorizing, storing.

What was the purpose of this science? If something was happening at the Institutes, if there was some covert activity, then what was the goal? And what, she asked herself, was the role of the Laboratory of Brain and Behavior? She turned on the ball of her foot and continued to march across the glossy white floor, thinking. The laboratory. The jungle. She understood Dr. Kalia's reluctance to publish unfinished work, but why this obsession with privacy? Why this—she nodded, admitting that the word fit—secrecy? What was it about the laboratory that justified the degree of isolation he so desperately protected?

She stopped in place. She crossed her arms, facing the blank computer screen. If there was an explanation, she would not find it here in this empty white room. She would not find it at all unless she looked. And, if Kalia's protectiveness was any guide, there was only one place to begin such a search. In the jungle.

Jennifer walked to the door and quietly pulled it part way open. The corridor was deserted. She stepped through the door and made her way down the hall to the tissue culture lab. Putting her ear to the door, she listened. There was no sound.

The young scientist eased the door open, then entered the lab, closing the door softly behind her. She began to search the room quickly, looking for one of the black jump suits that would make her nearly invisible in the dome. She checked cabinets under the countertop, drawers beneath the supply shelves, and a tall closet set into the wall. She did not find any of the black suits.

She pulled the door open quietly. Moving down the short stretch of hall, she approached the door at the end, the door to the hydroponic garden. Again, she pressed her ear to the door. She heard only the steady drone of the water pumps. She put her hand on the doorknob. Just as she started to turn it, voices came from within. One she recognized from its deep quality as belonging to Dr. Kalia. The other sounded higher. Layla?

Jennifer gently released the doorknob and retreated back down the corridor. This time, she passed through the other door, into the molecular biology area.

It too was empty. There was a quick tapping sound and she whirled. It was the printer, automatically typing out results from the scintillation counter. She shook herself, recovering from her fright, and started searching for a jump suit. Jars and bottles of various stock chemicals lined the floor-to-ceiling shelves. She checked the lower cabinets, but found only more chemical supplies. Then she saw another tall closet door and pulled it open. Black jump suits hung in a packed row.

Selecting what looked like a small size, Jennifer closed the door and rapidly made her way back to her own room. She took off her shoes and began to step into the suit, but found that her dress bunched up uncomfortably. She removed the black garment again, quickly took her dress off, and stepped back into the suit, carefully zipping it up to her neck.

The corridor was still empty when she left her computer room for the second time. Turning to the right, she passed along the empty hall, finally reaching the first steel door leading to the dome. Although she knew Kalia had installed a voiceprint lock to control the elevator, down here on the level of the laboratories there were no apparent security devices. The door opened easily. In front of her stretched the long dark tunnel, lit only by round green spots glowing in the floor. She swallowed once and entered the tunnel. When the door hissed shut behind her, she was left in nearly total blackness.

Walking between the glowing spots, the young woman moved through the darkness. Her heart was beating palpably faster. Then her reaching fingers came up against the cold metal of the final door. Moving a hand down the steel panel, she searched for the handle. She found it. Again she put her ear to the door. There was silence. She pulled open the door and looked through.

The jungle filled her view.

Through the transparent wall of the dome, that huge green splendor seemed incredibly close. She glanced quickly over to the observation post, but it seemed to be unoccupied. Then she looked back at the jungle as she stepped through the door. It clicked solidly shut behind her.

Jennifer was amazed again at the immensity of the place, the tropical wonders that went on and on. She began to move along the curving wall, letting one hand rub lightly against the wall as a guide, while her eyes searched into the primeval monsoon forest. Even in the dim light, its lush foliage was rich with every jungle color. The brush rustled and she started at the sight of a female lion, which ambled into a clearing, then made her stately way back into the jungle depths. Jennifer felt both entranced and vulnerable at the sight of the beast.

Jennifer came to the second observation post. Rounding the curve of the wall, she again looked at the post for signs of activity. The electronic panels winked their multicolored lights, but no one sat in the chairs before the console.

She walked along the dimly glowing runway, stepping carefully between the green spots, still guiding herself through the dark with one hand on the dome wall. The muddy stream curved close to the wall, trickling like a secret out of the depths of the jungle. Jennifer continued. Nearing the third viewing post, she tried to see through the long curve of the wall, but the tropical greenery was far too dense for her vision to penetrate. If any of the posts would be occupied, she thought it would be the third one, sitting opposite the big lake.

Jennifer thought she recognized the thick copse that came before the lake. Slowing, she craned her neck to peer around the wall, trying to approach the observation post in silence. Even stepping carefully, the click of her low shoes echoed against the dome. She stepped out of them. Barefoot, she covered the last thirty yards in a low crouch, her heart pounding.

The lights of the monitor console came into view. She stopped, holding her breath. Meters and dials glowed in the darkness, casting a dim red light over the electric panels, onto the vague outline of two chairs sitting before the console. They were empty.

She moved farther around the wall, almost beginning to breathe regularly again. When she passed the end of the dense thicket, the lake finally appeared.

It was as beautiful as she remembered it. The big stretch of open water lapped almost up to the transparent wall and extended for hundreds of yards to the waterfall. Across the lake at the clearing, there were no chimpanzees this time. However, even as she watched, the foliage at the edge of the clearing shivered, then bent down before an advancing dark form. She watched in fascination as a huge gray rhinoceros tramped out of the jungle and into the light of the open area. Although the beast looked fierce, Jennifer felt well protected by the broad stretch of the intervening water. The rhinoceros lowered its head to rub its big horn against the ground. She could see the exposed pink bulge at the top of its head. A cap of gleaming metal protruded from the center.

The animal stepped ponderously into the shallows, sending small waves rippling across the lake. It dipped its head to drink, then tossed it back, splashing a spray of water over its dusty flanks. Jennifer watched, oblivious to everything else, her gaze fixed on the big animal as she leaned against the clear wall.

Something moved to her right. She quickly looked around, up toward the waterfall. At the top of the cliff, two dark bodies came into view. Despite the distance, she could tell they were chimpanzees. The apes moved in a slightly anxious way, alternately digging at the ground and glancing around themselves. They pulled insects out of the ground and unceremoniously popped them into their mouths, all the while wary of any signs of danger. One of the apes rushed toward the other, knocking it over, and the two engaged in a brief spat of wrestling, which Jennifer recognized as part of the courtship routine. Then they went back to foraging for grubs in the low grass. She watched the scene with delight, feeling like a privileged audience at a remarkable play.

Suddenly, the scene changed. The apes' bodies stiffened. They looked around, swinging their heads in quick turns. Then they cried out in alarm, baring their teeth, and fled rapidly out of sight into the jungle.

Another figure came into view at the top of the cliff. When she saw it, Jennifer's hands closed in a frantic spasm. She started to tremble violently, unconsciously backing away from the wall. "No," she gasped.

Her body bumped into something solid. She screamed as two arms reached around her and grasped her wrists in a viselike grip.

"Yes, Jennifer," Kalia's voice spoke into her ear as she struggled uselessly against his strength. "How else would we know? How else would we ever know?"

— ▪15▪—

It was still raining when Jason reached the Institutes. The darkness was unnatural for an early summer evening, a gloom cast by the roiling clouds of the seasonal storm. He entered the campus on Lincoln Drive, and followed it around past Building 13 to find the service road.

Jason turned into the narrow alley, pulling his Land Rover into the black cover of a tree. He lifted the heavy gym bag off the front seat and stepped out into the rain. In his dark clothing, he knew he would appear as no more than a moving shadow in the murky night; nonetheless he stayed close to the building walls as he followed one side of the laboratory toward the red brick mass of the Center. He could just make out the guards at the main entrance, watchful in their glassed-in booth.

Jason walked down the steep truck driveway behind the building. It ended at a loading dock on the subbasement level. The doors that led from the loading dock into the center were locked. Jason guessed that the last workers to leave the center in the evening would be the shipping and receiving personnel, often on duty to await late deliveries of animals. It seemed likely that they would use these doors when they left. He hunkered down in the lee of the concrete wall, his collar turned up against the chilly rain, and began to wait.

Hardly five minutes had passed before voices approached from within. An obstreperous group of workers banged through the heavy double doors, swinging them wide as they stepped out into the night. When the rain hit them, they began to swear, and they held newspapers and jackets over their heads as they ran up the driveway toward the parking lot.

The doors were closing fast when Jason leapt from the shadows, swinging his gym bag between them. It caught. He slipped through the entrance and glanced around quickly. The big loading gallery was unoccupied. He moved past the shipping office, then pushed through a smaller door into the main tunnels of the subbasement. Once he entered the tunnels he had to slow his pace. Nearly all the lights had been extinguished, leaving only the lights above the stairwells to offer their weak glow.

He recalled the tunnel system from his daytime visits to central supply. But now, in the night, Jason had trouble orienting himself to the dark maze. He stepped with care, his hands out to avoid obstacles in the dark, his eyes fixed on the single light bulb glowing above a stairwell door ahead.

He arrived at the door. In the glow of the light, he read the black plastic panel identifying the stairway location. He knew he had to work his way to the north wing, at the far end of the Center.

In the shadowy light, the corridor appeared to be an impassable jumble. Huge crates had been left on their pallets, unloaded at the service elevators for morning delivery. Cartons of supplies stood piled in confused heaps. Forklifts and hand trucks sat where they'd been abandoned. From some of the dark boxes came the squeaks of rats and the mews and yips of cats and dogs awaiting transfer up to the labs.

Jason picked his way along the subbasement corridor, trying not to upset the balanced crates. His rubber-soled track shoes were almost silent on the dusty cement as he moved farther into the depths of the building. He came at last to the stairwell door marked North and pushed it open, passing through.

Heavy footsteps sounded on the stairs above, several flights up from his level. The stairwell door swung shut behind him with a loud click. The footsteps stopped. Jason didn't move. He could almost hear his heart in the hush of the stairwell. For a moment, the only sound was that of the air conditioning, a soft rush of cool air filling the basement with a quiet hiss. Then the footsteps continued, retreating into the distance.

Jason began running lightly up the stairs. He didn't stop until he reached the third floor—the floor that held his branch offices. He eased the door open, passed through, then closed the door, releasing the crashbar without a sound. The corridor stretched out before him.

Unlike the subbasement, the hall was still well lit, and a variety of sounds broke the silence of the night. Printers tapped out the data from unattended scintillation counters. Compressors for the heavy refrigeration units periodically boomed on. Voices carried faintly from a distant office. Jason crossed the hall, passed the labs, and reached the door to the Clinical Neuroscience branch office. It was locked.

He set down the gym bag, pulled out his pass key, and unlocked the door to the reception area. Moving through the secretarial suite and the file storage room, he reached the door to Dr. Murray's office. It too was locked. He inserted the pass key and started to turn it. It didn't move.

He removed the key and searched his bag. The lock was a standard spring-loaded type, its bolt hidden by the angles of the molding. He pulled the precut strip of tin sheeting from his bag. It took several seconds to work the strip of pliable metal into the crevice between the molding and the door. He inserted it several inches, then wiggled it down until the hook-shaped end was at the level of the doorknob. He jerked it back. The latch sprung open.

There was a loud bang. Jason dropped the gym bag and ripped back his sleeve. The hand of his watch was just sweeping past the fifty second mark. The compressor of the big freezer had just begun a cycle. He marked the time carefully. Then he lifted his gym bag and entered Dr. Murray's office.

—■—

The intercom buzzed suddenly. The white-coated scientist set down his trowel and pushed up a switch. A voice came through. "Dr. Kalia?"

"Yes."

"We have a reading."

"Where?"

"The Center."

Kalia glanced across the garden at the young woman tied to the chair. Her eyes met his for a moment, then darted away. The intercom buzzed again.

"Shall I notify our people?"

Kalia didn't respond immediately. He stroked his chin with his hand, his eyes closed, two deep furrows tracking across his brow. Finally, he answered. "Yes." He began to reach for the switch. "Yes, do that."

"Thank—" The voice was cut off as Kalia flicked the switch down, and carried on with his work.

———■———

Jason left the lights off and walked around to the far side of the desk. Again he set the gym bag onto the floor, and unpacked it quickly. He put the chisels aside and picked up a heavy cylindrical cannister. Its weight shifted from the liquid inside. He shook the cannister vigorously and felt it turn ice cold in his hand.

The bang of the compressor came again. He instantly checked his watch. One minute, eighteen seconds from the last cycle.

He trained his penlight on the edges of the vault door. Then he uncapped the cannister of coolant. He sprayed the visible sections of the deadbolts with the liquid, watching as a thick coat of frost rapidly built up on the door. He set the cannister aside and lifted a chisel, fitting it into the narrow space between the vault door and the frame, its point resting against the bolt.

This was the moment that worried him. The blow would be loud. Possibly repeated. He had no way to predict whether the sound would carry or whether it would blend indistinguishably with the bangs of the compressors out in the hall. He pulled his left sleeve up to his elbow and lifted the sledgehammer in his other hand. His eyes were trained on the luminous hands of his watch, counting down. Fifteen seconds. Eight. Four, three . . . He drew the hammer back behind his shoulder, then slammed it forward onto the chisel. "Don't move!"

The lights shot on in the room. A shock of surprise went through his rigid body. He raised his eyes to see over the desktop. Dr. Murray held a large black revolver in both hands, aiming at Jason's head.

"Lay your hands on the desk. Get up. Not too fast."

Jason put down the tools and stood slowly. The two scientists faced each other across the desk. Murray's eyes were narrowed to slits, and he breathed through teeth clenched in an angry grimace.

"Jason, I want to know what in hell you think you're doing here." The barrel of the gun wavered only slightly in his grasp. It remained centered on the young doctor's head.

Jason didn't see any point in dissembling. "I wanted to find out what this Institute is up to that the Central Intelligence Agency has seen fit to classify."

"Hah!" Murray laughed sardonically, still eyeing him with care. "I suppose you would!"

"Dr. Murray," Jason spoke rapidly. "I don't know what you have to do with this, I don't even know how to look for the answer, but something is happening at the Institutes, and I intend to find out what it is."

"Of course! Of course you do!" The branch chief was seething with anger. "The CIA will be very interested to know about your concerns!"

"I'm sure they will." Jason pressed his lips in a line. "Dr. Murray, you gave me an article by Steven Shay. He didn't send it to you. How did you get it?"

"Jason," the gray-haired man sputtered, "what in hell has that got to do with anything? I got it from one of the other researchers on the genetics project. As people like you well know, we are too goddamned free with our data around here."

Jason went on undismayed, "And just what is in that safe?"

"Hah!" His mouth drew almost into a bestial sneer. "Just for your information, my young friend, that safe is empty. The only thing in it was a bunch of old declassified papers on stress in navy pilots. When the CIA told me to watch out for spies, I cleared it out. It's ironic. You blew your 'cover' or whatever they call it just to break into an empty safe!"

"My cover? What do you—"

Murray snorted. "You know, Jason, I rather liked you. I never would have figured you for a KGB agent."

Jason stared at him dumbfounded. "A what? What in God's name are you talking about?"

"Don't try to pretend!" the branch chief shouted. "They told me the damn Soviets might be involved! They told me the Center might be infiltrated! You probably killed Tom yourself!" He raised the gun, his face twisted with rage, his finger tightening on the trigger.

Jason fixed his eyes on the black muzzle. "Dr. Murray,"— his hands tightened into fists—"I don't like guns."

"That's just too bad, Dr. McCane!"

Both men whirled their heads toward the voice.

An orange-jacketed figure came through the door, holding an automatic pistol. Jason recognized the cylindrical outline of a silencer. The man jabbed his weapon into the branch chief's chest.

Murray spasmodically dropped his revolver onto the floor and shrank back into his chair. Another guard joined the first man at the door. It was Billy, the north wing security man.

"Dr. McCane, it's good to see you," Billy said with grim jocularity, centering his gun on Jason's solar plexus.

Murray's voice was choked. "Billy, what are you doing? What are you men doing here? Arrest this man! He's a spy!"

Billy turned to the other security officer. "Shit. Tie and gag him. I'll have to get instructions about him." He turned back to Jason. "As for you, just don't breathe too loudly, understand?"

Jason watched as they bound Murray into a helpless bundle, his arms twisted back and fastened to his ankles with wire. Then Billy jerked his gun toward the door, signaling for Jason to precede them out of the office. Both men followed him out through the reception area, then flanked him as they entered the corridor.

"Which way, commandant?" Jason asked.

The steel barrel of a gun stabbed fiercely into his lower back, propelling him to the right. He glanced back, considering his chances of disarming them, but the men had stepped back to keep their distance. They walked behind him, six feet back and as far to the sides, both keeping their silenced weapons aimed at his spine. As he swung his eyes around, he managed to glance at his watch.

The group moved down the north wing, approaching the turn into the central hall. Jason could hear the tension in the hissed breathing of the gunmen. They matched him step for step, saying nothing, executioners escorting the condemned man, alert to his every move. They were coming abreast of the stairwell door now. Jason measured the distance with his eyes—at least two yards to the side. Too far. He increased his pace slightly, counting down. Five, four, three . . .

The compressor kicked on with a bang. The guards started to whirl toward the sound. Jason leapt to the side, both feet leaving the ground, and slammed into the crashbar of the door. Plaster exploded off the wall beside his right ear, but he was into the stairwell. He jumped down half of the first flight, checking his balance with the handrail, and swung around the corner as another bullet pinged off the landing floor.

He ran down the stairs three at a time. Voices were cursing behind him. The sound of footsteps clattered down the stairs in pursuit. As he sprinted down the four triple flights, he heard the squawk of their handheld radios. They were spreading the word. Another voice was added to the two, another pair of footsteps pounded above him. The echoes of the guards became a continuous clamor. Jason kept moving; he raced down the stairway, swinging himself around the landings with one hand on the rail and his feet flying wide.

The sound of his pursuers was beginning to fall behind. He finally reached the second basement level and stopped a moment to pull the door shut quietly. The click was lost in the clatter of running feet. He made his way along the north tunnel through the now-familiar gloom. He came to the main tunnel and turned down it, snaking rapidly among the crates on his way through the bowels of the Center.

A light flashed on. The alcove where the freight elevators arrived was just before him. Voices poured from the alcove, ringing off the concrete walls. He began backing up, keeping his track shoes close to the floor.

"You two take the right, OK?"

"Yeah."

"KLR three-eighteen Security," the radio squawked, "Report."

The hordes of crated animals mewed and yipped and squealed at the intrusion of the sound. Jason looked back. There were no intersecting halls, no exits at all from the long straight tunnel to the north wing. He looked forward. Four beams of light caught the suspended dust of the subbasement, sweeping out of the alcove into the darkness of the main tunnel. He heard one security guard sneeze from the kicked-up dust.

"Three-eighteen Security, we're at EB two, proceeding north and south."

Four black barrels poked from the alcove, followed by the guards who held them. He saw that the weapons were not revolvers. They were machine pistols. Two of the guards turned away down the hall, aiming their lights to search the dark space before them, weapons at the ready. The young doctor cast his eyes about desperately. The other two lights began to turn toward him.

Jason leapt straight up. His hands swung apart, each meeting the dirt surface at the top of an asbestos-covered pipe. The pipes gave out a muffled squeak. He threw his legs up, grimacing in the effort to land them silently. His body was a rigid board, spread-eagled between the pipes. The pipes were hot.

The two security men moved up the tunnel side by side, flashlights picking out the crates as they shuffled along warily. Boxfuls of frightened rats scrambled at the glare, their red eyes glinting between the slats of their galvanized prisons. The orange jackets were now directly under Jason. The doctor's arms and legs were burning from the heat. He gritted his teeth.

A piece of asbestos dropped from one of the pipes.

The guards thrust forward their machine pistols. The asbestos ticked its way down behind a wall of tin-lined wooden boxes. In each box, rats leapt in terror.

The two security guards frantically flashed their lights over the boxes. The lights arced and coursed over the stacked tower of wood, casting weird flights of shadows around the confinement of the tunnel. One guard stepped forward, still in a crouch, recovering from the startling sound and beginning a systematic search. "You check that side."

The other man moved toward the far end of the pallet stack, searching with his light. The first guard stayed just beneath Jason.

Jason's limbs were on fire. The pain raged straight through his spine and gripped his whole body in its furnace. He squeezed his eyes shut and bit into his lower lip.

The guard bent, peering warily over one pile of crates to the space behind them, his weapon ready. He slowly crept to the other side of the pile, then suddenly stabbed his light at the wall. The only response was the hungry cry of a pair of boxed cats. He straightened. Then he aimed the muzzle of his automatic weapon upward, working the beam of his light up the wall. Jason held his breath. The light swept toward his foot.

The guard sneezed. He sneezed again. "Goddamn it," he cursed nasally, drawing his sleeve across his nose. His light flashed across the wall. He sneezed once more. Waving his hands at the dusty air, he said, "Nothin' here. It's the fuckin' animals. Let's get out of here."

"Hey, Arnie!" The shout bounced down from the far end of the tunnel. "Give them south all clear! Meet you on B one!"

"OK!" the guard below him called. Then, at a lower tone, he spoke into his radio, "Three-eighteen Security, B two South all clear. Proceeding to surgery."

"KLR three-eighteen Security, ten four," came the static-covered answer.

The two orange jackets disappeared in the dark, flashing their lights, trailing the sporadic explosions of sneezes.

Jason dropped to the floor. He lay flat on his face, pressing his burning arms against the cool concrete, gritting his teeth as the agony slowly abated. Finally, he dragged himself up to kneeling and rubbed at the vicious ache in his legs. He lifted the front of his shirt to mop the sweat off his face. Then he slowly got to his feet and began to make his way down the tunnel.

When he reached the loading gallery, he halted at the door to look around. The area was deserted. He jumped off the ledge and ran across the floor. Reaching the exit, he took a last glance behind him up the dark tunnel. It remained silent, except for the squeals of the crated lab animals, destined for their brief careers in science. He pushed through the double doors and out into the rainy night.

━■ 16 ■━

Jason swept the rain-soaked hair back from his forehead and dialed Jennifer's number. The burr of the rings went unanswered. He cradled the receiver, frowning in puzzlement. She should be home by now, he thought. Perhaps the rain had delayed her.

He located his folder of orientation documents and took out a map of the area. He scanned it for several minutes. Then he dialed Red's home number. No answer. He checked his directory and reached his hand toward the phone again. He stopped, almost jerking away as from a hot iron. His jaw tightened. Then he lifted the receiver and punched a number. After a single ring, it was answered by a woman.

"Yes?"

"Is Red there?"

"Who?"

"Red . . . I mean agent James Gradov." He could hear a series of rapid clicks, overlaid by a thin, high whine. There was a muffled clatter and an expletive; it sounded as if the phone had been grabbed away from the woman.

"Jason, is that you?" Red's voice boomed on the line.

"Red, I want to talk to you. Right now."

"Jesus! Where are you calling from? Look, don't say anything, get yourself to a pay phone!" His voice was insistent. "Your line is being—"

"Never mind where I am. I want to see you in person, in twenty minutes, at the Cedar Lane entrance to Rock Creek Park. Come alone."

"Goddamnit, no, Jason, hold on . . ." Red stopped in midsentence. He realized he was talking to a dead receiver. Then the high background whine abruptly stopped, ending with a second, nearly imperceptible click.

"Shit!" Red exclaimed.

Across the CIA data center, the young analyst Jimmy took off his headphones and looked at the big agent. "What do you think, Red? Shall I call field ops?"

Red stared fiercely at the package on his desktop, a large brown envelope bearing Jason's name and address. The surveillance of Jason's apartment had finally paid off; the field operations unit had just brought this in. Red leapt to his feet and stalked back and forth across the data center floor, opening and closing his fists. "Shit, shit, shit!"

"Red," Jimmy said, "you're not thinking of going alone. . . Red!" But the big man had suddenly grabbed the envelope off his desk, shoved it into the pocket of his raincoat, and made for the door.

It took Jason only twelve minutes to reach the nearby urban park. He left the Land Rover on a small side street that had no direct access to the park, separated from it by a narrow stand of hickories. He had picked the spot not for its proximity, but for its direct connection with a feeder road onto the beltway. Although he had no idea what Red might do, he knew that he wanted an escape route.

Above him, supported on concrete pillars ninety feet high, the beltway cut like a black snake through the night sky. In front of him, the narrow road leading to the park wound in a curve of wet tarmac down a hill from the residential area into the dense band of woods. Jason stood in the shelter of a large tree. He was barely twenty feet in from the road, facing the rear of the modest frame homes across Cedar Lane. Two empty cars had been parked in driveways across the street when he arrived. None had pulled up since. From where he stood, there was a clear view of the occasional vehicles that wound their way through the ribbon of park.

The night had turned unseasonably cool from the gusting wetness. He checked his watch, then thrust his hands into his nylon slicker, drawing the fabric closer around him. Certainly Jennifer had returned by now, he thought. He resolved to call her as soon as he got the chance. His eyes swept the intersection, an open black plane washed by whirling spates of rain. Wind seemed to slap the water onto the road, lift it in twisting fingers, then slap it down again.

Jason was pulling his hand free to check the time again when a pair of headlights appeared. They paused at the cross street, then angled toward the park. The car didn't stop, but continued across the intersection, finally disappearing around a curve. He looked again through the scratched crystal at the luminous dial of his watch. Twenty-one minutes. Droplets landed squarely on the watch face, distorting the numbers into crazy blurs.

An engine sounded from the direction of the park. He looked back down the hill. As the vehicle moved into the lights of the intersection, he saw that it was the same one that had just entered the park, a small imported sedan. The car drew to the opposite corner and came to a halt. For a moment, there was no movement. Then Red stepped from the driver's side and shut the door.

The big man stood still in the street, peering around him through the storm. His loose raincoat was rapidly turned dark by the rain. He held his hands up to form a cone around his mouth. "Jason?" he called out to the empty intersection. He half turned, then called again, "Jason?"

The young doctor stepped deeper into the shadow of the tree. He faced at right angles to the street. "Open the car doors!" he called, deliberately shouting into the wind.

Red looked up, but the wind had carried the voice deceptively, and his eyes were searching the dark woods thirty yards away from where Jason stood. "Jason, where the hell are you?"

"The doors!" Jason called again.

Red hesitated a moment, then turned back to the car. One

by one, he opened all four of the doors. The vehicle's interior was well lit by its courtesy light. It was empty.

"Walk to the curb across from you!" Jason called again into the wind.

Red seemed to hesitate again, then slowly crossed the intersection, scrutinizing the woods as he walked. He stopped at Jason's side of the road. He was still thirty yards south.

"Jason, you bastard, where are you?" Red squinted against the highway lights, trying to see into the trees.

"Take off the coat. Now!"

The heavy CIA man swore, then obliged the doctor, removing the raincoat and dropping it onto the ground.

"Hands up!" the doctor commanded. "Do a full turn."

Again Red acquiesced. A crew neck sweater covered his broad frame. There was no sign of a weapon.

"All right, Red. Now we talk." Jason stepped out of the tree's shadow, letting the streetlights shine onto him. Red looked around a moment, spotted him, and started walking over.

One of the cars parked on the opposite side roared to life and screeched out of its driveway. It fishtailed around and raced toward them across the open space. Jason saw Red pull a black pistol from under his sweater. The agent started to run directly at him, his teeth clenched in a fierce grimace. The lights of the car raked the trees as Jason whirled around and started to run.

"Jason!" he heard Red shout at him. A gunshot sounded. The big man was barely ten feet behind him. "Jason, you fucking idiot!" Another shot. "Get down!"

Automatic weapon fire chattered from the speeding car, crashing around them through the trees. Jason felt his legs buckle as he was tackled from behind. Gunfire swept by inches overhead, cutting into the hickories, spraying bark chips. Red rolled off Jason's legs and sat facing the road, pulling his trigger again and again, shattering the car's windshield and blasting at the gunman on the passenger side. Jason caught a glimpse of blood exploding beside a thick mustache. The machine gun stopped firing, but another barrel sprouted from the window at the back. Red targeted the driver and fired again; his bullet creased the hood. The car skidded to a stop and a burst of fire came from the rear as the car was thrown into reverse and careened back across the intersection. It squealed in a full turn and sped off down the road.

Red remained sitting, his gun clutched in both hands pointed down the road, his breath coming in short quick swallows.

"What the hell is going on?" Jason shouted. He swiftly reached around Red and pulled the pistol out of his hands. Red didn't resist. The big man leaned back onto his elbows, still breathing heavily.

"Who were they?" Jason demanded.

The CIA agent's breathing started to slow slightly. He finally said between breaths, "Probably DARPA."

"Who? Red, what in God's name does DARPA mean?"

Red continued to stare down the road. He gritted his teeth a moment and exhaled. Then he answered, "The Defense Advanced Research Projects Agency. I mentioned them to you before."

Jason paused for a moment, then demanded, "Why do you say it's them, Red?"

"Because we picked up one of their men outside your apartment yesterday. He's a known agent, working under the control of General Simos. General Simos is the director of DARPA."

Jason became silent. He sat back and followed Red's gaze down the street. Red turned to face him for the first time. His face was flushed, his breath still came in ragged gasps. "Hey, Doc, sorry to bother you, but do you know anything about first aid?"

Jason shifted around to his side. It was then that he saw the bleeding hole in Red's upper leg.

———■———

After applying his belt as a compression bandage, Jason ran back through the trees to his Land Rover. He drove it straight through the band of hickory woods and backed it to within feet of the injured man. He lifted his friend into the rear of the vehicle, stretching him almost flat. At Red's insistence, he stopped to grab the fallen raincoat. Then he roared in the direction of the Bethesda Suburban Hospital.

En route, Red ignored his admonition to rest. The adrenaline surge of the firefight was still blocking his pain. His voice racing, the agent quickly filled Jason in on the CIA investigation. "We've known for a couple of years that something's up at the Institutes. Too many security irregularities. Too much data disappearing. We were sure it was the Soviets, trying to steal biotechnology. We never dreamed it was an agency of our own government. It wasn't until two months ago that we decided we had to go after this thing."

"What happened two months ago, Red?"

"A Normal Volunteer disappeared, a young woman. That's why we upped our contact with the scientists. Your Dr. Murray has tried to be helpful, but even he may be a pawn in this business."

"But how did you find out that DARPA was involved?"

Red ground his teeth as a wave of pain swept over him, then went on. He explained how the CIA audit uncovered evidence that the Institutes were spending a lot more than their appropriations: six hundred million dollars last year alone. The money supposedly came from private foundations—but all of it moved through the same Swiss bank, transferred from Washington, DC. "We just completed the trace; that Swiss account is controlled by General Simos."

"Christ! Six hundred million!" Jason skidded into a corner, gunned the engine, and straightened the car. "Who is this guy Simos, anyway?"

"A crazy man." Red shook his head. "He was nearly court-martialed for atrocities in Vietnam, although he never got convicted because of lack of evidence. The army thought they were putting him out to pasture when they gave him DARPA, but he's turned DARPA into the Defense Department's most powerful secret agency."

"But, Red," Jason asked, "how could DARPA pump that kind of money into NIH without anyone knowing?"

"It's wild. The Senate has a committee that oversees NIH funding; the guy in charge is Senator Bowie. But Bowie seems to be blocking our investigation. That's why we're . . ." Red paused. "Well, I might as well tell you: We're planning to move in on DARPA headquarters. Now, Jason, let me ask you something: What the hell is going on at the Institutes that the Defense Department would secretly fund for six hundred million dollars a year?"

Jason didn't offer an answer. He swung the car into the emergency drive of the hospital and backed it to the ambulance entrance. "Gunshot," he called to the orderly.

In moments, Red was transferred to a chrome-railed cart. It was lifted over the rainswept curb and pushed through the doors. Jason accompanied Red through the chaotic hallway, helping to wheel his gurney back into an examining room.

A young surgical resident with a pockmarked face followed them into the room, starting his questions even as Red was transferred to the table. "All right, all right, what's this? Where is it? Joyce"—he turned to a nurse, then back to Red—"No, you just lay flat, OK? Joyce,"—then back to the nurse—"hand me the scissors will you? And hang D5 normal"—to another nurse—"and a line, thanks, with an extension this time, right? And a couple of eighteens over here. What's this?" He began cutting up the leg of Red's pants, starting at the ankle.

"Gunshot," Jason answered. "Medial thigh about six inches down. It's been twelve or fifteen minutes. He's lost maybe a unit."

The surgeon's tone changed in response. "You a doc?"

"Pulse one ten, BP one thirty over eighty," one nurse called out.

"Yes."

"Hi, I'm Bill Poski. Susan, a line yet?"

"Jason McCane."

"Howdy." The young surgeon spread the leaves of Red's sliced trouser leg and bent to appraise the elliptical purple mouth, drooling bright red blood. With two fingers he gently spread the lips of the wound. Red sucked in a breath through his teeth.

"Sorry. Somebody call Sandy, all right?" The resident moved up from the leg, pulling a stool over with his foot and rolling up the sleeve of Red's shirt. "I'm going to have to start an IV here, OK?" he explained to Red as he snapped a length of red rubber tubing out of his belt and cinched it around the arm above the elbow. "So"—he looked at both of them, then down to Red's forearm—"what happened?"

Red answered quickly, "Goddamn punks!" He winked once at Jason. "Can't even walk your goddamn dog in the park anymore. Fuckin' punks!"

"Rock Creek?" the surgeon asked. "You get jumped? You'll feel a little stick now. Good." He quickly rotated a plastic syringe into place and drew up the plunger, filling it with blood, then twisted it loose. "Susan? Thanks." He exchanged the syringe for the IV line. The nurse passed him strips of tape. "Lytes, CBC and type and cross for four units, all stat. That damn park . . ." He looked up to Jason, shaking his head.

Jason frowned in agreement.

The resident returned to the leg. "Gotta stay clear of it at night." He passed his hand underneath, feeling for an exit wound. "Can you move this? Good. This? Good. Toes up? Good. Can you feel this? Fine. This?"

"Ah!" Red struck the cart beside him with his fist.

"Sorry. So how'd you . . ." He looked up to Jason again.

The neuroscientist hesitated. "I was—"

Red cut in, "Thank God this guy was driving by! Jesus! His headlights scared the fuckers off. Hey, what'd you say your name was?"

"Jason. Jason McCane." He accepted the free hand Red awkwardly extended for a shake.

"Jim Finnerty. Goddamn! Wait till the wife finds out about this!"

Jason started to answer the covert smile appearing on Red's face but was stopped by the way that smile distorted with pain.

"No major bleeders or nerves, but I want X-rays and maybe an arteriogram," the surgeon summarized his first impressions after the rapid exam. He addressed the nurse, "Keep it at a hundred for now," tapping the IV line with his finger. "And six of MS. Joyce, can we wash it up? Where the hell is Sandy?" He briskly left the examining room.

Red looked up at his friend. "You want to translate?"

"He says he may want to take a picture of your arteries to see if they're OK. And you're getting some morphine for pain."

"Right. I am starting to feel this sucker." He gripped Jason's hand and squeezed, lying back onto the cart. He gritted his teeth as a nurse began to irrigate the raw edges of his wound with betadine.

A tired radiologist appeared in the room, washing away his languor with black coffee as the surgeon marched in at his back describing the case. Then the radiologist and his technician together wheeled Red from the room, rapidly rolling his cart off into the basement of the hospital.

While his friend was gone, Jason found a pay phone in the lobby. He dialed Jennifer's home number. There was no answer. He dialed her lab at the center. No answer. He dialed the NIH switchboard and asked for the number of the Laboratory of Brain and Behavior. He was told it was classified. The woman began to ask who was calling.

Jason quickly cradled the phone and turned into the main hall. When he reached the examining room, Red had already come back from X-ray. The radiologist was standing at a view box in the hall.

"As you can see, the slug is sitting right up against the femoral artery." The radiologist pointed with a pen at the black and white image. "Could blow at any time."

The surgeon said, "I'll call my chief." He turned to Jason. "It looks like your friend has bought himself an operation."

Jason nodded once, then he stepped into the curtained room while the surgeon went off to make the call.

Red was perched on his elbows. "Hey Jason, I heard that. What's this operation bullshit?"

"Take it easy. Here, lay back down." He held the pillow as his friend eased down again. "That piece of lead is just kissing one of your big arteries, so they're going to pull it out for their collection. Nothing too dramatic, all right?"

Red shook in a quick spasm of pain. "Right," he rasped. Then he lifted his head up quickly. "Hey, I almost forgot! The guy we pulled in yesterday at your apartment: He was collecting your mail for you. I even left it alone." His attempt at a smile twisted again into a grimace of pain. "Check out my raincoat," he said exhaustedly, returning his head to the cart.

"Thanks, Red. I will." Jason paused. "Look, I don't know what's going on at the Institutes, I don't know what DARPA is up to, but I'm going to find out."

The big agent looked up at him. "Jason, if the most rabid gang in the Defense Department is running this show, this is no job for the Lone Ranger. Here, give me something to write with."

The young doctor passed him the paper wrapping from a gauze bandage and a pen. Red scribbled a number and passed it back to his friend.

"Call them, man. Don't leave here before you call them."

"Who will I reach?" Jason asked, buttoning the scrap of paper into his shirt pocket.

"Let's just say you call this number and you get the CIA's whole goddamned army. Helicopters, tanks, you name it."

A nurse and an anesthesia technician entered the room and unlocked the wheels of the cart. Jason gave his friend's hand a last squeeze as they wheeled his gurney out through the curtains. This time, they took him to the right, toward the surgery suite. Halfway down the hall, Red suddenly sat up on the cart. "Jason . . ." he said groggily.

"Hey, lie down!" The nurse put a hand on his shoulder.

"Got to tell him," the agent mumbled. The medication was rapidly taking effect. "They probably bugged his car. . . ." He collapsed flat.

When Red had gone, Jason ran out to his Land Rover. He lifted the mass of the rain-soaked coat from behind the seat, and searched the pockets. In an inside pocket, he found the package. Reentering the hospital, he located an empty on-call room and set the big envelope aside for a moment while he washed the rusty coat of dried blood from his hands. Then he cleared a work space on the desk and placed the package in front of him.

It was an Express Mail envelope, a flat rectangle of glossy cardboard, barely half an inch thick. He inverted the package to see the return address: A. Beimeyer, LLB, JD, Attorney at Law.

———■———

The paper was brittle with age, a crackling folio of yellow-edged pages, held together by the remnants of a fabric binding, its glue long dissolved by decades of travel and dank storage. But the rigid upright letters of his father's printing were hauntingly familiar, as clear as the day they were written. This was the journal of Dr. Lowell McCane. His single compulsion had been this nightly historizing; in a few words or a few pages, the anthropologist had always recorded a day's summary of events and moods, no matter where he was.

Jason sat at the desk, paging through the sheets, searching for one special week. As Jason had requested in his phone call, Beimeyer had sent him the volume pertaining to the spring of 1956. He skimmed through the earliest entries.

April 14, 1956: Camp IV, Omo

Preparations complete for traveling. Porters engaged for the trek to the river. Meeting Leakey in the north . . .

Jason flipped forward, skipping the details of the voyage. Then he began reading the entries relating to his father's historic Paris conference, "The Ascent of Social Man."

May 1, 1956: Paris

Arrived Paris. Mssr. Arambourg's provisions for the conference seemed extravagant, until I learned of the rather startling number of registrants. Dr. Kalia and his party are expected tomorrow.

Louise took Jason to the Jeu de Paume, where he devoted the better part of the afternoon to wreaking havoc with the Impressionists and the guards . . .

May 2, 1956: Paris

Conference opened gloriously. Met Paul Kalia for

the first time today. On first blush, his persona rankles a bit, though no one can deny the importance of his work. I remain convinced we have much to learn from these biologists. Perhaps my first impression . . .

May 5, 1956: Paris

Another solid day of discussion. The only thorn remains the rather troubling editorials of my cochairman. Not everyone shares his opinion that evolution has left most men unfit for equal participation in society. He goes further, predicting that the comparative fitness of different societies must inevitably be resolved in a struggle for ascendancy, a global conflict.

His point about genetic variation is well taken, of course, but the political implications of such a stance . . .

May 6, 1956: Paris

Conference closed. In most respects, I suppose it will be regarded as a success. Nevertheless, I pack for Nairobi with eagerness. It is Dr. Kalia's sort of thinking that has made me cherish my self-imposed exile from the cold-war mentality that grips my so-called civilized world. His private opinions exceed even his most brazen public statements. Kalia believes that the fittest men must ascend to dominate all others. He actually wishes that he could speed the process—press the course of human evolution! Make the perfect man! Thank God there is no science on earth that could ever bring to pass these evil dreams. . . .

Jason held the yellowed sheet stretched taut, staring at it as if it were alive. His father could not have predicted the arrival of gene transfers. Jason knew better. It was more than an evil dream. It was almost possible. He thought about Kalia's work. His own work. Tom Sherrington's work. The new genetics work all around the Institutes. If all of those efforts were harnessed, coordinated, linked together . . . He remem-

bered Tom's bold offer. "You map 'em, I'll transfer 'em!"
The paper shook in his grip. He corrected himself: It was
possible! Red's question cycled through his mind. "What's
going on at the Institutes that the Defense Department would
secretly fund for six hundred million dollars a year?"

Jason sprang to his feet and ran down the hall. As he
reached the pay phones, he jerked out the scrap of paper with
the number Red had given him. He lifted it, debating for a
silent moment. Then he shoved it back into his pocket and
sprinted toward the outside doors, passing through the waiting
room at a dead run, oblivious to the stares. As he dashed out
into the rain, his pulse was racing, his mind a montage of
furious thoughts. But one single thought burned brighter than
the rest: Jennifer.

⊸∎ 17 ∎⊷

The black-suited figure sat before a monitor screen—a large computer display terminal overlaid with a dim fluorescent map of the Washington area. A single green blip was blinking off and on, once a second, motionless just north of the District boundary. The watcher looked away, pulling a log book into the pale crescent of green light cast by the screen. He checked the time on his watch and made an entry. Then he rose and stretched, shaking the cramps from his legs. He turned and looked through the clear plexiglass into the jungle behind him.

A long green snake hung from the branch of a nearby tree, its scales irridescent in the twilight gloom, its red liquid tongue flicking silently in and out as it smelled the air for prey. The man pressed up against the plastic wall, watching the reptile. The thick ophidian body curled around the branch, slithered halfway down the trunk and poised, rigid in space. There was a tiny movement in the grass, a barely visible shivering of the blades. The snake whipped downward, flashing its open jaws toward the movement, yellow fangs glinting for a split second, then its body tossed about in the grass, trying to swallow the jungle rat whole.

The bleeding rat twisted frantically in the jaws, working its legs in a hopeless parody of running, throwing its head back to try to bite its way free. The snake's needlelike jaws crushed together steadily as the animals thrashed about at the base of the tree. Suddenly the rat stopped moving and hung limp, something precious broken inside. The snake adjusted its grip, then slipped away, disappearing in the tangled undergrowth.

The man turned back to his task. However, when he reached the screen, he could not find the blip of light. His eyes swept the quadrants rapidly. Finally, he sighted the light moving toward the extreme left edge of the monitor. He pushed a button, keying in a grid with a larger scale. He pushed another button, measuring the velocity. Then he reached for the intercom switch.

"Dr. Kalia?"

The voice answered through a small speaker. "Yes?"

"The car has started moving again."

"Direction?"

"West, sir. He's moving pretty fast."

"I see." There was a pause. Then the voice returned. "So, we may have a visitor tonight. Well, we know what to do, don't we?" There was a click, then silence.

———■———

Senator Bowie was expecting the call. He grabbed the phone on the first ring. "Yes?" he said.

The authoritative voice on the other end was familiar. As the senator listened, a smile began to break out across his face. He said only, "Yes, Doctor. It would be a great pleasure. I'll be there as soon as possible." He cradled the phone momentarily, then he lifted it again to call for his limousine.

———■———

In a building in central Washington, DC, in a room with windows that overlooked the Old Executive Office Building, a man stood at attention. The man was known outside of this building as "Mr." Williams. His actual title was colonel. He was the principal aide to the director of DARPA.

A second man was seated in a chair, facing out the windows.

All the colonel could see of him was his head, clipped almost bald in a military cut, supported by a neck as thick as a column.

"Sir," the colonel began, "we have the situation under control—"

"Shut up!" the second man roared. He rose from his chair and whirled around. His face was coarse and dark below his narrow eyes, his jacket stretched to contain his heavy shoulders, giving him the overall appearance of a bull dressed in the uniform of a general. "One man captured. Two men killed. And McCane and the girl are still alive!"

"But, sir—"

"Ten years I've worked to make this project happen. I will not have it jeopardized! I'll see that this is done right. Get the car."

"Where are we—"

"To the laboratory, you fool!"

—■—

Lightning crashed down through the night sky, lighting the road in a quick blaze of white before it was plunged again into rainswept darkness. The engine whined, pushed to its limits. Jason tried to see through the water-battered windshield as the car flew along the highway, but the wipers were no match for the deluge. The line painted down the middle of the road was his only guide. It shined as a streak of white between his headlights, like a silver snake leaping out of the stormy night.

He saw the mouth of the laboratory access road, a deeper blackness between the thrashing trees, and jerked the wheel. The Land Rover sprayed gravel as it careened in the turn. With a lurch and a scrape, the Rover plowed into the woods.

Despite its four-wheel drive, the vehicle rocked and skidded as he gunned it along the muddy tunnel. The headlights were almost useless, their beams shooting wildly about as the car bucked through the forest, pitching and yawing like a boat in a typhoon. The boulders at the edges of the track were invisible, lost in the dark and rain, and he glanced off them, caroming from one collision to the next.

When he finally estimated that he'd gone about halfway to the lab compound, Jason stopped. He sat in the car, trying to remember what he'd seen at his last visit—the fence, the gate, the guardhouse—as rain pounded like timpani on the flat metal roof. Then he slammed the car into gear again, twisting the wheel, deliberately aiming for a narrow space between two trees off one side of the lane. Branches slapped against the windshield, totally blocking his view. With a bang, the car jolted to a stop after twenty feet. He got out and pushed his way forward through the brambles to find the obstruction. It was a birch tree, solidly rammed up against the front bumper.

Jason made his way back to the door, reached in, and cut the ignition. He left the keys dangling in place. Then he pushed through the brush back to the road. From there, the Land Rover was nearly invisible. He pulled on the hood of his slicker and started to run up the lane toward the laboratory.

Jason splashed along the road, lifting his knees to clear the jumble of rocks and roots, his feet sucked in by the viscous grip of the mud. After half a mile, he slowed as the track began to widen. Through the trees, around a curve in the road, the guard station came into view, a squat peaked box before the high metal gate. Jason left the road and cut into the forest. He moved carefully, stepping through the trees in a low crouch, until he reached the wall of the station. He lifted an eye to the rear window and peered into the hut.

A man sat in the darkened box, his face lit by the orange tip of his cigarette. From his posture, the man seemed intent on the road. The guard reached forward and stubbed out the butt. For a moment there was darkness. Then a match flared, briefly lighting the hut as he lit another cigarette. Jason saw what he expected: an electronic panel for one of the locking devices that responded only to a precoded voice. Light also glinted off a cylinder of blued steel, the barrel of an automatic weapon.

Jason silently drew back into the trees. When he judged that the sound of his footsteps could no longer carry to the hut, he moved more quickly, pushing his way through the woods. Fifty yards from the guard station, he finally reached the tall fence. It was easily fifteen feet high, with a spiral of barbed wire running along the top. He moved closer, flexing his fingers for the climb.

There was an angry hiss and a small flash of light. He jumped back. At the top of the metal lattice, a tendril of smoke was curling up from a ceramic plug. Looking down the length of the fence, he saw that the woods were lit with flickering bursts of light: As rain fell onto the fence, sparks were jumping from its wire mesh.

Jason looked once more toward the guard's hut, considering his options. He turned away from the hut and forced his way deeper into the woods. Thorns tore at his pants as he worked through several hundred yards of thick brush, paralleling the electric fence. He leapt down a slope, waded a rushing stream, and began to climb up the opposite side. Halfway up, he saw what he was looking for.

A maple tree was rooted in the embankment. One thick limb angled out over the barbed wire. Jason looked up at the tree limb, wiping the rain from his eyes. Even if he got across, the drop on the opposite side would be daunting, maybe twenty feet.

He clambered up to the level of the tree. A small bole grew out from the trunk four feet up. He jumped onto it, hugging the tree. Using the tips of both shoes, he shifted to the top of the bole, then bent carefully, his eyes on the first branch above him. He leapt, falling backwards away from the trunk. His fingers barely touched the branch. He forced his slipping fingers into the bark. The grip held. He swung himself quickly up to stand on the branch. Without hesitating, he jumped again. His hands slapped around the wood, and he pulled himself up onto the big limb.

Quickly, he stepped out along the limb, crossing above the fence. Sparks buzzed and spat below him, crackling fingers of blue-white light. Five feet beyond the barbed wire, he lowered himself and circled the limb with his hands. He flipped his body out into midair. The ground rushed at him. He hit with his muscles bunched, rolling away from the fence. Jumping to his feet again, he ran through the rain, across the meadows toward Kalia's Laboratory of Brain and Behavior.

Jason dodged under the portico leading to the lab entrance and put his back to the wall. Several cars were parked under the portico, including Kalia's Lincoln. He recalled Jennifer's laughing description of her rattly American car; he spotted her little Dodge, neatly sandwiched between the other vehicles. He pulled off his noisy slicker, tossing it aside. Carefully, he approached the glass doors. No lights were on in the lobby. There was no sign of life in the reception area, no noise but the subdued rumble of the storm. He searched the edges of the door, running his eyes around the perimeter. No beams of light or obvious wires led from the frame. He braced himself, then pulled the door handle quickly outward. It opened easily. Still there was no sound. He slipped inside.

Jason crossed the marble floor of the lobby. His eyes were everywhere. In the darkness he could barely see the two halls that led from the lobby, but he remembered that one led to Dr. Kalia's office. He passed the midpoint and stepped onto the carpet runner that spanned the reception area.

A siren shattered the night.

Jason rushed toward the far side of the lobby, vaulted a couch, and sprinted for the side hall. Out of the corner of his eye, he saw a black figure entering the lobby from the other side, running toward him, holding a weapon. Jason got to the corner in a moment and turned to run down the long corridor. The siren's scream obscured the sounds of his pursuer as he raced down the hallway toward the open door of the outer office. With a leap, he covered the last few yards and tumbled through the doorway. Then he jumped back to his feet and reversed direction, crouching against the wall.

A second later, the black-garbed figure swung through the doorway, his machine pistol held at the ready. Jason came up from the crouch with his forearms forming a wedge. He shot the wedge up between the man and his weapon, spreading his fists as he went, wrenching the gun out of the man's grasp. Then he planted a foot in the man's chest and slammed him toward the door of Kalia's inner office. The door crashed open under the hurtling body. Jason followed him, and ran past the prostrate form to face the man seated at the desk.

"Where's Jennifer?" he demanded.

Two more black-suited figures rushed into the room, leveling their weapons at the young doctor. He whirled toward them. The third man rose unsteadily to his feet. Kalia quickly raised a hand, signaling for the guards to hold their fire. He looked up calmly from his desk, his lips in a slight grin. The siren began to moan down to silence.

"Jason," he said, leaning back in the leather chair, his thick white eyebrows raised in a look of amusement. "Good evening. Won't you take a seat?" He nodded at a chair in the center of the room.

The younger scientist stood across from Kalia, his body tensed, his fists clenched, hair matted and clothes still dripping from the rain. He drew quick breaths through his teeth as he eyed the director of the laboratory. "Where's Jennifer?" he demanded again.

"Ah, yes." Kalia smiled. "Jason and Jennifer. I should have guessed. The irony is stunning: Here we are, two educated men of science with something rather critical to discuss, and the young gentleman must know about his lady. I must admit, I had never figured you for the warmhearted type. But the mating instinct is a powerful one." He gave out a short laugh. "Our DNA makes us all victims of love. Sit down, Jason."

Jason didn't move. He fixed the man with a look of steel. Kalia sighed. "I see. Well, since you must know, Jennifer is fine. She has not been harmed in any way. We will bring you to her soon." He signaled again to the black-suited guards, who turned and left the room, pulling shut the door.

"But first," Kalia continued, "we must talk."

The elder scientist again angled his head toward the chair. Jason eyed him warily for a minute, then sat down. The two men faced each other across the expansive desk, Kalia sitting forward, his hands clasped before him. Jason remained alertly still.

"Jason," Kalia began, "let us not pretend. I think you know what I'm doing here in the laboratory."

The younger man continued to face him guardedly. He nodded once.

"Yes, good," Kalia said. "I thought as much." He looked briefly toward the pair of tapestries on the wall, as if searching for the right words, then went on. "You know what my true goal is, but do you know why? Do you have any conception of why this work must be done?"

"Dr. Kalia, I only know that the first obligation of science is to humanity."

"Humanity?" Kalia stood up rapidly. "Humanity? Jason, what is 'humanity'?" His voice rose as he stepped around the desk. "Humanity is the flawed product of a collection of genes selected through trillions of generations. Genes to make an organism breathe and grow. Genes that make that organism fit for scraping out survival on this earth of ours. Most of all, genes to make us reproduce and reproduce and reproduce more genes. And for what? So that the next generation can carry on, surviving, reproducing, mindlessly to infinity!"

"Mindlessly?" Jason looked up at the elder man pacing before him. "I will not debate the rest, but how can you call humanity mindless? You, who have spent a lifetime studying the complexities of the brain?"

"Mindless. That's exactly what I mean." Kalia continued pacing back and forth, his eyes lost in the distance. "Yes, the human brain is an amazing organ. But it exists only for one purpose: to ensure the perpetuation of the genes that created it. Every facet of human nature, all our dreams and hopes and passions, are just the by-products of that fertile instinct orchestrated by the genes for their own benefit, to go on and on forever."

"Yes," Jason interjected, "the *process* is mindless. But the organism is not. There is no other product of evolution as incredible as the human mind."

"Precisely!" Kalia held up a finger, then went on with his rushed speech. "Don't you see? Human nature hasn't changed in fifty thousand years! Since the birth of *Homo sapiens,* we have been slaves to our DNA. We are still the same pitiful beasts we've been since the beginning of the Pleistocene!

"Jason, as I'm sure you know, there's less than a six-percent difference between the genetic codes of chimpanzees and humans. Just think: What extraordinary beings we could be if we just made another six-percent advance! For the first time in the world, we would be able to truly ascend. To control evolution. To choose which human characteristics we should keep or discard. To give man any strength, any mental ability, any perfection we desire. Not just *Homo sapiens,*" his voice rose to a shout, "but *Homo perfectus!*"

"And who will choose?" Jason responded. "Who will decide the direction of human evolution? You? The Department of Defense? The warped leaders of DARPA?"

The old scientist looked at him with irritation. "Jason, don't you understand? Of course the military is supporting my project, because the future of America depends on it! America needs the best gene pool if we are to be the leaders of this world. And the National Institutes of Health are the perfect place to do this research. I've got the labs, the scientists, the experimental subjects—eighteen branches at five different Institutes are working on it right now, and they don't even know it! *I'm* the only one who knows the master plan. But unless I had DARPA to control the Institutes and bring me data from other scientists, how could I get the resources I need?"

"So you've simply sold out to a crazed group of Defense Department madmen who want to breed an American master race!"

"Damn you!" Kalia bellowed. "You don't understand. Just as your father didn't understand. Only genetically superior men will survive the final competition! That's the way of evolution. We're talking about the ascent of man!"

"The ascent of man? Damn it, Dr. Kalia, you're not talking sense! How could a handful of mutants—no matter how superior—compete with the wild type?"

Kalia sat back down. His face was lined with a strange solemnity. He looked down to his tented fingers, then up. "Jason, what do you know about the origin of clams?"

"Clams? What in the hell are you talking about, Dr. Kalia—"

"We studied clams for years, baffled by the record: Two hundred and twenty-five million years ago, they suddenly replaced the brachiopods. What happened to all the brachiopods? There is only one answer. . . ." Kalia smiled, seeing Jason's expression. "Ah, so you do know. You know that evolution is not always such a gentle process. You know that even a small number of mutants can prevail, can ascend to dominance, when their competitors are suddenly eliminated by—"

"Mass extinction."

Kalia laughed out loud. "Yes! Mass extinction! The past has taught us the lesson of our future. Jason, how long do you imagine that this insane race for nuclear superiority can go on before the final moment? A decade? Three? Does it matter? The military is preparing."

"Dr. Kalia, no!"

"Don't you understand why we built the dome underground? Once the new race is born, we have nothing to lose by launching a first strike."

"No!"

"Mass extinction will clear the way. The wild type is doomed. The mutants will be protected from the conflict. Then the superior species, *my* superior species, will ascend to rule the world!"

Jason stared at him with utter dread. His eyes were almost as wide as Kalia's.

"Jason, don't doubt for a moment that I will succeed." The laboratory director fixed his wild gaze on the face of the young man before him. "Gene splicing is an established technology. Test-tube fertilization is an established procedure. The only thing we're doing that's new is to combine the two. With your help, it won't be long. In two years—three at the most— the first of the new race will be born." He leaned forward across the desk, speaking with urgent zeal. "Join me, Jason. I can protect you from DARPA. I already have. You can be part of the most important scientific advance in the history of the world. Join me."

Jason's gaze was locked on Kalia's. The men faced each other in the tense silence, their eyes yoked in wordless interplay. Jason's voice sounded utterly calm when he finally spoke. His words came barely above a whisper.

"Where is Jennifer?"

Kalia continued to watch him for a minute. Then he leaned back slowly, venting a long sigh. As the famed scientist looked at Jason, a change came over his eyes. A hardening. He shook his head and turned slightly toward the paired Chinese tapestries that hung down one side of the room.

"All right, Layla," he said.

Jason whipped around to face the tapestries. In the space between them, he saw the hand with the weapon, and he started to leap backwards over his chair. The girl appeared as he twisted in midair. There was a sharp crack. Crashing back, he felt a pain explode in his chest just before he hit the floor.

With one hand, he clawed at his chest, found the dart, and pulled the needle out of his muscle. Trying to rise from the floor, he realized that his limbs would not respond.

"It's just a short-acting anesthetic. Don't bother trying to move," Kalia was saying.

The words came to him through a ringing sound that filled his ears. Looking up, he saw the scientist and his dark-haired daughter standing over him. She was speaking to him, smiling, thanking him for his help with the automatic gene sequencer, but he heard nothing. His eyes were aching to focus but he saw only two shapeless forms. Then their images were lost in a rushing gray-black haze.

— ∎ 18 ∎ —

aves washed onto the beach in Java, starting with a deep rumble, splashing up into a whitecapped wall, rolling as a flat hissing stream up across the sand, then rolling back out to meet the next wave in a cycle that went on and on. Each one sent a salty spray of droplets into the air, landing on him, cooling his naked skin as he lay drowsing in the equatorial sun. He heard his name called, "Jason!" and he slowly turned in the heat, feeling the sand rub against his body. "Jason!" the voice came again. A vision appeared before him. A brown-skinned figure, approaching up the beach, long legs swinging her sarong. She moved with deliberate leisure, sensual, eager, smiling at him as she came. Somehow, he wasn't surprised as the vision shimmered, changed, metamorphosed by the blurring waves of heat that rose above the island sand. As the figure neared, he saw a girl with skin as pale and fine as an Englishwoman's, hair so long and bright it seemed to float like a golden veil around her head, moving toward him like a dancer, reaching out for him. He smiled, recognizing Jennifer.

"Jason!" The voice seemed frightened, not fitting the vision at all. "Please wake up!" He didn't want to stir. The image was so warm and close, he felt paralyzed by heat and languor, waiting for the girl.

"Jason!" Another voice. A man's voice. "The drug should be metabolized in the next few minutes."

He listened to the voice, tried to place it as he took in a deep breath. He felt confused, halfway from dream to waking, shifting his stiff limbs slightly where he lay.

"There, he's moving. You see, Dr. Darien?" The man spoke again and Jason's mind struggled to the present: Kalia. He opened his eyes, but a film seemed to blur his surroundings.

"Jason!" Jennifer called again.

His vision began to clear, and he saw her at last. She was standing before him, wearing a black jump suit, barely six feet away. Her figure seemed to float in a sea of emerald green. She looked terrified.

"Ah, Dr. McCane. I see you are recovering," spoke the white-haired scientist.

Jason tried to get up. He barely managed to kneel before he fell back to the floor. Dragging himself up again, he staggered toward Jennifer, but his eyes didn't see the obstruction. He slammed into it, collapsing against the transparent wall. Looking through it, he finally realized where Jennifer was. Inside the dome.

"Ah yes," Kalia was saying, "now you begin to wake up. I told you you would get the chance to see your true love."

Jason crouched against the wall, dazed, trying to stop the roaring chaos of his mind. He shook his head, then looked behind him, his brain gradually clearing from the drug. He had awakened at one of the observation posts outside the dome. Dr. Kalia was standing with Layla, silhouetted by the blinking mosaic of the computer console. Two of his black-suited guards stood beside him. Behind them stood three more men: one was hugely fat, one was square-jawed and broadly built, the third was as short and stout as a bulldog.

"Allow me to introduce you," Kalia was saying. "This is Senator Bowie. This is Colonel Williams. And this is General Simos, the director of the Defense Advanced Research Projects Agency." Each of them nodded to Jason in turn.

Jason stared at the men, then turned to face the scientist.

"Kalia." He spoke the single word, his tongue still thick from the drug.

A roar sounded from the distance. Jason twisted his head toward the jungle, looking at Jennifer for a moment, then scanned his eyes rapidly over the glossy plane of the wall.

"Yes, Jason," Kalia said. "I think you understand the situation now. Your lady friend was lowered through the access port, so don't waste your time looking for a way to reach her."

Jason's chest filled in quick expansions. On hands and knees, he clawed his way up to the dome wall, trembling, struggling to control his still anesthetized muscles. He looked up. A rope sling with a net at the end led up to the access port almost forty feet up the glass-smooth wall. The young doctor's eyes came down to Jennifer. He took in her ripped jumpsuit, her tear-streaked face. She seemed almost to be in shock, staring at him through the wall, standing with her hands pressed flat against the transparent barrier of armored plexiglass.

Jason shook himself and stood unsteadily. He placed his hands against the wall opposite Jennifer's, as if to touch her. His eyes met hers, which were bright with terror. Then he turned to face the white-haired scientist. His words were slowed by the drug, but his tone was clear. "Let her go, Kalia."

"Let her go?" Kalia smiled. "Have no fear, you will be joining Dr. Darien shortly. But first, she will serve a most valuable purpose."

"What purpose?" he demanded. He pulled himself erect, tipping against the wall, catching himself with a hand. "What in hell are you going to do with her?"

The older scientist just shook his head. "Don't be naive. What purpose have scientists always served? To give their lives for the sake of knowledge!" His mouth curved into an ironic grin. "Jennifer is about to become the subject of a little experiment. All of us have come down here to watch. Since your turn is next, we thought you should be interested."

Jason lurched toward the older scientist. "I'll kill you, Kalia!"

The two guards rushed in and grabbed Jason, viciously twisting his arms behind his back. He struggled furiously, but the drug still made him too weak to resist.

Kalia had involuntarily dropped back a step. He composed himself. "Hah! My young friend, you don't seem to understand.

You see, things shall be rather the other way around. First we shall see how long Jennifer survives. Then you will have your chance to show us what the wild type can do!" The scientist nodded to Layla, who stepped over to the electronics panel and began to manipulate the controls of the computer. Kalia turned back toward Jason. "Can you imagine what would happen if every large animal in that jungle were to lose its fear? If, for just a few hours, every aggressive drive were totally stimulated? To hunt, to dominate, to kill, to feed!" The scientist's eyes fairly glowed.

"Kalia! No!" Jason shouted, struggling with the guards.

Kalia stepped to the recorder beside the computer. He spoke: "This is Dr. Paul Kalia dictating a primate experiment. . . ." As he spoke and Layla worked the computer, the sounds of the jungle were changing. The jabbering of the colobus monkeys turned into strident screeches. The quiet snorts of prowling beasts changed to louder growls. The jungle seemed to be coming alive, turning into a wild cacophony of bellows and screams.

Jennifer looked frantically around her, searching for a door, an opening, any way to get out. A sound came from the brush covering the bank of the jungle stream. Jennifer whirled and saw the leaves moving. There was a low growl. Then a hyena appeared in the clearing.

The spotted animal lowered its belly to the ground, ears pinned back, snout wrinkled in a snarl. A metal cap protruded from the center of its skull. "Jason!" Jennifer screamed. She began backing away from the animal, sliding along the wall.

"*Jason!*" she cried again. The animal stalked slowly toward her, baring an ugly set of yellow teeth. The hairs stood up along the ridge of its back. Muscles bunched, ready to attack, it started to lope after her.

Jennifer turned with a cry and began to run. "*Jason,*" she shouted, "help me!" Then she plunged into the green depths of the jungle. The hyena followed her into the brush.

Jason's rage exploded. Like the bursting of a dam, it crashed out of the darkest corner of his heart. A sound ripped through his lungs and tore its way out of him as a roar.

He ripped his arms out of the grip of the guards, slamming one of them to the floor. He went for Kalia. The other guard tackled him from behind, bringing him down with a crash, but instantly Jason twisted free and began to rise. The guard swung a fist toward his head. Jason blocked the blow, ducked under the man's arm, and threw him headfirst into the wall. The man crumpled like a sack. Jason turned again to advance on Kalia. "Get her out!" he bellowed.

"Not so fast, Dr. McCane," spoke Colonel Williams as he stepped between Jason and Kalia. He was pointing a pistol at Jason's chest.

"Get her out, Kalia!" Jason yelled again over the growing roars of the jungle.

Dr. Kalia was laughing. "It's too late, my young friend. You can't help her now. The program is entered. We couldn't stop it if we wanted to!"

They all heard a scream, a woman's voice, coming from the depths of the jungle. Jason spun to face the glossy wall. There was only one way in or out. He ran directly toward the wall. He leapt, catching onto the rope sling dangling from the access port. He began to climb.

General Simos spoke quietly to Colonel Williams, "Kill him." Williams lifted his pistol to aim at Jason's back.

"Let him go!" shouted Kalia. "Let him go, let him go. He'll die soon enough!" The scientist's laughter echoed through the tunnel, following Jason as he pulled himself up hand over hand, straining every muscle in his arms to climb as fast as he could. "You and your damned father. He thought I was a fool, just because I had the vision to see the future of mankind and the courage to change it. And now you!" He shook his fist with fury. "You dare to challenge the ascent of the fittest? You dare to defend the wild type? Jason, you are the wild type! You are the wild type! Now try surviving this!"

Finally Jason reached the lower edge of the access port. He pulled himself up to balance in the opening. His nostrils were immediately filled with the hot musty smell of the jungle. He coiled up the rope sling from outside the dome, then threw it down on the inner side. He didn't hesitate a moment, but swung himself over the lip of the port and slid down the rope to the jungle floor.

The moment he was down, the men outside pulled the rope sling back up. It caught for a moment on one of the cameras mounted on the inner surface of the dome wall. They jerked it free, ripping the camera off the wall. It landed with a crash at Jason's feet. Then the ropes were gone.

"Jennifer!" Jason called out. He began to run toward the edge of the clearing where Jennifer had disappeared. He was almost into the brush when he saw the animals.

The first hyena must have been part of a pack. Four more of them slipped through the undergrowth to face Jason. Their eyes were wide with the effects of the brain stimulation. Their mouths were twisted in snarls, their teeth flashing as they advanced toward him. Each of them bore an inset cap of shining metal.

At some instinctive level he thought *weapon*. He ran to grab up the fallen camera. Grasping it by its mounting bracket, he swung the camera down onto the rocks, shattering the camera into a mangled box of rattling electronics and broken glass. He brought it down again, until the camera broke entirely free from its tripod. He hefted the longest piece of the tripod, a rod of steel ending in a jagged point.

The first hyena was moving in. Jason feinted toward the hyena with his steel spear. The animal didn't even flinch, but came at him at a dead run. It leapt. Jason whipped the rod around, catching the animal on one flank, knocking it to the ground. It got back up.

Another hyena moved up beside the first. Then another. And another. The pack moved toward him as a unit, crouching, wet teeth bared in their slavering mouths. Jason bellowed at them, shaking his makeshift spear. They seemed to hesitate a brief second. Then they rushed at him all at once.

He sprinted away from them, heading for the bank of the jungle stream, thirty feet away. The hyenas were snapping just behind him. The leading one leapt at his back, teeth flashing. It bit at one arm, barely missing the muscle, ripping a small bloody patch of skin off his elbow.

Jason reached the stream bank and jumped out. The hyenas followed him in. He landed in shoulder-deep water halfway across. With fast strokes he made for the far bank while they came swimming after him. Splashes from their paws landed on his back as he hauled himself out, gripping a root with one hand, still holding the steel rod in the other.

One of the hyenas let out a terrible scream. Jason looked around and saw the animal lifted half out of the water. Its body was shaken like a rag doll, clamped in the jaws of a ten-foot crocodile. The reptile bit down, and blood spurted from the hyena's mouth as its ribs gave way with a crack. The other hyenas began to climb the bank. Jason turned and ran into the jungle depths, fighting his way through the foliage. "Jennifer!" he called. "Jennifer!"

—■—

Jennifer clung to the branch of the tree, her arms quaking with tremors of exhaustion as she hung suspended over the ground. The hyena frantically circled beneath her. It jumped to gnash its ugly yellow teeth in the air beneath her, scrabbled at the trunk of the tree, then circled again, snarling and giving out its weird high barks.

Suddenly she heard it. A chorus of howls coming from the direction of the dome wall. The hyena beneath her pricked up its ears, then ran off toward the sound of its baying pack. Jennifer shuddered with relief as she released the branch and slumped to the jungle floor against a log. She squeezed her eyes shut and pressed her hands over her ears, trying to block out the terrible cacophony of the jungle, trying to think. It didn't help. The roars and screeches that filled the air were like a physical force, attacking her with their brutal power. She felt something touch her arm. She opened her eyes and discovered a huge green snake slithering over the log beside her. She leapt to her feet and ran on blindly, using her hands to slap away the vines that blocked her path, keeping her knees high to clear the matted greenery. She ran as fast as she could, trying to put the sounds of the hyena pack behind her.

—■—

"Jennifer!" Jason called. There was no answer but the wails of a hundred wild animals. The jungle was a riot of sound. As the hyenas fell momentarily behind him, their howls began to blend into the general commotion. All around him through the green gloom of the rain forest came the cries of raging beasts. The sounds of their fury excited the birds and smaller monkeys, whose caws and screeches added to the pandemonium. Dodging and weaving through the bush, Jason tried to find a clear path. His face and legs were ripped by thorns, but he ran on. "Jennifer!" he called again.

He broke into a small open space where the light almost penetrated through to the forest floor. Running across it, something caught his attention. He slowed, then stopped and bent to examine the ground at the base of a tree. The undergrowth seemed ripped and matted, covered with scattered shards of bark. A hiss sounded behind him and he whipped around. He saw a thick green snake, just disappearing over a log. Then he saw it: a fragment of black cloth, hanging from a stubby branch protruding from the log. He rushed to grab up the shred of cloth. Then he looked carefully at the ground. It was nearly impossible to be sure, but he thought the grass was flattened in a rough path across the open space. He set his jaw and ran into the jungle in that direction. "Jennifer!" he shouted as loud as he could.

——■——

Off to her right, the light seemed to be brighter. Jennifer turned in that direction. The dense scrub gave way to sparser ferns, then grasses. She broke into a clearing. The yellow grass rattled under her feet as she crossed the meadow, startling birds from their nests. She ran much faster in the open, but the clamor of the hyenas was rising again. She was almost across the clearing when she heard the other sound, a drumming crescendo. She looked to her left and screamed.

The black mass of a heavy antelope hurtled toward her, two curved horns pointed forward, aiming for her middle. She had no time. She flung herself to the ground and the big wildebeest galloped over her. One hoof tore into her lower leg.

Jennifer cried out at the sudden pain. She rolled over and painfully jumped back to her feet. The horned beast had already turned. It lowered its head, scraped the ground twice, then began another charge.

Jennifer raced for the edge of the clearing. A fiery pain shot through her leg every time it hit the ground. Behind her, the pounding of hoofbeats grew inexorably. She whirled her head around, glancing back for a moment at the pursuing beast, then ran even faster. She lifted her legs in a furious rhythm, her heart pounding like a triphammer as she sprinted. She flew across the clearing, leaping over rocks and fallen branches. Her legs were shooting, aching. Her teeth were clenched, her hands balled in white fists which moved in rapid arcs. The drumming hoofbeats rose to a crescendo behind her. Run, she told herself. Please God run. The safety of the trees was only yards away. Faster.

"Oh!" She hadn't seen the fallen branch, and tripped face forward onto the ground. "No!" she screamed, facing the galloping wildebeest as it rushed in, its head lowered, its horns gleaming. "No!"

There was a flash as something flew through the air. The wildebeest stumbled as if thrown off balance, then spun around. It was then that she saw the rod of stainless steel sticking out of its shoulder.

"Jennifer!" Jason cried out as he ran into the far side of the clearing, following the path his makeshift spear had taken. "Jennifer, get to the trees! Climb one if you can!"

"Jason," she cried with relief. She leapt to her feet as the wildebeest circled and ran to the jungle's edge. This time, she found a tree with a low fork and climbed up it quickly.

Bellowing furiously, the wildebeest whirled in a circle, trying to shake off the pain. The spear was dislodged by its frantic movements and flew to the edge of the clearing near Jennifer's tree. The big animal turned back to face Jason.

Howling, the hyenas rushed into the clearing. Before the antelope could even change direction, they were upon it, leaping at its back, biting into its flanks, rushing their slavering mouths toward its neck. Two of them continued toward Jason.

He dashed for the trees. The hyenas were snapping at his legs when he left the ground. He caught a branch and swung away from them. The wild dogs gave out their weird high yelps, circling the tree, jumping up at him. But he was out of reach. The two hyenas quickly turned back to take part in savaging the wildebeest.

The pack surrounded the horse-sized antelope, attacking it in twos and threes. It swung its horns in fierce arcs, kicking out, trying to defend itself. But they came from too many directions. Blood from a dozen wounds marked its body in ragged red patches. The antelope's struggles were slowing. Then one hyena got to the neck, ripping the jugular vein, and all hope was gone. The antelope fell to the ground, snorting and bellowing horribly, kicking at its attackers as they began to tear it apart. The caps on their heads gleamed in the twilight.

"Jennifer," Jason called from his tree at the opposite side of the clearing. "Stay where you are! I'm going to try to get that spear back."

"Jason, be careful!"

He clambered out along a branch, moving higher in the tree. A stiff vine was slung from his tree to the next one, halfway across the clearing. He tested the vine with a hard tug, then jumped out. The colobus monkeys screeched at him, shaking the leaves in outrage as he flew through their high territory. He reached the next tree and caught himself in the fork. With an eye to the bloody scene in the clearing, Jason dropped to the forest floor. He ran to the perimeter of the clearing and pulled his weapon out of the ground. So far, none of the hyenas had discovered him. He quickly backed away from the meadow toward Jennifer's tree. "Come on," he said quietly, lifting his hand to help her down. She slid from the fork of the tree to land beside him. He took her hand and they left the field of carnage, running together into the wild depths of the jungle.

⚫19⚫

Jason and Jennifer fell against each other as they stopped to catch their breath. They held each other, panting from the run, gazing at the towering foliage around them. Direction was meaningless. In the depths of the jungle, there were no landmarks. There was only the formless maze of the rain forest, the green, and the heat, and the echoing cries of the beasts. Their eyes met. They were both thinking the same thing: There was no safety in either the dense or the open areas. There was no safety anywhere. They had to get out.

"The first thing is to find out where we are," Jason said.

Jennifer wiped hot sweat from her eyes and looked around in the gloom. To their left, the floor of the jungle seemed to rise. "Jason, maybe we could see the way if we could get up high enough to see over the trees."

Jason nodded. "Let's try it." He reached for his spear with one hand and took her hand with the other. Quickly, they began moving again, following the upward slope.

They ran on, fighting their way through the bush. Jason held his steel spear at the ready. The hot air seemed to weigh on them, to hold them back, to sear their lungs. They fought the urge to rest, and simply ran. The slope was getting steeper.

A sound that they could not identify was coming from ahead, a loud steady whisper. They climbed to the top of a ridge and halted.

Before them was a grassy plateau. The open area was divided by a thin stream, which began in a pool at the summit of the hill. The stream rushed across the plateau, then seemed to disappear into space. Beyond, and much lower down, was a broad expanse of shimmering water. Treetops were visible below and hundreds of yards away.

Jennifer realized where they were. "Jason, this must be the top of the waterfall. You know, where it drops over the cliff into the lake!"

"I'll bet you're right," he agreed, scanning the plateau. It looked deserted. He stepped out from the cover of the trees and called for her to follow. Together, tentatively at first, they began to cross the open meadow. They headed for the high point at the edge of the cliff. Lifting their knees to clear the yellow stalks of savannah grass, they began to trot. As they ran, the expanse of the lake below came into view, glistening in the distance.

Jason's right foot struck something, throwing him off balance. He caught himself and quickly turned. His eyes darted about. Then he saw it. He halted in terror. "Jennifer,"—he drew her to him—"don't look."

The young woman drew in a breath as her eyes found what Jason had seen. "Oh my God!"

The body lay naked and bloody in the grass. A girl or young woman, it was hard to tell. She was flayed open across the back and legs, where the flesh had been ripped away, leaving raw red gashes and exposed bone. Her scalp with its black hair was attached to her skull only by a thin flap of skin. One arm ended in a bloody stump at the elbow. She had been killed—and partially eaten.

Jason felt his head pounding with the rhythm of his heart. Laying aside the spear, he knelt beside the girl's body and reached for her head. Gently, he turned the face up from the ground. It wasn't a face. The cheeks had been gnawed away from the facial bones. One eye hung from the oozing black socket by a thread of nerves. Protruding from the top of her skull was an inset cap of shining metal.

Jennifer screamed. Jason let go and went to her. "I knew it! I knew it!" she cried, her eyes fixed on the body of the girl.

Jason held her close. "Jennifer, what do you mean?"

"Just before Dr. Kalia and his men caught me, I saw something up here!"

"You saw her?" he asked.

"I saw . . . a person. It was so far away, so much of a shock. It must have been her! My God, my God! That's what my research is really about! Jason, they're testing their theories on human beings!"

A high-pitched wail cut through the other sounds of the jungle. Jason and Jennifer looked up. At the top of the plateau, a leopard was circling the pool. It was coming toward them rapidly. Returning to its kill.

"Get back!" he shouted. "I'll try to stop it. You run for the trees!" Jason bent to grab his spear, then rose to face the jungle cat.

"Like hell I will!" Jennifer replied. "If you're not running, then neither am I!"

His eyes never left the leopard. He spoke urgently, "Jennifer, we can't both outrun that cat. Please, my love, get out of here. Now!"

The leopard screamed again. It was running at them, its claws digging into the ground as it bounded over the grass, three hundred pounds of killing power. Jennifer clenched her teeth. She reached down and hefted a rock, standing her ground beside Jason.

Jason let out a terrible yell, then rushed straight toward the cat, holding his spear out before him with both hands. The leopard was ten feet away when it leapt, jaws open, claws spread. As the cat flew toward him, he crouched down, wedging the back of his spear into the ground and holding the point upward.

The animal landed before him, screaming, raking his arms with bleeding stripes. But the teeth were held away from him by the spear, buried in the cat's ribs. Furiously the leopard fought to get off the steel rod. Jason ignored the claws that tore at him and heaved the spear forward, twisting it, searching for the heart. One claw swiped at his forehead. Blood poured down into his eyes. Then the cat reached his leg and ripped into the muscle, knocking Jason onto his back. The beast clambered on top of him, four sets of claws reaching, its mouth inches from his face, its flashing yellow teeth and hot breath filling his eyes. Jason heaved up on the spear with all his strength. Red foam appeared at the cat's teeth, but still it ripped at him with its razor-sharp claws. It shot its bloody jaws down to reach for his neck.

There was a sudden thud. The cat's head twisted to the side. Through the red veil of blood, Jason saw Jennifer swinging the big stone again. This time, the leopard dodged her swing. The cat leapt off Jason, dragging the spear, and went for Jennifer. She threw the rock with all her strength at the charging animal, then turned to run. The leopard was on top of her in an instant. She screamed and fought the beast.

Jason leapt up and flung himself onto the cat's back. He circled it with his arms, gripping its powerful forelegs with his hands. He fell backwards, jerking the animal away from Jennifer. Frantically the beast tried to shake free of him. Jason caught the cat's head in his hands, trying to hold the deadly jaws shut. He braced himself and used all of his strength to pull the cat's head back. There was a sudden crack. The leopard convulsed, thrashing wildly. Then it fell across him, dying. Its hot blood poured over Jason as he lay beneath it.

Jason pushed off the leopard's warm body. He stood staggering, bleeding, and walked toward Jennifer. "Jennifer, are you all right?" he began to say. Then he sat down heavily and flattened onto his back.

Jennifer was beside him in a moment. "Oh, Jason," she said, taking in the blood seeping from his multiple wounds. She ripped one sleeve off her jumpsuit and used it to mop the blood from his face. She ripped off the other sleeve and pressed it against the wound on his calf, then bound it around his injured leg. She took his head in her lap. "Jason, my Jason."

He lay on his back, his heart pounding, too exhausted to

speak. On that high plateau, the deadly roars of the jungle sounded almost dreamlike. There was a terrible music to it, a thousand colliding rages that sounded like the keening in some hellish kennel. Jason stared upward. Above him was the top of the dome, soaring in perfect concavity. His eyes followed the wall, as if mesmerized by its perfection, its startling likeness to sky. They traced its curve down and down, until the wall disappeared behind the thick green barrier of the trees. The wall. The access ports. If a tree grew near enough . . .

"Jennifer," he said in a rough voice. He wiped his mouth with his hand, cleaning away the drying blood. "Jennifer, I think I have an idea." Jason climbed painfully to his feet and looked around him. From where he stood, the wall of the dome was mostly obscured by the trees. However, in several directions, sections of wall were visible at the level of the access ports, forty feet above the ground. One such section lay at the far end of the lake, where he remembered the observation post sat beyond the dome wall, but the trees there were sparse.

"What are you thinking?" Jennifer asked. She stood up beside him and encircled him with her arm.

"The only way in or out of here is through one of the access ports," he replied. "Let's say I could find a tree close enough to the wall; maybe I could climb it and reach one of the ports."

Jennifer looked around. "There!" She pointed at an exposed section of the dome wall on the far side of the plateau. "That might do it." Where she pointed, it looked as if the jungle grew flush up to the wall. It was at least half a mile distant, across the stream that divided the plateau. A single faint shriek came from that side of the jungle, but nothing moved under the dark tangle of the trees.

Jason shook himself, trying to forget his pain. Although flesh had been ripped open on every limb, Jennifer's bandage was working well to slow the bleeding of his wounded leg. He bent over the dead leopard, planting one foot against its chest, and jerked his spear free. Then he and Jennifer started across the wide plateau. They leapt the stream in turn, then joined hands and made their way toward the wall of foliage.

The shriek came again. Then again, louder. A chimpanzee broke out from the trees at the far edge of the plateau. It ran, knuckles rapidly alternating with feet, glancing behind as it went. Two more apes appeared. At first, they seemed to be chasing the other chimpanzee. But they too were shooting their eyes back over their shoulders as they ran.

The three apes crossed in front of Jason and Jennifer, running frantically. They splashed across the stream barely twenty feet away, but didn't seem to see the man and woman. One of the apes slipped as it crossed the rushing water. It lost its balance and was rapidly swept toward the waterfall. With a final howl, it disappeared over the edge of the cliff.

"What the hell . . ." Jason said.

Jennifer's eyes were wide as she watched the apes. "Jason, chimps only run like that from predators!" She tugged at Jason, pulling him back toward the trees.

Another ape ran into the meadow from the trees. It too came shrieking toward the stream. It never made it. Two lions, a male and a female, sped out of the bush side by side. They caught the chimpanzee immediately. Together the lions mauled the ape, rending its black belly apart even as it screamed, pulling the shining intestines out of the dying body within seconds. Not content with their first kill, the lions left the twitching remains and started after the other apes, which were now more than halfway across the plateau. The lions looked around for their next victim. They saw the running man and woman.

Jason and Jennifer frantically looked over their shoulders. The lions were coming after them, gaining fast. It was too far to the trees. Jason grabbed Jennifer's hand, changing direction, running with her straight toward the edge of the cliff. The waterfall shot out over the lip, cascading at least seventy feet down the rocks to the lake below. They leaned over, quickly scanning the cliff face. The drop was sheer, overhanging, with no possible handholds.

They looked back. The lions were dashing across the clearing, two tan blurs of motion, their bloody jaws open, their eyes fixed on the two young scientists. Bright caps of metal stuck up from the centers of their skulls. They were almost upon them.

"Come on!" Jason shouted. He grasped Jennifer's hand, "It's the only way. Hold on tight!" Together they took three running steps away from the waterfall, then sprinted to the edge of the cliff.

Their bodies hurtled out into space. The rippling surface of the lake filled their vision. Helplessly, they watched the rocks and the green lake loom up at them as they plummeted through the open air. Wind rushed past their ears in a whine. The frothing water at the bottom of the falls seemed like a huge boiling cauldron, waiting for them below. And then they struck.

They plunged down through the green water. Jennifer was blinded by the rush of silt past her eyes. Her feet collided with the muddy bottom, and she began fighting her way back up. Desperately, she swam toward the dull glow of the surface. A green wall of water seemed to block her way. Her lungs were bursting. Slowly, terribly slowly, the glow above became brighter. She kept her eyes focused upward, but her kicks were weakening.

At last their heads broke free of the water. They both took in immense breaths. A shadow crossed their eyes and they looked up. Two golden figures were falling rapidly toward them. They backstroked furiously. The lions had followed them over the cliff, their brains robbed of natural fear by the chemical stimulation. The lions twisted in space, roaring, then crashed down among the rocks at the base of the waterfall. Their bodies lay broken and still, showered by the spray from above.

Jason and Jennifer treaded water, staring at the shattered beasts, mesmerized by that unblinking vision of sudden death. They held onto each other, floating together in the warm green water.

"Ready?" he asked, tilting his head toward the far bank of the lake. Jennifer nodded. Side by side they began to stroke across the open water. Remembering the crocodiles, Jason lifted his head to search for any movement, but the water was still. In several minutes, they finally felt their knees brush the soft mud of the shallows and stood. Dragging one leg after another, pulling their feet out of the sucking mud, they waded the last few yards in, then climbed up the steep sandy bank. They collapsed together on the sand.

The wall stood before them. Black. Sheer. Implacable. Jason knelt before it, dripping, and looked up. The dome wall was a polished plane, featureless except at two points: More than nine feet up the wall was one of the tripod-mounted video cameras. Forty feet up the wall was the access port.

The access port. Jason stared up at it, his head tilted back. He shook his head like a dog, scattering droplets of water and blood, and slowly stood. He glanced around them. There were several trees rooted in the narrow stand, but all were thin-trunked, their limbs too sparse for the tree-dwelling monkeys, too weak for the larger apes, suitable only for the birds whose nests dotted the upper branches. None of the trees seemed to be close to the section of the wall that held the access port.

Jason walked to the wall, laying his hands flat against it. His head craned backward as he stared straight up at the hinges forty feet above him. He looked both right and left. The nearest trees had branches that reached to perhaps five feet below the port. But with his weight on them, those branches would simply dip, bending ten feet too low.

"What about this one?" Jennifer said. She was standing beside a tree almost twenty feet from the wall. Its willowy branches tapered to nothing more than seventy feet overhead. "I know it's farther back, but if your weight bends it down . . ."

Jason didn't let himself think. He trotted to the base of that tree and began to climb up, using whatever knots he could find to give advantage to his raw hands. He climbed, moving by sheer impulse, scrambling with the instincts of an animal. He reached the first fork and movement was easier, calling on balance that he learned as a boy, but based on something more ancient. He clambered like an ape up to the topmost branch, then out along it as far as it would hold him. He clutched it to his chest and started to shift his weight.

Rhythmically he pushed into the branch, then out again,

pumping it like a swing, his eyes on the wall, the access port now twenty feet away. Moving through the air, he closed his eyes and pumped, squeezing the branch between his blood-stained fingers, clenching his teeth in a grimace of need that would not dare become hope, swinging with the branch, thin as a baby's arm, out toward the wall, back to the center, out again. Eight feet away. Back to the center. Six feet away. Back to the center. Two feet away and he stretched out his arm toward the latch on the door as the tree whipped him out through the air toward the wall . . .

There was a crack. "Jason!" Jennifer screamed. As he fell, the cry that escaped him had nothing to do with fear. His thrashing embrace of the lower branches was a twitch, a reflex of the animal saving itself, but for nothing. His face twisted with pain, fighting the tears. For nothing. He clutched the tangled web of branches that had saved him, oblivious to the rips in his hands and face, to his wounds, to his precarious perch, aware only of the cracking sound of the instant before, that single final sound and what it meant. The branch was broken. There was no other. He was filled with a terrible rage that was, at last, rage at himself. Deliberately, he clamped his fists shut on the sharpness of the branch, driving the points of wood into the raw flesh of his fingers, into the bare nerves, wanting only the pain, needing the brutal bleeding pain.

It was the scream below that made him open his eyes. The leaves blocked his view, but he saw Jennifer stumbling backwards, her eyes on something he couldn't see, her face white with terror. Jason dragged himself along the branch, frantically pulling the leaves aside to clear his view.

It was Tony, the weight lifter. His teeth were bared, his huge muscles rippled, his naked skin was marked by multiple red abrasions. He held a thick branch raised in one hand like a club. Then Jason saw the man's head. The scalp had been cut away over the top. In its place, a gleaming cap of metal stuck up from the center of his skull. Tony suddenly rushed forward, grabbing Jennifer by the arm. He began dragging her toward the bush.

"Tony, stop!" Jennifer cried, twisting vainly in his iron grasp. She slapped and punched at him furiously.

Jason swung himself down from the tree limb, flying through the air. He caught the branch below with one hand, swinging his body out from the tree and falling free. He landed in the clearing just behind the big weight lifter.

Tony whirled. Eyeing Jason, he threw Jennifer aside. She landed heavily against a tree and slid to the ground. Tony came to his full height. He inflated his chest and pounded it with his fist, bellowing in fury. He raised his club above his head with both hands and rushed forward, swinging the branch down as he came.

Jason rolled to one side, lashing out with his foot. The club crashed down where his head had just been, and Tony went sprawling to the ground. In an instant, both men were on their feet. Neither one hesitated a second. They rushed directly at each other. Tony swung his huge branch at Jason's head, but the doctor blocked it, knocking it away, and threw a punch that caught Tony in the center of his abdomen. It had little effect on the man, who reached for Jason's throat with both big hands. Jason dodged below the grip, whirling around, slamming a heel into Tony's ribs. Tony stumbled a moment but quickly regained his balance and came after Jason again. Jason brought his fists up together, knocking the arms apart and battering his opponent's head between the hard edges of both hands. Again it seemed to have no effect. Tony caught one of his wrists and furiously twisted the arm up behind Jason's spine, driving his head down toward the dirt. He snarled as he jammed the young scientist's neck into the ground.

The sound of mocking laughter echoed through the dome. As Jason struggled to free himself, Dr. Kalia and his party appeared through the dome wall as if they floated in black space. They were gathered at the observation post, watching the battle. "Now you will see!" Kalia shouted. "Now you will learn the power of my creation!"

Agony swept through Jason as his neck bent further. He jerked from side to side, trying to break free. He flipped his lower body over, still in Tony's tight grip, unable to escape. Then Jennifer leapt onto Tony, grabbed the sides of his head and twisted.

Tony let go of Jason with a gasp. He ducked out of Jennifer's hold, caught her by the wrists, and slammed her to the ground. Then he jumped at Jason again. His head collided with the edge of Jason's rocketing foot, and he went down, blood pouring from his twisted nose. He leapt up again without a pause, but Jason was already upon him, following his kick with a flurry of punches, shooting the tips of his fingers with incredible speed into the vulnerable spots of torso, head, pelvis. Tony roared and swung his hands like a sledgehammer. Jason dodged under the double-fisted attack and spun his heel across the wrestler's ankles, his mastery of the art at one with his instinct, instinct at the call of his bloody final need—survival.

But Tony was not human. Fingers of chemical stimulation ripped through the centers of his brain, accelerating reflexes, blinding him to pain, recruiting every muscle to the single task: *kill.* Tony rolled away and rose again, reaching out for a weapon as he did, lifting a log and holding it like a battering ram, running straight at the lanky scientist.

Jennifer threw herself across Tony's legs. The weight lifter went sprawling. He quickly rose and backhanded Jennifer across the face, drawing blood. Jason rushed in and slammed his knee directly into the huge man's solar plexus. As Tony fell backward, he shot out his gripping hands and closed one over the bleeding open wound on Jason's calf.

It was too much. The pain that lanced through Jason was like lightning stabbing into his spine. He lost his balance, then fell, his temple slamming into the edge of the fallen steel tripod.

Black and gray and brightness swam before his eyes. He only felt and couldn't see the huge form land on top of him, the hands encircle his neck with the brute force of a noose, the arms shaking his head as if he were a rag doll. He barely saw Jennifer as she leapt on Tony's back. Tony slammed an elbow into her head, knocking her aside, and continued throttling Jason. "At last, my young friends," Kalia's voice boomed into the dome, "at last you discover how weak and pitiful the wild type is!" Jason could only grope blindly at the monstrous thing that was attacking him, desperately fighting off the equally desperate urge to let unconsciousness carry him out of the pain, out of life, trying to remember escapes and blows, his mother and father and Jennifer, as his occiput struck the ground again and the medical school dissection class came back to him—"These are the carotid arteries . . ." in the gray flesh of the flayed open old man–cadaver's neck as his head struck the ground again—". . . must avoid putting pressure on both of them at the same time because you could literally stop the flow of blood to the entire anterior brain." He could see the balding anatomist's smile that turned into Dr. Kalia's evil grin as his head hit again, and he palpated the throbbing tubes above him and with every last drop of strength he *squeezed.*

Jason pushed off Tony's unconscious form. He got to his hands and knees, taking in huge lungfuls of air, fighting to catch his breath. He saw the big weight lifter's chest rising and falling, and he knew he was alive. "Jennifer," he called as he crawled over to her where she lay in the dirt. Gently he lifted her head. She moaned and opened her eyes. For a moment, a look of panic came over her.

"No, no," he said, stroking her head. "It's all right."

"Oh, Jason . . ." She reached for him.

Kalia's voice came through the loudspeaker. "You fools!" he shouted. "Do you think you will survive forever? You are just defenseless beasts in a world that will not suffer your presence much longer. The wild type is doomed to die!"

Jason looked around. Night was rapidly coming on in the jungle. He slipped an arm under Jennifer and carried her toward the mossy bed at the base of a slender tree. He set her down on the soft moss. "We're not going to make it out of here, are we?" she asked. Jason held her to him, rocking her in his arms, as Kalia raved on, his ravings mixing with the raucous sounds of a jungle gone mad, the sounds of their living and inescapable hell. "Die!" Kalia screamed. "It's time for the wild type to die!" Kalia reached for a switch. The wall went black.

━ ■ 20 ■ ━

In the observation post, Kalia turned to the assembled group. His face was flushed. "Ah, my dear friends, could you ask for a more perfect experiment? The wild types display their primitive nature, slaves to the brutal instincts that hold back human progress!"

Senator Bowie stood at the dome wall, leaning forward to see through the plexiglass. Sweat glistened on his fat face. He was breathing heavily. His eyes were on Jennifer.

General Simos and Colonel Williams were also staring with rapt excitement. They stood side by side, arms folded, watching through the dome wall like spectators at a sport. The two guards sat in the chairs before the computer, nursing the injuries they'd suffered. Money changed hands between them, a wager on the outcome of Jason's life-and-death battle with the brain-stimulated weight lifter.

"Layla, my dear,"—Kalia turned to his daughter—"this will not take much longer. Perhaps you could go to the Center and collect the notes from Dr. McCane's desk?"

Layla got up, briefly kissed her father on the cheek, and left the observation post.

Kalia turned back to face the jungle. "Such magnificent specimens of the doomed breed," he said. "It will be almost a pity to see them die."

—■—

Jason rose gingerly and walked to the bank of the lake. Cupping his hands, he filled them with water. He climbed back up the bank, trying to hold the water in the hollow of his hands. He brought it to Jennifer where she lay. She drank greedily. He brought her more, then returned to the bank and splashed water onto his face before dipping his head to drink. He rejoined Jennifer at the base of the big tree. She was shivering despite the musty jungle heat. He drew her close into the crook of his arm.

"Jason,"—Jennifer's eyes lifted toward the far end of the lake—"look!"

He followed her gaze. Across the lake, on the open sandy shore, the black forms of apes were rushing about. They were fighting. At least ten of them were waging a pitched battle. They seemed to be attacking each other indiscriminately. Two or three would gang together, forming momentary alliances to overcome one of the larger apes, then just as quickly turn on their allies. Biting and gouging, the apes tore at each other, leaving red traces of their attacks, madly using their incredible strength and their stained yellow teeth to rip away the flesh of other members of their own troupe, and in turn were ripped apart. The battle was moving, even as they watched. The troupe of apes was coming their way.

Jason and Jennifer struggled to their feet. "It's insane!" Jennifer cried. "Apes don't kill each other for . . . for nothing!"

"These apes do," Jason said grimly.

The battle was rapidly running toward them around the lake. Screams of rage and agony filled the dome as the fighting apes chased one another through the jungle toward the clearing.

Jennifer whipped her head around to face Jason. "They're not using the trees!" she shouted. "Come on, we have to climb!" She turned to the slender tree nearby. Jason boosted her up into the crotch of the tree, then rapidly followed. As he left the ground, two big apes ran into the clearing, screeching, ripping at one another with their teeth. Jason and Jennifer moved higher into the branches.

In moments the clearing was filled with fighting chimpanzees. Their black bodies flew about, biting and scratching at each other in a bloody battle, caps of metal glinting on their heads. Jason and Jennifer watched, awestruck, as the beasts fought on top of Tony's unconscious form as if it wasn't there. The chimps tore into one another, using their powerful jaws to deadly effect. One ape chased another into a neighboring tree. The first ape followed. They were swinging from branch to branch when they saw the two humans. They let out a howl.

The troupe of chimpanzees looked up. Three large males broke off their fight to face the tree. They screeched, pounding the ground, ripping up patches of grass, their eyes on Jason and Jennifer. Moving as one, they headed for the base of the tree.

"Higher!" Jason shouted as he followed Jennifer up toward the next branch.

Drained, aching, the two of them climbed. The angry guttural exclamations of the apes followed them as Jason and Jennifer dragged themselves up through the tangled web of branches. The first big chimp reached the tree. He eyed the climbers above, baring his yellow canines, and reached for a branch. The second ape was close behind. "Jason, we'll never be able to outclimb them!" Jennifer cried. "What's that?"

A trumpeting sound cut through the dome. Jason and Jennifer looked down. A loud thudding noise was coming from the depths of the forest. The thudding rose to a boom as the huge black mass of a rhinoceros ran into the clearing. The rhino whirled around, searching for a target, ripping into the ground with its hooves. Shrieking, the troupe of chimpanzees scattered into the undergrowth.

The rhinoceros saw one ape perched in a tree and dipped its big horn as it galloped head-on into the tree trunk. The bang was like lightning striking. It tore a thick slab of bark from the tree, almost shaking the chimp loose.

Jason and Jennifer watched, amazed. The rhinoceros was

an Indian one-horn, a solid ton of armored muscles. A film of brown dust coated the steel cap protruding straight up from the center of its skull behind the thick horn. It shook its horn, recoiling from the collision with the tree, and stamped in rage. It threw back its head, trumpeting, then lowered its horn again. It ran like an unstoppable force aiming for an immovable object, blind to its pain, maniacal, galloping, and slammed into the tree. The tree bent at the assault. The chimpanzee caught itself by wrapping its arms around the branch.

Jason's eyes were fixed on the rhinoceros. His jaw was set, his breath came quicker, his heart was pounding in his chest, seeming almost to skip beats, racing against his fear. "Jennifer, that's it!" he shouted.

"Jason, what do you mean? Jason!"

He waited no longer. He jumped to the ground with a yell.

The big horn whipped around. Two black shiny eyes peered at him in utter fury. The rhinoceros lifted both forelegs off the ground, stamping down where the man had landed, but Jason had already moved. The animal shot after him, propelled by rage, barely a yard between the tip of its horn and the sweaty muscles of Jason's sprinting back, chasing him straight toward the wall.

Jason leapt. His hands closed around the camera mounted on the wall. They stung with the vibration as the rhinoceros crashed into the wall below the remote-control camera. Jason hung from the still-vibrating mounting tripod, his muscles bunched. Had he heard it?

The rhino was jarred, thrown off balance as it recoiled from the wall. It caught itself and shook its thick head, snorting as it trotted back from the wall. In the trees at the edge of the clearing, the troupe of chimpanzees howled with bloodthirsty excitement.

Jason flung himself to the ground and instantly turned to face the wall. Black, opaque, solid. He heard the snort, almost palpable on the back of his neck, as he played his hands frantically over the surface of the wall. Yes. A slight indentation. "Jason!" he heard Jennifer shout in warning. The hooves were drumming now, crashing toward him. He turned to face the enraged beast, staring into the eyes of the oncoming rhino, only feet away, robbed of its instinct of self-preservation, an express train of gray-black flesh concentrating its energy in the point of that horn, aiming for the young man's chest. Jason forced himself to wait, timing the ultimate moment, sweat pouring into his eyes.

"Kiyah!" He jumped and felt the rush of air below him. He caught the steel tripod and jackknifed his legs upward. Shock waves of vibration shot through his forearms. He almost screamed in relief. He heard it! A crack. Hanging from the camera support, he could feel the wall shake, the rhinoceros twisting its horn in the gap, struggling to escape. Jason heard the high-pitched screeches of the armored plexiglass, wrenched by the power of the beast. Another crack. One arm of the tripod broke loose from the wall. Jason caught himself and pulled up on the shivering camera. The rhino broke free, stamping in fury. The black hairy back passed underneath Jason, and he dropped to the ground, whirling to inspect the wall.

Six inches wide. The men on the other side of the wall were staring through the gap in speechless shock. "Have no fear," Jason heard Dr. Kalia shout to his group. "You are perfectly safe!" Jason wrapped both hands around the edges of the damaged wall and pulled. There was no movement. He jumped up, forcing both feet into the crack, his hands just across from them, suspending himself on the wall, and pried with all his strength. The cooler air of the observation post played across his body, taunting him, inaccessible. The men on the other side seemed to be paralyzed with amazement. Still too narrow and no time left. The pounding of the rhino's charge began. He dropped to face that onrushing horn.

A black blur shot across the clearing. One big chimpanzee rushed in and bit the rhino's leg. The huge beast whirled at the attack, sending brown dust flying with its hooves. It eyes found the ape even as it changed direction, and it charged directly at the sprinting animal, racing into the stand of trees. The ape swung its way up another tree just as the rhino slammed into the trunk, showering bark and moss. The chimp howled down at its pursuer while the thick-skinned rhino stamped and snorted with fury beneath the tree.

Jason wasted no time. He dashed away from the wall and hefted a thick fallen branch, then ran back. He ignored the shouts of the men on the other side and the shrieking of the chimpanzees. Using the branch as a lever, he anchored one end into the gap in the wall, then threw his body against the free end. A screech of straining plexiglass wailed through the dome. Nothing. The gap was still just six inches wide. Colonel Williams drew his pistol.

Jason heard Jennifer scream, "Get off of here, goddamn it!" He whirled to face the jungle. The big chimpanzee had leapt across to Jennifer's tree, landing just beneath her. Jennifer was punching away the ape's reaching hands. The rhinoceros followed the ape. Its first assault on the tree trunk shook the chimpanzee down to a lower branch. Jennifer held on fiercely. The rhino charged the tree again and again, systematically ripping it out of the earth as Jennifer and the ape clung to the quaking limbs.

Jason lifted his branch as he ran straight toward the rhinoceros. He entered the trees, not even slowing when the animal began to turn at the sound of his running approach. He swung down the club at the last moment, slamming the wood into the thick gray skin of the rhino's back.

Even as he leapt away, the branch was ripped out of his grasp by the whirling horn. His balance was gone. Jennifer cried out. With one hand Jason pushed off from the ground like a sprinter in a bad start. Then his legs pumped like never before, propelling him through the jungle, the hot breath of the rhino just behind him. Forty feet. He feinted left then dodged right, hearing the crash as the beast was thrown off course. Twenty feet. The beast was just behind him. The thunder of the hooves drove out all other sound. The hissing of the rhino's breath was hot on his legs. Five feet. He took one quick, long stride and catapulted off the ground.

A crack ripped through the dome. The sting of the steel tripod he clasped in his hands was replaced by another sensation. The tripod was falling away from the wall. Flailing to catch himself, he landed on the ground. The sound of screams filled his ears. He looked up and let out one of his own, a scream of triumph.

The rhinoceros had broken through the wall. In the narrow space of the observation post, Kalia and the others were wildly dodging its lethal charge. The animal whirled about, scattering chairs and stamping in fury.

Colonel Williams moved forward, thrusting his pistol before him. He emptied the small-caliber weapon into the rhino's tough hide. The bullets did nothing to slow the beast. The rhinoceros rushed in, pinning him to the computer and crushing his chest in an instant. It whipped around, seeking the next target for its bloody horn. The two guards fired on the animal. One screeched in pain as the horn caught him, flinging him against the wall. The other dropped his weapon and tried to escape.

With wild howls, the troupe of chimpanzees left the trees and raced for the hole in the wall of the dome. Jason rolled out of their path, but the animals paid no attention to him. Kalia screamed as the apes came through the wall. He lunged for the computer. Frantically, he jabbed at the keyboard, trying to turn off the signals to the brains of the animals. He screamed again as two apes dragged him to the floor.

"Come on!" Jason ran to the tree as Jennifer quickly clambered down. He took her hand and sprinted with her toward the gap in the wall. They leapt together through the jagged gap, out of the dome.

The observation post was a madhouse. The chimpanzees were swarming over Kalia and his men. General Simos and Senator Bowie jumped to the side just as the rhino rushed toward them. The huge animal crashed into the computer console, setting off a shower of sparks. A thread of acrid smoke rose from the console, which then burst into flame. The rhino turned on Simos. The general grabbed the fat senator, holding him before himself as a shield. "No!" screamed Bowie. The rhinoceros plunged its horn into the senator's belly. He slumped to the floor, clutching at the bleeding hole in his abdomen, dying. General Simos turned and ran screaming, the big animal chasing him down the tunnel that led away from the exit.

Jason held Jennifer's hand, moving toward the exit door through the smoke and flames that were billowing from the wreckage of the computer. They dodged through the melee in the observation post, jumped over the grisly remains of Senator Bowie, and began to rush along the tunnel that led around the wall of the dome, speeding between the green luminescent spots that marked the way.

"Don't move!" Blood dripped down Kalia's face from a head wound. He was holding the gun dropped by the fleeing guard.

Step by step, he advanced on them. "So, you dare to interfere. You dare to toy with the most important work in the history of science. You dare to spoil my dream!" He backed them against the wall of the dome, his face outlined by the red glow of the growing inferno, clutching the pistol in both hands, his finger tightening on the trigger. "My work must go on! The wild type must die! The wild type must—"

His words were choked off to a strangled gasp. He fired wildly into the air, then dropped the pistol and reached up to try to pry loose the immense fingers that gripped his throat from behind. Tony had staggered out of the dome and approached from behind. The huge weight lifter's eyes bore a look of wild animal fury. "No!" choked Kalia. Tony lifted him off the floor and began to shake him by his neck. "No!" An explosion ripped apart the computer console. The gap in the dome wall had expanded in the flames, and the trees nearby were catching fire.

Jason pulled Jennifer behind him down the tunnel. They ran around the dome, making their way past the first two observation posts, out the door and down the hall of glowing green spots. The smoke was around them as they ran past the laboratories to the elevator. They leapt inside just as the hall behind them burst into flame. Fingers of flame reached for them as the doors of the elevator closed. The elevator car shot up through the mountain, shaken by a series of booms. The lights in the elevator blinked, then went out as the doors groaned open. They had stopped short; the floor level met the middle of the open elevator doors. The car shuddered, beginning to slip back down the shaft. Jason made a stirrup of his hands for Jennifer, and she jumped up out of the elevator. As Jason followed, she tugged on his belt, helping him through the doors. The elevator rattled violently, then plummeted back down the black hole.

Hand in hand, they raced past Kalia's office, across the lobby, and out into the darkness. Suddenly, the ground heaved under them and a thunderous crash split the night. They were thrown into the air. Jason clutched Jennifer to him as they fell, trying to cover her with his body. They shut their eyes against a storm of flying debris and held onto one another as they hit the roiling ground. They clawed away the dirt that was covering them and opened their eyes to see the center of the mountain sinking, wreathed in a black cloud of dust, roaring and rumbling as it sank into a crater in the earth.

―•21•―

Jason! Get me out of here!"

Red glared up from his bed as Jason and Jennifer stepped into the hospital room. His face was eloquent with disgust. "They took away my clothes, they stuck this thing in my arm—hi, Jennifer—The food is terrible, the entertainment is terrible, and these nurses simply have no idea of their extraordinary luck in getting a prince like me."

The sturdy matron in white who was adjusting his intravenous line cut in. "Prince? Why, my lord, I've seen prettier frogs." She moved to the door and smiled sweetly. "If you need anything—"

"Out!"

". . . just write to your congressman." The door swung shut behind her.

"You see what I mean! Rescue me from this antiseptic prison!"

"OK, OK." Jason came around the bed. He hooked his cane on the bedrail. "You tie the bedsheets together, I'll drive the getaway car, and Jennifer can create a diversion."

"I'll say she can." Red grinned up at her.

"Oh, Red," Jennifer said, laughing. "How are you doing,

really?" She stood beside Jason, linking her fingers into his hand.

"Good as new. Watch this." Red cocked his eyebrows twice in a show of bravado, then gritted his teeth as he grasped the side rails and gingerly lifted his leg off its nest of pillows. He set it back down with a proud smile. "See! Everything works. How about you guys? Jennifer?"

"I'm fine. Jason's the one . . ."

"I'm okay. A few stitches here and there." He glanced up to the white square of bandage covering half his forehead. "Surgeon says I'll be running around in no time."

"Great! Hey, you guys, have you seen this?" Red pulled over his nightstand and grabbed a newspaper. It was an early morning edition of the *Washington Post.* Jason and Jennifer read the headline: "Heart Attack Claims Senator Bowie." "And this here," Red said as he pointed. Their eyes skipped down the page to find a smaller article: "Explosion Rocks Virginia Countryside—Nobel Prize Winner Missing."

Jason began reading the text aloud: " 'Distinguished National Institutes of Health researcher Paul Kalia is missing and feared dead today after a freak accident at his laboratory in Virginia.' "

"Like it?" Red grinned. " 'Freak accident'?"

Jason smiled, shaking his head. "I'll never trust a newspaper again. I suppose the CIA deserves the credit for this?"

"Hey,"—Red put aside the paper—"we may not have class, but we try to do the job."

"Yes," Jason agreed, "you do." His face grew solemn. He reached his free hand for Red's. The two men looked into each other's eyes. "Red," Jason began, "I'm sorry I—"

"Now, come on, partner." Red squeezed his hand. "You had your reasons and I had mine. I wish I could have told you more. We just didn't talk too good, right?" His eyes twinkled, smiling up at his friend.

Jason returned the grip. "Right."

"Red?" Jennifer asked, "I mean, if it wouldn't be violating official secrets or anything, do you mind telling me just what the CIA has to do with all this?"

"To hell with official secrets!" He reached for his bedside

phone and lifted the receiver to speak to the outside guard, instructing him to seal the room. Then he put it down and turned back to Jennifer. He told her quickly about the CIA's investigation, up to the moment when they discovered that DARPA—the Defense Advanced Research Projects Agency—was pouring millions of dollars into the National Institutes. "Hell, General Simos controlled almost half of NIH!"

"General Simos?" she asked. "That squat little man at the dome?"

"The director of DARPA," he replied. Red explained how General Simos had gained covert control of NIH, funding labs throughout the Center. He had even installed his own agents there, posing as security guards. The CIA had moved troops in to arrest them. "And that's not all: General Simos was sending agents all over the country, stealing data for Dr. Kalia, killing scientists such as Harkus and Shay simply because they got in the way."

Jennifer looked up at Jason. He put his arm around her as Red went on.

"We raided DARPA headquarters and picked up most of the DARPA staff, but a few of them got away." Again he pulled over the rolling nightstand. This time, he pulled the plastic drawer out from underneath, extracted a photograph, and laid it before them. Jason and Jennifer bent to examine the picture, blurred, grainy, obviously taken through a tele-photo lens. It showed three people rushing through a door. Jason couldn't identify the two men, but the tall attractive woman was easy to recognize.

"This picture was taken at the airport," Red explained. "Our cameraman saw these three escaping on a Berlin flight, but he didn't have the backup to stop them. The two men in the photo are DARPA agents. The young lady"—he tapped the picture—"is Kalia's daughter." The CIA man set the picture aside. "Now, Jason, I've got a question for you: Could Dr. Kalia have done it? Could he really have bred a new human race?"

Jason didn't respond at once. He stood still, looking at the floor. Finally, slowly, he began to nod. "Yes, definitely. Kalia was right, you know: All of the technology is available right now. Once he found the genes, all he'd have to do is to transfer them into human eggs."

Jennifer was nodding. "And my own project fits right in: That research on ape behavior wasn't just theoretical—he was using Normal Volunteers for live experiments!"

The three of them looked at one another, silent for a moment, sharing the thought. Red shifted in bed, but the movement sent a jolt of pain through his leg that registered on his face.

"Red?" Jennifer asked. "Maybe we should come back later? Is there anything . . ."

"No, no, hold on, I'm fine. I just have to find the right position." He reached for the trapeze dangling from a bar above him. Jason and Jennifer both moved to adjust his pillow. "Christ, you two," he protested, but he couldn't help grinning as they settled him into place. Red lay back, his eyes going from one to the other. Then, hesitantly, he spoke. "Hey, Jason, so what's on your agenda? It looks like the Center's going to be closed down for a while, so you guys are out of a job." He left the thought unfinished, watching his friend.

Jason looked briefly at Jennifer. "I don't know. I've been thinking about doing something different for a while." He walked to the window and stood facing out. "Maybe get back to my art."

"Jennifer?" Red looked over to her.

Her eyes were on Jason. "I . . ."

"Well, look, you guys, I don't mean to sound like an advertisement, but we sure could use a few good men—ah, persons." He grinned as they both turned to face him.

"You don't mean . . ." Jennifer began.

"The CIA?" Jason finished.

"Sure, why not?" He eyed them both. "Not to give you swelled heads or anything, but I should say that I'm not making this offer on my own. The authorization comes straight from the . . . from pretty damn high up! You're wanted. Both of you, if possible."

Jennifer joined Jason at the window. For a minute, they looked out through the glass. It was a warm morning, the sky azure blue, the sun bright on the trimmed lawn of the hospital, which stretched in green perfection before them. Slowly, in unison, the two young scientists turned to face each other. Both were smiling. Jason kissed her lightly on the lips, then turned toward his friend. "Sorry, Red."

"You're sure?" He looked glum, seeing their unchanging smiles. Sighing, he lay back. "Well, just remember, the offer will always be open."

"Thanks, partner." Jason nodded to him. "And relay our thanks to . . . whomever."

"I will." Red just shook his head. "Well, where do you go from here?"

Jason grinned. "Oh, I think I'll just be taking this young lady home with me."

"You'll . . ." Jennifer's eyes went wide. "Now wait a minute, Doctor. I haven't agreed to . . ." Jason had moved closer, holding her hand to his lips. "Jason, don't you imagine you can sweep me off my feet. Oh!" He did exactly that, holding her in his arms, kissing his way up her neck. "Jason! You—" His mouth covered hers. "Mmm!" She pushed at his chest, her arms outstretched, then becoming laxer, finally circling him as she returned the kiss.

A knock sounded tentatively at the door.

"Go away!" Red shouted.

The door opened slightly and the guard looked in. "I'm sorry, Red, but this . . ." A young woman was peeking around his shoulder.

"Cindy!" Jason and Jennifer broke their embrace and quickly crossed the room to meet her.

"Stop . . ." The hapless guard was close behind her.

"Come in here, young lady!" Red called out, his face in an amazed grin. "It's okay, Frank," he said, waving the guard back out.

Jason and Jennifer began asking, "Where have you been?" "Are you all right?"

"Hold it, hold it!" Red shouted them down. "I'm the interrogator! I'll take care of this!" The outburst quieted momentarily. "Now"—he faced her sternly—"just where have you been?"

Cindy stepped toward the bed, unperturbed, flanked by

Jason and Jennifer. "No place special," she said, smiling. "I just went to stay with my aunt in Baltimore after I left the Center. Everything was so crazy that day, nobody paid any attention when I took off."

"You . . . your aunt . . ." Red's bluster was lost in his relief.

"How are you, Cindy?" Jason interrupted.

"Oh, I'm okay." She shrugged off the question. Then she caught herself, and answered more carefully, "I mean, I think I'll be all right."

"And how on earth did you find us?" asked Jennifer.

"Easy," she answered. "I called Dr. Murray. He figured you'd probably be here."

"Well." Red had almost regained his composure. "Welcome to my very humble . . . You have no idea how worried . . ." He caught himself with a hint of embarrassment. "I mean, it's good to see you."

"It's nice to see you, too." She grinned at him in a way that brought a faint red blush to his ears. "So, tell me what's been going on around here. The whole Center looks like it's an army camp! I went by to pick up my stuff and . . ."

"Ah yes. Well,"—Red clasped his hands behind his head and nodded toward a chair—"it's a long story."

"Oh, no, I can't stand it! The posture of the great storyteller! Jennifer, maybe we should get some lunch?" Jason suggested, reaching for her hand.

"What? Oh, sure, good idea." She smiled. "Red, we'll come by a little later. Cindy, would you like to come with us?"

"That's all right," the girl answered casually. "I guess I'll stay here for a while." The blush, somehow, had spread from Red's cheeks to hers.

"Okay, we'll see you later." Hand in hand, Jason and Jennifer walked to the door. They could just hear Red's next words as they passed into the hall:

"Cindy, are you good at keeping secrets?"

Acknowledgments

The Wild Type is fiction, a story, but it is also the product of a very real odyssey through biopsychology, neurology, and psychiatry—a thrilling journey of discovery for which I owe credit to many.

First, I want to thank the dear friends who shared the joys and trials of my adventure combining writing with medicine through their warm and valiant support, especially J.S. and R.G.

I want to thank the bold thinkers who have trained and inspired me, including Dr. Jerry Levy of the University of Chicago, Drs. Joe Foley and Robert Daroff at Case Western Reserve University School of Medicine, and Drs. Jonathan Cole, Jeffrey Gilbert, and Marsel Mesulam of Harvard Medical School.

I want to thank the many scientists who shared ideas with me about the wonders of neuroscience, genetics, and human behavior, including Jenya Grinblat and Tod Woolf of the Harvard Biology Department.

I want to thank my patients, who daily remind me of why this journey is so important. And I want to give credit to the many brave spirits at NIH and elsewhere—neurologists, psychiatrists, researchers, clinicians, and nurses—who devote their days to exploring the mapless frontier of the human brain and to treating those often neglected patients who suffer its disorders. If this book excites discussion or moves a young person toward joining our adventure of discovery, it will live a life beyond its story.

Finally, I want to thank my extraordinary literary agent, Jean Naggar, and my editor, Betty Prashker, whose unflagging energy and wisdom have made this story a book.

Jeffrey Ivan Victoroff, M.A., M.D.
Los Angeles